If only he could stop thinking of her as a woman....

If he could just enjoy Shelley as a friend again. But he couldn't. He couldn't stop noticing the sleek curves of her calves beneath the hems of her conservative skirts and dresses. He couldn't stop noticing the golden shimmer in her hair, the breathtaking clarity of her eyes, the fullness of her lips. Every evening he would kiss her cheek or pat her arm and say good-night, and he would dive into his bed and groan over its emptiness, over his loneliness.

He wanted her. Not because he and she lived under the same roof. Not even because she was the mother of his child.

He'd wanted her long before he relocated to Block Island. Now that he was there he was forced to acknowledge the truth: he had moved to the house for Shelley as much as for his son.

He'd moved because he loved her.

ABOUT THE AUTHOR

Judith Arnold received inspiration for *Safe Harbor* from two sources: a family vacation to the picturesque Block Island and a Billy Joel album. The lyrics on the album *STORM FRONT* not only gave her the book's title, but one particular song, "And So It Goes," gave her the inspiration for the mood and characters. Judith makes her home in Massachusetts, with her husband and two young sons. A full-time writer, she is the author of over twenty American Romance books.

JUDITH ARNOLD

SAFE HARBOR

Harlequin Books

TORONTO • NEW YORK • LONDON
AMSTERDAM • PARIS • SYDNEY • HAMBURG
STOCKHOLM • ATHENS • TOKYO • MILAN

Block Island is a spot of land, approximately eleven square miles, located twelve miles south of Rhode Island in Block Island Sound. In describing the island I have tried to be as accurate as possible, naming beaches, streets, landmarks and shops. In particular, I have described Block Island's one pharmacy, which opened in 1986 and is located on High Street.

I wish to emphasize that while the Block Island settings of *Safe Harbor* are genuine, all the characters are fictional.

Special thanks to Skippy Sanchez of the Block Island Pharmacy for answering my questions. Also, thanks to the friendly clerks at the National Hotel's ice-cream shop, who told me what it's like to be a resident teenager on BI during the winter.

Finally, thanks to my husband, who ignored me when I said I couldn't afford to take a few days off from my writing, and dragged me to Block Island. "I bet you'll fall in love with the place," he said, "and wind up setting a novel there." He was right.

Published September 1991

ISBN 0-373-16405-X

SAFE HARBOR

Part One
Shelley

Chapter One

"Shelley?" her mother hollered up the stairs. "Kip's here."

Shelley gave the reflection in the mirror above the dresser a final, anxious inspection. She fussed with the skimpy crocheted triangles of the bikini, rearranging them along the woven string that circled her rib cage just below her breasts. On the one hand, she was afraid the triangles didn't cover enough of her; on the other, she acknowledged dolefully, she really didn't have much worth covering.

Some girls expanded out by the time they reached fifteen. Shelley seemed only to expand up. This past winter was the first during which she hadn't grown any taller—although at five foot nine, she was quite tall enough. Not only was she tall but she was built like a basketball player, with broad shoulders, long limbs, large hands and lean hips. Her limp hair was a bland shade halfway between brown and blond. Her eyes, an equally bland shade of gray, were set too close together. Her nose was too big, her lips too fat; her fingernails refused to grow and her feet were callused from too many summers spent running around barefoot.

And she was flat-chested.

Whatever had possessed her to buy a string bikini? She should have just pulled her bicycle out of the trunk of her father's car when they'd reached the Old Harbor ferry dock, kissed him goodbye and biked straight home. She should never have stopped in at the boutique on Water Street and blown thirty dollars on a scrap of crocheted turquoise yarn. She should have stuck to her old familiar one-piece suits so the entire universe—to say nothing of Kip Stroud—wouldn't have to contend with the pathetic sight of her straight-as-a-board figure.

She'd wandered into the boutique because she'd been melancholy yesterday afternoon, desperate for the kind of pick-me-up she got from buying something she didn't need. Seeing her father off on the ferry back to New London always put her in a funk. She understood that while she and her mother were free to spend all summer in their cozy vacation house on Block Island, at the end of each weekend her father had to "go to America," as the islanders called returning to the mainland, so he could put in time at his office. "Even bank executives have to work, princess," he'd tell Shelley. "I'll be back Friday night. I promise."

But this year, for the first time in the eight years they'd been summering on Block Island, Shelley's father didn't always keep that promise. Sometimes he didn't join Shelley and her mother until Saturday. One weekend he didn't come at all. "Things have been difficult at work," he would say, although Shelley couldn't fathom how he could make things any less difficult by hanging around in Connecticut on weekends when the bank's corporate offices were closed.

She missed him, but it wasn't for herself that she wished he would come to the island every weekend. It was for him. If anyone needed a strong, curative dose of Block Island it was her stressed-out father.

The island was the best remedy Shelley knew of for all the hassles and tensions of winter in "America." Maybe it was the sea breezes, maybe the slower pace of life, maybe the morning fog and the midday heat and the heavy scent of honeysuckle that permeated the air. Maybe it was magic. Whatever it was, Shelley was always happier on Block Island than she was back home in Westport. So was her mother, and so was her father when he was here.

"Shelley?" her mother hollered again.

"Coming!" Turning her back on the mirror, she grabbed her oversized Yale T-shirt, threw it on and pulled the hem halfway down her thighs. Then she smoothed the frayed edges of her denim cutoffs, grabbed her backpack and bounded down the narrow stairs to the first floor of the tiny cottage.

Kip was waiting for her outside at the bottom of the porch steps, his ten-speed bike balanced between his legs and a battered red backpack riding his shoulders. Like her, he wore a baggy T-shirt—his featured the Harvard crest, in deference to his Boston-area roots—and cutoffs. A month and a half of summer had imbued his skin with a golden glow, and his thick brown hair was long and rich with sunbleached highlights. He'd grown at least four inches and gained at least thirty pounds over the winter. He looked a lot more like a man than a boy.

Shelley shouldn't have noticed. She had known Kip too long and too well to think of him as a *guy*. He was her buddy, her best friend on the island. Ever since her first summer here, when she'd been at Scotch Beach with her parents and a scrappy eight-year-old kid with goggly eyeglasses had marched over and said, "Hey, you wanna see a dead snake?" they'd been pals. She had eagerly tramped through the dune grass with him to check out the reptile carcass, and they'd argued heatedly about whether a person could get poisoned from touching a dead snake, and by the end of the argument he had called her a dumb girl and she'd called him a poop-head, and they'd made a plan to meet at the beach again the next day.

For the next seven summers they'd been spending their days together at various beaches, in town, or biking along the cliffs. They'd been whiling away their afternoons licking ice-cream cones in Old Harbor and making pests of

themselves on the porch of the National Hotel, listening to
the folksingers hired to entertain the beer-drinking clien-
tele. They'd been winding down in the evenings sipping
lemonade and playing backgammon on one of the breezy
verandas of his parents' house. They'd been having pic-
nics, trading secrets, exploring hidden coves.

During the winter Shelley rarely thought about Kip. They
never called each other or wrote letters. She had her home
friends and he had his. But every year as June rolled around
and her mother embarked on preparations for the family's
annual migration to the island, Shelley experienced a quiet
thrill at the comprehension that soon she and Kip would be
tearing around the island again, bickering, swapping secrets, spying on his older sister and acting as if they'd never
been away from each other.

Kip Stroud was right up there with the sea breezes and the
honeysuckle when it came to things that made summer special.

"Come on, slowpoke," he called to her as soon as she
tossed her mother a perfunctory kiss and raced out of the
house. "You're getting as bad as Diana, taking forever to
get ready."

"I didn't take forever," she said, refusing to take his
needling seriously. She swung one leg over the seat of her
bike, shouted through the screen door that she'd be home in
time for supper, and then lifted her sandaled feet onto the
pedals and coasted down the rutted dirt driveway to the
street. A year ago she wouldn't have bothered to wear sandals, but now that she was fifteen she thought she ought to
do something about the unsightly calluses rimming her
heels.

"Wanna go up by Dorie's Cove?" Kip asked, then turned
right without giving her a chance to answer. Not that she
minded—they had discovered a well-hidden inlet near Dorie's Cove on the west shore, and it was their favorite beach.

Kip's bike boasted five more gears than Shelley's, but he took the hill slowly so she could catch up. "Those are your new sunglasses," she observed once she'd pulled alongside him.

"Yeah. My dad picked them up at the optician's and brought them down this past weekend."

"I like them," she said. They were similar to his regular glasses—tortoise-shell, aviator-style—and a vast improvement over the hinged clip-on shades he used to attach to his glasses.

"I look real cool now, don't I," he said with a self-mocking smile.

"Oh, yeah, real cool."

"Beat you down the hill," he challenged her, then shot ahead as the road veered left and descended down a steep, twisting slope.

Shelley cursed, but her voice was lost in the wind. She sped past weathered cottages with tiled roofs and wind-blanched shingles, past rolling green acreage, gnarled maples and dwarf pines, past potholes and picket fences and quaint signs hanging from porch railings, reading Sea View and Windlass and Queen of the Mist. For all their fancy names, none of those houses was anywhere near as nice as Kip's. His family owned a rambling Victorian year-rounder, more than one hundred years old, with upstairs and downstairs porches, a full dry basement and a cupola. They'd never bothered to name the house. It was simply the Stroud place, a glorious gray structure trimmed with white gingerbread, perched on two verdant acres surrounded by dense hedges and stone walls bordering a narrow road as hilly and serpentine as the road on which the Ballards' much smaller cottage stood.

Shelley loved the Stroud place. She loved the painstakingly restored woodwork inside, the fresh paint outside, the breezy verandas with their flower boxes and Adirondack chairs, and most of all the cupola with its breathtaking views of both Old Harbor and New Harbor. The house her parents owned was an unwinterized four-room Cape Cod furnished in a style her mother called "Goodwill Modern." Shelley was grateful that her family could afford the house, no matter how modest it was. But still...the Strouds' house was wonderful.

At the bottom of the hill she caught up to Kip again. The wind flattened his hair back from his face in a way that, combined with his dark-lensed glasses, gave him a mysterious, dashing appearance. The sun played over his cheeks, revealing the faint outlines of his shaven beard. His jaw seemed thicker than it had been last summer, his brow higher, the bones of his face more solid. Once again Shelley was forced to acknowledge how much he'd matured over the past year.

Maybe she was the one who had matured so much. Last summer she hadn't been at all conscious of how good-looking he was. Then again, last summer he'd had those doofus clip-on sunglasses, and he'd been skinny. Instead of a real, razor-worthy beard his jaw had been covered with peach fuzz, and his voice had squeaked like a clarinet in an amateur's hands.

Last year she'd adored Kip because he was her friend. This year, though... This year she kept getting hung up on stupid things like whether he was going to laugh at her when he saw her in her new bikini.

Nearing their private cove, they steered off the road and dismounted. After stashing their bikes behind a boulder, they picked their way down the rugged slope to the sheltered beach below. As always, it was unoccupied. Shelley sometimes wondered whether anyone else on the whole island knew of its existence.

Kip swung his pack off his shoulders, dropped it onto the sand and kicked off his leather mocs. "Man, it's hot," he complained, even though a brisk westerly breeze swept the humidity from the air. "I need some R&R. My old man made me help him paint the deck chairs this past weekend."

"Life's tough," Shelley said unsympathetically. She wished her house had a deck to put chairs on.

Kip tugged a blanket out of his pack and spread it on the sand. Then he pulled off his T-shirt and sprawled across the blanket. "Life *is* tough," he declared, although his broad smile gave him away. "My father's a slave driver, Shelley. You know how he can be."

"Oh, yes. He carries a whip with him wherever he goes." Actually, Shelley considered Kip's father an absolute teddy bear.

"What I want to know is, how come I had to help him paint the deck chairs and Diana didn't? Doesn't that seem sexist to you?"

"Very." Shelley sat on a corner of the blanket and opened her backpack, from which she pulled a towel and a bottle of suntan lotion. Sooner or later she was going to have to remove her T-shirt and shorts, but she stalled by searching for her sunglasses. "What was Diana doing while you were slaving away on the deck chairs?"

"You wanna know what she was doing?" Kip rolled onto his side and propped himself up on one arm. "She was down in Old Harbor, flirting with this college guy who's got a job renting mopeds at Aldo's for the summer."

"Oh, yeah?"

"Yeah. She says she's in love." He smirked.

"Why shouldn't she be?" Shelley said, although she felt a little disloyal taking Diana's side. Diana was three years older than Kip and Shelley, and summer after summer they'd snickered over her adolescent moods, her taste in clothes, her coquettish hip-swaying walk and her melodramatic sulks. But during the past winter Shelley had experienced a few intense sulks of her own, and she'd started experimenting with new fashions. She hadn't fallen in love, but she'd spent an awful lot of time squealing with her girl-

friends over Bruce Springsteen and dreaming about Danny
Clayburn, a gorgeous senior at her high school who didn't
even know she existed.

"If what Diana's in is love," Kip joked, "I hope they
come up with a vaccine before I come down with it. She just
sits around sighing all the time. When she's not sighing she's
working on her tan, and when she's not doing that she's
bitching at me."

"You probably deserve it," Shelley teased. Having ex-
humed her sunglasses from her pack, she'd run out of delaying tactics. The moment of truth had arrived. Taking a
deep breath, she unzipped her cutoffs and slid them down
her legs. Before she pulled off her T-shirt, she discreetly adjusted the bows of the skimpy straps that held the bikini
bottom on her hips. Then, acting as nonchalantly as possible, she peeled off her shirt and braced herself for Kip's response.

He didn't whistle. He didn't blurt out "What the hell have
you got on?" He didn't say "What a coincidence! I spent
the past winter growing a beard and a smattering of chest
hair, and you spent the past winter turning into a foxy
babe."

He would never say that—not only because she hadn't
turned into a foxy babe but because Kip didn't seem to be
into boy-girl type stuff. Like Shelley, he was fifteen, and
everybody knew boys matured later than girls. If he could
ridicule his sister's infatuation with a summer employee at
Aldo's, he undoubtedly had no idea what infatuation was
all about. His full ration of hormones hadn't kicked in yet.

Which was fine, Shelly decided. She herself had just
started dating this year, and so far she'd found the experience to be more hype than payoff. It was nice having some
guy take you to the movies, and it added to your stature at
school. But kissing was a pretty messy business, all in all,
and anything beyond kissing generally led to her shoving the
guy's hands away and the guy whining that all the other girls

do it, or that after he blew all that money on the movie he'd earned the right to paw her, or—the ultimate insult—that if she didn't like it there must be something wrong with her.

Maybe what was wrong with her was that she could barely fill a B cup. If she had bigger breasts, she'd probably have more nerve endings and being touched would feel more exciting.

In any case, while she wanted Kip to think she was a knockout, she didn't want him to kiss her or try for a feel. That would spoil their friendship.

He might have at least *noticed* the bikini, though. He might have at least said something like "Hey, you got a new swimsuit."

What he said, after the grand, anxiety-producing unveiling of her bikini, was, "The water sure looks great today." Then he pulled off his sunglasses, hoisted himself to his feet and jogged down to the water, splashing through the shallows until the waves were lapping his thighs and then taking a clean, graceful dive into the gently rolling surf.

Shelley glanced down at her body and shuddered. The tan lines left by her other swimsuits emphasized how sickly pale her belly was. Her chest was truly an embarrassment, revealing only the faintest shadow where a more fortunate girl would have cleavage. With a small groan, she folded her shirt and shorts in a neat pile and then stood and picked her way down to the water's edge.

The tide was low. Kip had surfaced and was standing a good thirty yards from shore, where the waves reached only up to his waist. His skin glistened with drops of water, and the newly sprouted hair on his chest looked darker and less curly. "Come on in," he beckoned, slicking his hair back from his face and waving to her. "It's not too bad."

It was icy, but Shelley hadn't come to the beach to squeal and snivel and act like a coward. Certainly braving the chill waters of Block Island Sound wasn't as daunting as stripping off her outer clothing had been just a minute ago. She filled her lungs with air, then raced headlong into the water, refusing to stop. Once the water was at her hips she dove under, feeling her skin erupt in goose bumps. Before she emerged she ran her hands briskly over the triangular cups of her suit to make sure they were still covering what they had to cover. Reassured that everything was in place, she bobbed up to the surface and let out her breath.

"It's freezing," she complained, just for the hell of it.

"Is not."

"You could build a snowman out here."

Kip laughed, then vanished under the surface again. In less than a second Shelley felt his hand around her ankle, giving her a sharp tug. She barely had time to take a breath before she tumbled backward and the foaming water closed over her head.

She and Kip had wrestled in the water more times than she could count. They had dunked each other, raced each other, splashed and tickled each other. This time, though, the horseplay seemed different. His fingers felt so strong on her leg, and when she floated back up and felt him behind her, his chest brushing up against her back, it was . . . well, different.

"What happens if I do this?" he asked, toying with the bow that held her bikini top on.

"You die," she said simply, spinning around and slapping his hand.

He was laughing. "In that case, I'll stick to the safe stuff." Before she could stop him he dove under water again, wrapped his arms around her knees and gave a jerk. She grabbed his shoulder, holding him down as she went under. He poked her ribs, she prodded his stomach with her knee, he shoved her away and shot back up into the air a split second before she did.

"You're a creep," she scolded. This wasn't as much fun as it had been last summer—or as recently as last Friday. For one thing, she was afraid of his accidentally pulling off her bikini. For another, she was afraid of his pulling it off *not* by accident. Maybe he thought there was something silly or affected about her wearing a swimsuit she had no business wearing. Maybe he resented the fact that she could get herself up in something sexier than usual, even if it didn't look particularly sexy on her.

"What's the matter?" he asked. He was standing solidly, his hands on his hips, his chest heaving as he caught his breath. His dark eyes peered at her through water-spiked lashes. He had lost his playfulness; obviously he could sense her anger.

Suddenly she was ashamed of herself. What a narcissist she was, to be so obsessed with a stupid bikini. "Nothing," she said apologetically. "I just . . . I'm a little tired. I'm going out."

Kip accompanied her, slogging through the water until they reached the beach. Shelley gave herself a quick wipe with her towel, then dropped onto the blanket, slipped her sunglasses on, bunched her towel into a pillow and stretched out on her stomach.

Kip spent a bit longer drying himself before he donned his sunglasses. "You want me to put some suntan lotion on your back?" he offered.

"No. I'm too wet. Maybe later."

He shrugged and stretched out beside her, cushioning his head on his crossed arms. "Are you okay?" he asked.

"Never been better," she said tersely. She didn't like lying to Kip, but since she honestly wasn't sure what was bothering her she figured she might as well not go into it.

He stared at her. She closed her eyes, but she could still feel his gaze on her, assessing her. "Have you got your period or something?"

Shelley laughed. She couldn't imagine discussing something like her period with any boy back in "America," but with Kip she felt perfectly comfortable talking about things like that. When she was eleven he'd told her he'd seen Diana buying tampons at the general store, and he and Shelley had snuck into Diana's bedroom, found the box in the closet, and stolen a tampon. Carrying their loot up to the cupola, they had examined it and decided that the very concept underlying such an object was gross. The following summer, when Shelley had begun menstruating, Kip had questioned her on why she didn't get grumpy the way Diana did, and whether the cramps hurt as much as Diana claimed they did, and whether she used tampons.

Shelley had answered all his questions honestly. She knew he'd reciprocate. When she'd asked him what a wet dream was he'd told her. When she'd overheard a couple of guys down at the harbor using crude language, Shelley had asked Kip what their words meant and again he'd told her. It was part of the magic of the island—the magic of her friendship with Kip—that they could talk candidly about things.

"No," she said now. "I don't know what's wrong with me, Kip. I think..."

"What?" he coaxed her, lifting a wet strand of hair that had unraveled from her braid and tucking it behind her ear.

"I'm upset about my father."

"Oh?"

A warm, soothing wind swirled around the cove, bouncing off the cliff behind her and dancing across her shoulders. She twisted her head so she could view Kip. "You won't tell, will you?"

"Of course not."

"Well... I think something's wrong with him," she confessed. It felt so good to put her feelings into words. She'd tried to raise the subject with her mother last night as they'd nibbled on salads and watched a *60 Minutes* rerun on the tube. Her mother had immediately cut her off, insisting that nothing was wrong with Shelley's father other than his being overburdened with work.

"Is he sick?" Kip asked. He shifted so his head was closer to hers on the blanket.

"No, nothing like that. It's just . . ." She exhaled. Maybe her mother was right; maybe she was imagining things. "He didn't come to the island till Saturday morning," she said. "Last summer he always came Friday afternoon, but this summer he doesn't come till Saturday—if he comes at all."

"He only missed one weekend," Kip reminded her.

"Your father never misses a weekend."

Kip shrugged. "If he missed a weekend, my mother would miss her weekly bee shot. He's got to come." Last spring Kip's mother had gotten stung by a bee and gone into anaphylactic shock. As a result she was on a regimen of desensitizing bee-venom injections. Since there was no pharmacy on the island, Kip's father had to bring her weekly dose with him when he came down from Boston.

But Shelley knew that wasn't the only reason Mr. Stroud came without fail every weekend. He came because he wanted to be with his family. She and Kip rarely saw each other on the weekends because Mr. Stroud wanted to spend as much time with his son as possible—even if all they did was paint deck chairs.

The Stroud family was wealthier than Shelley's, and their wealth went back several generations. But they weren't zillionaires; Mr. Stroud worked for a living. Yet Shelley suspected that even if things were difficult for him at his real estate management firm he would never miss a weekend on the island with his family.

"Has he said anything?" Kip asked. "I mean, about how come he can't come on Fridays?"

"Just that he's got too much work to do."

"Well, there you have it," Kip said. "He's working."

She wished she could accept her father's vague explanation as easily as Kip could. "I don't know. There's something about him. He seems so wired. When I talk to him about the stuff we've been doing all week, he just nods and says 'That's nice.' He's distracted all the time." She paused, searching Kip's deep-set brown eyes and finding in his sincere gaze the courage she needed to continue. "He and my mother fight."

Kip absorbed the declaration. "You mean, like, physically?"

"No—they argue."

His lips relaxed into an easy smile. "Big deal. All parents argue."

"I bet yours don't," Shelley contended.

"Of course, they do."

"About what?"

He had to think long and hard. "Well, my father likes French roast coffee and my mother doesn't."

"Wow. World War Three," Shelley muttered. She had been at the Stroud place a few Friday evenings; she'd seen the way his parents behaved with each other. The closest they'd ever come to a fight was when Mrs. Stroud would ask Mr. Stroud to do something he clearly didn't want to do— repair a broken piece of molding on the stairs, for instance. He would invariably give her a plaintive smile and say, with just enough sarcasm to be hilarious, "Yes, *dear*." Then they'd roll their eyes at each other and laugh, and Mr. Stroud would wind up kissing his wife on the cheek.

They were so openly affectionate, so obviously in love with each other. They must have been married at least twenty years, yet sometimes they acted like dating teenagers. They held hands and communicated with their eyes, and Mrs. Stroud fixed the collars of Mr. Stroud's rumpled shirts and he gave her loving pats on her behind when he thought no one was looking.

"What do your parents argue about?" Kip asked.

"I don't know," Shelley admitted. "That's the worst part of it, Kip. They wait till I'm upstairs and they think I can't hear, and then...they talk to each other in these tense, strained voices, and my father says things like 'You push me too far, Mary. There are limits. I can only go so far before the whole thing falls apart.'"

"What whole thing?"

"I don't know." She realized she'd answered too many of his questions this way—and that was part of the problem. She wished to God she knew what was going on. "They argue in the winter—but that's in 'America.' They never used to argue here. We'd come down to the island and everyone would mellow out. This summer, though—" she fought against the quiver in her voice "—my father isn't mellowing out. He needs to, Kip. And my mother just says he's just overworked and I shouldn't worry."

"And you're worried."

"Yes."

Kip sighed. "Maybe your mom's right, and it's just some mess at work or something." He must have read disbelief in Shelley's expression because he added, "Or maybe it's something real." He reached across the blanket to give her hand a gentle, reassuring squeeze. "I don't know what to say, except that I'm here if you need me."

She smiled. What Kip had said was exactly what she wanted to hear. He was with her, willing to listen, willing to be her friend. Knowing that she could count on him and confide in him was far more important than having him compliment her on her daring new swimsuit.

If he'd complimented her, he would have been lying, anyway. Instead Kip gave her his honesty—the most precious gift in the world. No matter what trouble was brewing with her parents, Shelley had Kip. She was a remarkably lucky girl.

Chapter Two

"What do you mean, you aren't coming?"

"Shelley..." Her father's voice emerged through the long-distance static on the telephone line. "Princess, don't make it harder on me than it already is, all right? I'd come if I could, but I can't."

"Why not? Couldn't you at least come on Saturday?"

"Don't nag." He paused, then asked, "Did your mother tell you to call me?"

"No. She told me *not* to call. But I thought maybe, if I could only talk to you myself..." Her voice wavered as she battled the urge to cry. When her mother informed her he wasn't going to come to the island that weekend, Shelley decided not to give up so easily. Perhaps if she let him know how very, very much she wanted to see him, he might change his mind. "Please, Dad. Please come."

"Shelley, you're making a mountain out of a molehill. The earth isn't going to stop spinning if I skip a weekend. Now pull yourself together. I'll see you when I can."

She closed her eyes, stung by his harsh words. He made it sound as if wanting to be with her father was selfish, as if she was being totally unreasonable by asking him to spend the weekend with his family.

What he'd said was true—the earth wouldn't stop spinning if he didn't come. And yet... more was at stake than one weekend. Shelley sensed, from the tense undertone in her father's voice and the grim set of her mother's mouth as she turned a page of the *New Yorker* magazine she was perusing, that something was gravely wrong, and that if her father didn't come to Block Island it would get worse. She was fighting for something far more consequential than whether she would get to spend time with her father that weekend.

If only she knew what it was.

"I miss you, Dad," she whispered into the phone.

After a brief silence he said, "I miss you, too, Shelley. But you've got to grow up and face reality. I can't come."

She sighed. Bad enough nagging and pleading. She wasn't going to beg. "I'll talk to you later, then," she mumbled before lowering the telephone into its receiver.

To her chagrin, several tears seeped through her lashes and skittered down her cheeks. Her father was right; she ought to grow up and face reality. The reality, in this instance, was that he would rather work than spend time with his daughter. Surely there must have been some way he could have contrived a trip to the island—even if he'd arrived on the last ferry Saturday night and departed on the first one Sunday morning. He could have managed it if he'd wanted to come badly enough.

But he hadn't managed it, because he didn't want to come. She suddenly felt cold, abandoned.

"I told you not to call," her mother chided without looking up from her magazine.

Shelley gazed through the doorway separating the kitchen from the parlor. Her mother sat on the sagging couch, her feet propped up on the ugly wrought-iron table in front of her. Clad in a T-shirt, jeans and espadrilles, her figure trim and her shoulder-length ash-blond hair brushed casually back from her forehead, she looked younger than her forty years. Closer examination of her face revealed the truth, however. Her eyebrows were indented in a perpetual frown, the smile lines radiating from her eyes had evolved into squint lines, and the corners of her mouth seemed frozen in a permanent downward turn. There was a hardness about her, a shadow of discontent darkening her features.

Shelley slouched in the doorway, swallowing the lump in her throat. Maybe if her mother weren't so grumpy her father would come. Maybe if someone told Shelley what was going on, she would be able to solve everything and make everyone happy.

"Why won't he come?" she asked her mother, detesting the tremor in her voice.

"Who knows?" Her mother reached for the glass of sherry balanced on the table next to her feet. She took a sip and shrugged. "Maybe he's having an affair."

Shelley gasped.

Her mother looked up from the magazine. "That was a joke."

"It wasn't funny."

"Well, nothing is funny this summer, is it?" Her mother's tone was wistful when she added, "I'm sorry. I'm not happy about your father's absence, either. But it's nothing for you to worry about."

"If he's having an affair—"

"He's not," her mother said with enough certainty to persuade Shelley. "It's just that there are lots of things going on at the bank."

"He could bring work with him if he had to. Other people do. Kip's father—"

"Kip's father is in a much more secure situation, Shelley. The Strouds are a solid family. They've got lots of money behind them."

"Are you saying we aren't solid?" Shelley asked, even though she didn't think she wanted to hear the answer.

Her mother took another sip of sherry. "I'm not saying that, no," she clarified. "I'm just saying, we didn't inherit what we've got. Your father has to work hard for every nickel. He's gone far and climbed high, but it isn't like he can tap into a family fortune when times are lean."

"Are times lean?"

"No." Her mother sounded infinitely weary. "Times are fine. It just takes your father a little more effort to get what's coming to him." She rolled her head back on the cushions and stared at the ceiling. "I'm sorry, Shelley. I should be trying to cheer you up, and I'm not doing a very good job of it. I'm angry, too. I'm angry with him for not coming, and I'm angry with myself for wanting him to when he obviously can't. And now I'm angry with you for whining to me about it. I'm sorry."

Gnawing her lip, Shelley turned away. She felt bad for having pestered her mother. She should have expressed sympathy instead. Her mother probably missed her father even more than Shelley herself did.

"I'm going out for a while," she announced, searching the kitchen for her sandals.

"Going out where?"

"Kip's house." He would comfort her. He would say whatever she needed to hear. Unable to locate her sandals, she pocketed her key and strode barefoot out to the porch, listening to the hiss of the screen door as it whipped shut behind her. The sky was fading as the sun slid below the horizon, and the air shimmered with the summer song of crickets.

Shelley padded down the steps and straddled her bike. She took a rubber band from a pocket of her jeans and pulled her hair into a ponytail so it wouldn't blow into her face. Then she cruised down the rutted driveway and steered toward Kip's house.

Five minutes later she reached the break in the stone wall where the Stroud driveway met the road. She slowed and turned onto the property, then pedaled along the edge of the broad carpet of lawn that spread in a gentle incline toward the front veranda. Lights spilled from first- and second-floor windows; through an open window came the sound of a Baroque flute concerto. The Adirondack chairs glowed in their new coats of white paint.

She alighted and stood her bike against the wooden lattice that underpinned the porch. Then she climbed the steps and tapped on the screen door. Within a moment Kip's mother appeared in the front hallway.

"Shelley! Hi, come on in," Mrs. Stroud welcomed her, holding the door open. Shelley's mother was arguably prettier than Mrs. Stroud; certainly she was more chic. But Kip's mother exuded maternal warmth. She did nothing to camouflage the silver streaks in her dark hair; she dressed with shabby gentility, in cotton chinos, baggy blouses and canvas sneakers. Her eyes were gentle, her smile genuine. Shelley always felt comfortable in her house.

"Is Kip home?" she asked.

"Last time I looked, he was. Kip?" she bellowed, her voice echoing against the high ceiling of the center hall.

Kip swung through the kitchen door, a half-eaten apple in his hand. As soon as he saw Shelley his face broke into a surprised smile. "Hey, Shelley!" he greeted her, then abruptly stumbled to a halt, his smile fading. Despite Shelley's brave expression, he must have realized that she wouldn't have bicycled over unexpectedly unless something was wrong. "Want an apple?"

Something might be wrong, but coming here definitely improved her spirits. "I'm not hungry," she said.

His mother tactfully disappeared through the arched doorway leading into the living room. Once they were alone in the hallway, Kip approached, his bare feet noiseless on the faded runner. "Wanna go upstairs?"

"Yeah."

He held up a finger, signaling her to wait, and then vanished into the kitchen to discard his apple. Once he rejoined her, they climbed the stairs to the second floor, entered the smallest bedroom, opened an inner door, and scaled the steep ladderlike steps behind it, first into the dusty unfinished attic with its dormer windows and cobwebbed corners, and from there up another ladder to the cupola.

The cupola was a cramped square space, no more than six feet on each side, but Shelley and Kip fit in without crowding each other. They sat diagonally, their backs nestled into opposite corners and their legs extended across the tiny floor. Through the open windows a balmy wind blew, and in the distance Shelley could hear the eerie reverberation of the Pt. Judith ferry's horn, announcing that it was about to pull out of Old Harbor for its last daily excursion to the mainland.

Kip linked his hands behind his head and leaned back, watching Shelley patiently. She pulled the rubber band out of her hair and raked her fingers through the tawny waves. Then she lifted her face to him. "My dad's not coming this weekend," she said.

Kip nodded, waiting, knowing she had more to say.

"He called while my mom and I were having supper, and my mom talked to him and then she told me what he said. I was upset, Kip, so I called him back and tried to talk him into coming. Was that such a terrible thing to do?"

"Of course not."

"Well, he acted like it was. So did my mother. My dad told me to grow up and my mom made jokes about how maybe my father was having an affair."

Kip cursed. "Do you think that's what it's about?" he asked, taking her concern as seriously as she did.

"No." She toyed with the rubber band, twisting it into figure-eight shapes and then letting it snap loose. "This is going to sound really crazy, Kip, but sometimes I think it's something worse."

"Like what?"

She shook her head. "I don't know. It's not fair, Kip—this is supposed to be my happy time, the summer on Block Island. But...I mean, for my mom to even joke about such a thing . . ." The tears she'd been suppressing ever since her mother had relayed the news about her father's phone call finally broke free. Shelley pressed her hands to her eyes and sobbed.

She was scarcely aware of Kip shifting, reversing position, wedging himself next to her with his legs forming a bridge over hers. He arched his arm around her and pulled her against him, and she wept into the soft cotton of his shirt, into the firm strength of his shoulder. A girl ought to be able to cry on her mother's shoulder, but Shelley couldn't.

She had Kip, though. Maybe that was even better.

After a long while she sniffled to a halt. Her shoulders rose and fell in a final shudder, and she pulled back from him and wiped her cheeks with her palms. "Sorry about that," she murmured hoarsely.

He smiled. As the sky darkened, the three-quarter moon grew brighter, reflecting off the lenses of his eyeglasses. "Sorry about what?"

She recalled the first time they'd met, so long ago, when he'd dragged her through the dune grass to inspect the dead snake he'd discovered. His motivation had probably been to shake her up, but she'd been tough and courageous. She'd squatted down and stared the corpse straight in its lidless black eyes. No doubt Kip had been testing her, trying to find out whether she was a sissy. He'd found out she wasn't.

But here she was, falling apart, blubbering, her courage gone and her emotions overblown. Here she was, leaning on him and acting like a dumb girl.

"I'm sorry I cried like that. I'm scared, Kip. I know there's no reason to be, but—"

"Maybe there *is* a reason to be," he countered, twirling his fingers through her hair. She understood that he didn't mean to alarm her, but rather wanted to reassure her that her reaction wasn't as dopey as she seemed to think it was.

"If my parents get a divorce, I'll die," she declared.

"No you won't."

"But I love them both."

"Well, maybe...maybe that's not it at all. Maybe your dad just has some problems to work out, and he wants to work them out by himself."

"Yeah—or with another woman."

"Maybe he just wants some time alone. I mean, every guy needs a little time to himself now and then."

"He has time to himself all week long," she reminded Kip. "We're here. He's all alone in Westport."

"But he's at work most of the time."

"Whose side are you on, anyway?" she snapped.

Kip groaned and socked her gently in the arm. "Girls," he muttered, an all-encompassing complaint. "Of course I'm on your side, Shelley. I'm just trying to explain..."

"Explain what?"

"He's a guy. There's no way you can understand everything that's going on in his head."

"You *are* taking his side," she accused, supremely annoyed.

"I'm trying to talk you down, Shell."

"You're a creep. And I can too understand everything that's going on in his head. Same as your head. They're both empty. What's going on inside them is zilch."

Kip laughed. So did Shelley. Arguing with him felt good; they both knew where they stood and what the situation was. It wasn't like arguing with her parents, where so much remained unspoken, unacknowledged.

From four stories below came the wind-borne drone of a moped engine. Shelley and Kip scrambled to their knees in time to see a two-seater bounce up the driveway to the front porch. The engine died and the two passengers—Diana and a strapping young man with black hair and a thick mustache—climbed off.

"That's him?" Shelley whispered.

"The love of her life," Kip whispered back.

Her personal woes momentarily forgotten, Shelley slipped into her spying mode. Spying on Diana was a summer tradition for Shelley and Kip, although this summer Shelley found herself spying on Diana less out of mischief than out of admiration. Diana was so pretty, so sophisticated. In her tank top and shorts, with her hair cut in an expertly styled shag and her eyes enhanced with tinted contacts and a subtle touch of makeup, with a narrow strap of braided leather circling one bare, slender ankle, she looked awfully cool.

In less than two months she would be heading off to Middlebury College. Maybe she was moody and sulky and she took forever to get ready. But she knew things Shelley longed to know, things that had to do with life and love and being a woman. Spying on her with Kip was entertaining, but sometimes Shelley wished she could spend a little time at Diana's feet, learning important things.

"I think he's kind of cute," she said of Diana's boyfriend.

Kip made a face. "He's a geek."

"He's got a mustache. He must be old."

"I could grow a mustache if I wanted," Kip said.

Shelley glanced at him and wrinkled her nose. "Nah. It wouldn't suit you. You're too clean-cut."

He gave her another playful sock in the arm. "*You're* a geek."

"Shh." She rose on her knees to watch as Diana and her date paused before the porch steps. He wrapped his arms around Diana's shoulders, and she wrapped her arms around his waist. Their lips met in a kiss.

After a prolonged minute the porch light flickered off and on. Diana and the guy sprang apart. "My mother," Kip murmured. "The guardian of virtue."

"What's she going to do when Diana goes off to college?"

"Pray a lot." He and Shelley watched as Diana squeezed the guy's hand in farewell and backed slowly up the stairs to the veranda, gazing dreamily at him as he climbed onto the moped and revved the motor. Not until he had vanished beyond the stone wall did she turn and enter the house.

"Have you met him?" Shelley asked.

"Who, Romeo?" Kip turned from the window and settled back onto the floor. Shelley sat, as well, the tight quarters forcing her into the curve of Kip's arm. "Not really. My mom invited him over for a barbecue Saturday evening, so she and my dad can check him out. My dad's going to be coming down with my grandmother, my Uncle Ned and Aunt Martha and their kids, so the guy will be just one face among many. Hey," he said, pulling back to look at her, "maybe you and your mother can come, too."

Shelley shook her head. "To a Stroud family gathering? We wouldn't fit in."

"Of course you would. It's going to be a mob scene. And if your father isn't coming to the island, what are you and your mother going to do all weekend, sit around and mope? Wouldn't you rather come to our house and eat some charred meat and soggy pickles? It'll be a good time."

"I don't know," Shelley hedged, although it did sound like a lot of fun. Much more fun than watching TV with her mother in their stuffy little cottage and wondering what Shelley's father was up to back in Connecticut.

"You'd get to meet Romeo," Kip pointed out.

Shelley was tempted. "Don't you think you ought to ask your mother first?"

"You know she'll say it's a great idea."

Of course she would. Kip's mother wasn't the sort to get hung up on two guests more or less at a barbecue. "Well...if it's okay with my mother, then, sure, we'll come."

"Good." He gave her an affectionate hug, then hauled himself to his feet. "How about let's go get some lemonade and bother Diana?"

"Okay," Shelley agreed as Kip grabbed her hand and hoisted her off the floor. Once again he had made her feel better. As they descended the ladder into the house, she could almost forget about the problems that had sent her crying into his arms.

"DO I LOOK ALL RIGHT?" Shelley's mother asked.

Shelley turned from the mirror where she'd been trying futilely to do something interesting with her exceptionally uninteresting hair. Her mother had on white jeans and an oversized blue silk blouse that gathered in a knot at one hip. From her ears dangled large gold hoops; her wrists were circled by gold bangles.

"You look very classy," Shelley said, meaning it. She didn't add that the Strouds had too much class to worry about looking classy.

Shelley's mother had met Kip's parents on a few occasions, and they'd exchanged small talk on the usual subjects—the names of house painters, the outrageous cost of electricity on the island, the most recent incident of vandalism at the lighthouse up at Sandy Point. They'd never actually socialized in a big way, though. When Shelley's father was on the island the Ballards did family-type things—going out to dinner at the National Hotel, picnicking at Mohegan Bluffs or just hanging out at the house, being together. And when Shelley's father wasn't on the island her mother felt peculiar about venturing out in public without him. "I'm a married woman," her mother would claim. "I'm not used to traveling solo."

After much urging from Shelley, however, her mother had decided to attend a party without a proper escort. Three cheers for independence, Shelley had muttered under her breath when her mother finally accepted Kip's invitation. Just because her mother had married her father at the age of twenty-one, just because she'd never had an outside job—let alone a career—or an identity apart from "Mary Ballard, wife and mother," just because she'd never done *anything* solo didn't mean she couldn't go to the Strouds'.

She was nervous, though, and because she was, Shelley couldn't be. Giving up on her hair, she tossed her brush onto the dresser and stepped into her sandals. She wore a polo shirt, khaki shorts and a thin gold chain about her neck—a birthday present from her father. The best thing she could say about her appearance was that, six weeks into the summer, she had acquired a dynamite tan.

"Well, let's go," her mother said brightly. It was obvious that she was trying hard to be cheerful despite the absence of her husband.

Downstairs, Shelley's mother stopped in the kitchen to pick up her purse and a bottle of zinfandel. When her mother had purchased the wine Shelley had tactfully reminded her that people at barbecues drank beer and soda, but her mother wouldn't listen. "When someone invites you to dinner," she explained, "it's correct to bring a bottle of wine."

Her mother handed her the bottle once they were both seated in the car. Shelley recited the directions, and her mother drove. Her grip on the wheel wasn't too tight, but Shelley could sense the anxiety in her mother's slender arms, in her taut jaw, in her rigid posture as she squinted in the early evening sunlight. As much as Shelley missed her father, she realized her mother missed him in different ways: not only because she wanted to see him and talk to him, but because she felt insecure and exposed without him.

Shelley had always admired her parents' marriage. Some of her classmates had divorced parents, and they seemed sad and confused about it. But until this summer, when strange, ominous undercurrents kept churning through her family, Shelley had considered her parents an ideal couple. George Ballard conquered the world and Mary Ballard organized the home front. George earned the money and Mary spent it wisely, not on trinkets and junk but on the sort of clothes, household furnishings and jewelry that would earn the family a respectable place in the world. Shelley's parents strove hard; they looked good together; they complemented each other.

It had always seemed to work so well—until this summer. Something was amiss, a gear out of alignment, a clamp broken, two pieces of metal rubbing together, creating friction, setting off sparks. For the first time in her life Shelley found herself wondering whether being in such a tight, self-contained marriage was a good thing, after all.

At least, she resolved, when she got married she would have her own career. None of this not-used-to-traveling-solo stuff for her. She would marry, of course—a strong, ethical, handsome man like her father, a man devoted to taking care of her, even if she would require less care than her mother. She would marry a wonderful guy and live happily ever after, but she would never let herself become dependent on him.

"That's the driveway over there," Shelley said, gesturing toward the opening in the stone wall. She'd pointed out the Stroud place to her parents before, but she didn't blame her mother for not remembering. There were so many pretty stone walls on the island, so many tangled hedges of rose and honeysuckle, so many charming Victorian houses crowned with cupolas.

The sounds of laughter and conversation wafted through the car's open windows as Shelley's mother steered up the driveway, braking to a halt behind a mud-spattered Jeep. Outside the car, her mother took the bottle of wine from her and they started around the house to the emerald stretch of lawn at the rear. There they came upon a crowd of some twenty people: older folks seated on lawn chairs, sipping beer and iced tea; two youngsters playing badminton with profound ineptitude; a cocker spaniel streaking through the yard, happily terrorizing chipmunks and squirrels; a toddler roaming across the grass on fat, wobbly legs; a girl of about eight standing beneath a crab apple tree, hollering to someone hidden in the branches above her. Beneath another shade tree Diana and her boyfriend stood, holding hands and watching the chaos with wary amusement. On the patio, Mrs. Stroud was arranging bottles of ketchup and mustard at the center of a long table, which was covered with a festive red-checked tablecloth and several citronella candles. Mr. Stroud held court over a huge barbecue grill, armed with elbow-high hot mitts and long-handled utensils and sporting an apron with the words Treat Me Right Or I'll Burn Yours printed across it.

Shelley's father wouldn't be caught dead wearing an apron like that. On Mr. Stroud, though, it looked cute. A tall, robust man with a full head of silver hair and a pleasantly lined face, he was the kind of person who could wear the silliest things and not look silly. That, Shelley believed, was true class.

Mrs. Stroud finished setting up the condiments and turned. Spotting Shelley and her mother, she beamed, waved and hurried over. "Hi! Shelley, and—Mary, is it? I'm so glad you could come!"

Shelley's mother relaxed a little bit. "It was so nice of you to invite us. Here, this is for you." She handed Mrs. Stroud the wine.

"Oh, my, you shouldn't have! Well, thank you so much!" Mrs. Stroud cupped her hand around Shelley's mother's elbow and ushered her away, chattering enthusiastically.

Shelley let out a long breath. This was going to be fine. Her mother was going to enjoy herself. They both were going to survive this weekend without her father. They were going to prove to themselves—and to him, too—that they didn't need him to have a good time.

Reassured that her mother was all right, Shelley searched the yard for Kip. She recognized his bare feet dangling from the branches of the crab apple tree.

He jumped down to the grass below with the gracefulness of a trained acrobat. He had on a kitsch Hawaiian print shirt, cutoffs and his new sunglasses, and he was holding a

Frisbee. Like his parents, he seemed utterly at ease about himself and his appearance. Shelley envied his confidence.

She approached him as he and the girl emerged from the tree's shade. "Now listen," he instructed the girl, "you've got to throw the Frisbee level or it's going to go up in the tree again. Can you do that?"

The girl shrugged.

"Because the next time it gets stuck in a tree, *you're* going to get it. Hi, Shelley." Kip grinned at her. "This is my cousin Becky. Wanna play Frisbee with us?"

"Sure." She circled the yard with her gaze. "Are all these other people your cousins, too?" she asked.

"Some of them. Sally—the baby—and Michael—the kid whose shoelace my mother's tying—are."

"And so is the dog," Becky declared solemnly.

"Hey, the dog may be your brother, but he's *not* my cousin," Kip teased. "The gray-haired lady chugging beer straight from the bottle is my grandmother, and those kids stuffing their faces with potato chips are the Sussmans— they've got a summer place up near Grove Point. Their mother is that lady pouring lemonade, and their father is the one demonstrating golf swings to my Uncle Ned. And last but not least . . ." He shot a swift, sidelong glance at Diana and her boyfriend. "There's the man in the spotlight."

"He looks like the man in the shadows," Shelley observed.

Kip chuckled. "He can run, but he can't hide." He turned to Diana and her boyfriend and beckoned them with a wave. "How about it, guys? Wanna join us for a game of Frisbee?"

Diana shook her head, but after a quick conference her boyfriend said, "Count me in," and jogged across the lawn to them.

"Shelley, Mark. Mark, Shelley," Kip said briskly, presenting them to each other. "Come on, spread out, everyone. We've got to turn Becky into a champ before my father burns the hot dogs.''

They began tossing the plastic disc around. Naturally Kip and Mark showed off, making dramatic catches when ordinary ones would do, flinging the disc behind their backs and catching it between their legs. Becky's tosses were wobbly, and more often than not they veered off course, but she managed to avoid the tree branches.

Shelley had always been a decent athlete. While not as flamboyant as Kip and Mark, she threw with an efficient, accurate snap of her wrist, and she wasn't afraid to chase down an errant toss.

Within a few minutes she was sweating. She shouted words of encouragement at Becky and derisive remarks at the two male hotshots. Occasionally her vision would snag on Diana, seated by herself under a tree, watching the game. Diana appeared cool and composed, not a single glossy hair out of place, not a hint of perspiration on her brow. Her hands were clean, her fingernails polished. She looked fabulous.

Back home in Westport, Shelley probably would have sat out the game, too. She would have been concerned about her appearance, her demeanor. She would have wanted any boys present to understand that she was a girl, a breed quite different from them, someone they should desire from a carefully cultivated distance. She would not compete athletically with boys, or yell playful insults at them, or sprint and leap. She would never, never sweat in front of them.

But here the only boy she really cared about was Kip, and there was no point in acting like a girl with him. He hadn't even noticed her female attributes when she'd had on her string bikini. To him she was just another guy, a pal, someone to elbow out of the way when they raced each other to catch one of Becky's wild tosses. Acting ladylike around him would be a waste.

Seated primly on the sidelines, Diana looked infinitely more attractive than Shelley. But darting around the lawn, laughing and panting and playing with all her might, Shelley was having infinitely more fun.

Chapter Three

Dear Shelley,

I know you're mad at me, and I don't know if writing this letter will help. I wish I could explain things in a way you'd understand, but I'm not sure that's possible.

I can't always be with you, even when I want to be. But you're growing up, and accepting that fact is part of becoming an adult. Even though I'm your father I have a life separate from you, and sometimes it makes demands on me that I must act on, whether I want to or not. This is a hard lesson, but you're a smart, mature young lady and I think you can handle it.

I will again be unable to come to the island this weekend. There are too many pressing matters here in Connecticut. But I'm glad you're spending your summer on the island, and I hope you're enjoying it "to the max," as you might say.

I love you, Shelley. I know you're disappointed that I've missed these weekends with you, but I hope you can find it in your heart to forgive me.

Be good.

Love, Dad

Shelley reread the letter again and again. Her father's handwriting was atrocious, a slanting, aggressive scrawl. But she deciphered every scribble, every loop and slash; she let every word imprint itself in her heart. It was such a rare thing for her father to send her a letter. That he had, that he'd taken the time to write and beg her forgiveness, gratified her as nothing else could—short of seeing him.

He claimed she was smart and mature, able to accept disappointment, able to forgive. Because he viewed her with such respect, she felt compelled to live up to his praise. She would stop resenting him, stop pleading with him. She would be the daughter he loved.

"What did he write?" her mother asked. She had already skimmed her own mail and was now looking across the kitchen table to Shelley, who clung to the single sheet of stationery on which her father had penned his brief letter.

"Nothing," Shelley said automatically. This was between her and her father. If he'd wanted her mother to know, he would have sent her a copy of the letter.

Still, Shelley realized that being secretive would only feed her mother's curiosity, so she added, "Just that he's sorry he can't come to the island every weekend."

Her mother pursed her lips, as if she didn't quite believe Shelley. Rising from the table, she crossed to the sink and busied herself fixing hamburger patties for their dinner.

Shelley scowled at her mother's back for a minute, then carried her letter upstairs to her bedroom under the eaves. Stretched out on her bed, she read the letter one more time. She *had* told her mother the truth about what it said—an abridged version, maybe, but essentially the truth. What mattered most to Shelley, though, were the personal nuances, the father-daughter stuff, the parts she hadn't told her mother: *"I love you, Shelley. You're growing up. I hope you can find it in your heart to forgive me."*

"I forgive you," she whispered, folding the letter carefully along its original creases and slipping it back inside the envelope. She hid the letter in the middle drawer of her dresser, tucked between two folded shirts. Then she smiled at her reflection in the mirror and went back downstairs to help her mother fix dinner.

An hour later, the dishes done and the table wiped, Shelley told her mother she was going to Kip's house. Ensconced in the parlor with her usual props—a magazine and a glass of sherry—her mother nodded without looking up.

Terrific, Shelley thought sourly as she pocketed her key and left the cottage. Her mother was angry with her. She'd simmered all through supper, picking at her food, responding to Shelley's conversational gambits with terse answers. When Shelley finally said, "What's the matter, Mom?" her mother had grumbled about how tragic it was when girls couldn't trust their own mothers.

Shelley trusted her mother. It was just that... Climbing onto her bike, she sighed. The letter was between her father and her. He'd written it to her. No matter how much she trusted her mother, she didn't have to share it with her.

The last time she'd been to Kip's house, Saturday evening, the place had been swarming with guests. Tonight, except for the single light in an upstairs window, it appeared vacant. The air was still and mild, fragrant with the scent of mowed grass. Evening mist was beginning to rise off the water and drift across the land, giving the world a delicate soft focus.

Shelley parked her bike by the front veranda, climbed the steps and knocked on the door. Kip's voice drifted down to her from the illuminated second-floor window. "Who's there?"

She walked to the far edge of the veranda and craned her neck. She saw his backlit silhouette in the window. "Me," she shouted up. "Shelley."

"Oh, hi! Hang on, I'll be right down."

He vanished from the window. Ten seconds later he was opening the door to her. "Come on in," he said.

"Where is everybody?" she asked as she entered the house. Its silence unnerved her. Whenever Mrs. Stroud was home she had the stereo on playing one of her classical music tapes.

"The Rosses invited my mother over to see the slides they took of their sailboat trip to Nantucket. They invited me, too," he admitted, then jabbed his finger toward the back of his mouth to indicate that he found the idea nauseating. "I forced myself to say no."

"I can't imagine why," Shelley said with a grin. "Where's Diana?"

"Where else? With Romeo."

"His name is Mark," Shelley declared, "and I think he's very nice."

"Oh, great. Now you're in love with him, too."

"Don't be ridiculous," Shelley retorted. "I just thought that, considering how embarrassing Saturday might have been for him, he held up quite well."

"Embarrassing?" Kip exclaimed, leading Shelley up the stairs. "What was embarrassing about it?"

"Oh, come on. There he was, being evaluated by not just your parents but by you, your grandmother, your aunt and uncle, friends from Grove Point—"

"Hey, if he wants to date Diana he's got to pay the price."

They had reached Kip's bedroom. In summers past Shelley had spent many rainy afternoons in this room. It was almost as large as the entire two-bedroom second floor of the Ballard cottage, and perfectly adequate for hanging out in. But although it was already the third week of July, this was the first time she'd been inside Kip's bedroom that summer.

She wasn't sure why that was. Part of her suspected it was because this summer she and Kip were fifteen, and that made everything different. Boys' bedrooms suddenly took on a new meaning.

Not much in the room had changed since last year. The bed was made—but sloppily, with the spread uneven and the sheet under it wrinkled. The hardwood floor was clear—but only because a variety of junk was heaped haphazardly on the bookshelves and the top of the dresser. The oval braided rugs lay on either side of the bed, and the red-white-and-blue kite Kip and Shelley had launched every year on the Fourth of July was rolled and propped against a corner of the window seat overlooking the side yard. The only alteration Shelley noticed was that Kip had removed the poster of the solar system that used to adorn one wall, and hung in its place a framed parchment map of Block Island with pen-and-ink sketches of clipper ships sailing around it.

"I was reading," he told her, rummaging through the clutter on his dresser top for something that would serve as a bookmark. He settled on a scrap of paper covered with gin rummy scores, stuffed it into the copy of *The Catcher in the Rye* lying face-down on his bed, and put the book on the night table.

"I read *The Catcher in the Rye* in English this year," Shelley remarked, lifting the dark red paperback from the night table and flipping through the pages to see how far Kip had gotten into the story.

"We were supposed to read it," he told her, "but I got stuck in Mr. Goober's class—"

"Mr. *Goober?*"

"Well, his real name is Mr. Goebler, but everyone calls him the Goob. He said he wasn't going to teach *Catcher* because it was a dirty book. He made us read *The Turn of the Screw* instead. You ever read anything by Henry James?"

Shelley shook her head.

"He sucks eggs," Kip said. "Anyway, first thing I did was take the T into Boston and buy a copy of *Catcher*. I figured, if the Goob thought it was dirty, it was something I wanted to read. So far it's great."

"You think so?"

"You didn't like it?"

Shelley shrugged. "I thought it was okay. I know it's supposed to be this classic and everything, but..." She gazed thoughtfully at the book, tracing the stiff edge of the cover with her fingertip. "Well, it's just...it's about a boy. I mean, everything we read in school is always about boys coming of age. We read *Huck Finn* and *The Red Badge of Courage* and *Billy Budd,* and they're all about boys. Boys growing up, boys facing crises, boys becoming men and all that. We never read anything about girls."

"Maybe nobody's written a good book about girls."

She gave him a withering look. "You want to read a good book about a girl coming of age? *To Kill a Mockingbird.* The best book I've ever read," she told him. "It won a Pulitzer prize, it was made into a movie, it's a great book. I don't know why they don't teach it in school. They should. I'm really sick of reading about boys coming of age all the time."

Kip frowned. It dawned on her that he was a boy coming of age; maybe he took her comments as a personal insult. "On behalf of boys all over the world," he said sarcastically, "I apologize for inspiring such boring literature."

"I didn't say it was boring," Shelley hastily clarified. "I just said it would be nice to read about girls sometimes, too."

"Boys who are coming of age read lots of stuff about girls," he said, grinning mischievously.

"In *Playboy,* right?"

"You know me too well, Shelley," he said with a sigh. His smile became sincere and he held up his hand to make a pledge. "I promise that I will read *To Kill a Mockingbird.*"

"Good. And then you can read *The Diary of Anne Frank,* and *Little Women,* and—"

"Hey, why don't you just write me a list?"

"I will," she resolved. "Better yet, let's bike down to the library tomorrow and I'll pick out some books for you."

"What a vacation," he protested. "I'll read your books if you'll read *Guadalcanal Diary*. You turn me into a wimp, and I'll turn you into a marine."

"Yuck," she said bursting into laughter.

Kip laughed, as well. "You wanna play backgammon?" he suggested.

"Okay."

He reached up to pull the box down from the shelf in his closet when the sound of a moped motor rumbled through the open window. "Uh-oh," Kip murmured ominously. "The lovebirds are about to make the scene."

Shelley tiptoed to the front window, ducked down so as not to be visible from the front yard, and looked out. She saw the moped coasting up the driveway, with Mark steering and Diana perched behind him, her arms wrapped around his waist. "Maybe we should go downstairs and turn the porch lights on and off," Shelley said.

Kip shook his head. "They aren't going to get in too much trouble. Diana knows I'm here. Whatever they do, they're going to have to do it outside." He knelt beside Shelley and peered out the window. "I can't see them anymore—can you?"

"The angle isn't good."

"Let's go upstairs." Kip helped her to her feet. Together they hurried out of his room, down the hall to the small bedroom and up the ladder through the attic to the cupola.

From the tiny room atop the roof they had an unobstructed view of the front yard, the moped, and Diana and Mark, who were seated on the porch steps, talking. "See?" Shelley said in Diana's defense. "Your mother doesn't have to flash the lights at them. They know how to behave."

"Sometimes." Kip and Shelley arranged themselves on their knees, resting their arms on the sill in front of them and gazing out through the open window. The cupola was dark, so they didn't have to worry about being detected from below. "After you and your mother and the Sussmans left Saturday night, my father had one of those disgusting little chats with Mark,'' Kip informed her. "You know, 'What are your intentions, young man?' That kind of stuff.''

"Oh, God, how embarrassing! I'd die if my father did that to a guy I was dating.''

"That's the trouble with you, Shelley—you're too introverted. You've got to learn how to direct your hostility outward. Diana didn't threaten to die—she threatened to kill my father.''

"What did Mark do?''

"He had the script memorized. 'I like Diana, we're good friends.' The whole thing was really gross.''

"You were eavesdropping, I take it?''

"I couldn't help myself," Kip said, feigning innocence. "I was in the kitchen with my mother, cleaning up. They were in the living room, right across the hall. Besides,'' he added with a grin, "my *mom* was eavesdropping. Every time I made a noise she'd shush me and strain to hear what Mark was saying.''

"Like mother, like son," Shelley scolded.

"Yeah? Well, here you are, spying on them.''

Shelley mirrored his smile. "I don't feel so guilty. They aren't doing anything worth spying on.''

It was true. Diana and Mark sat quietly, Mark's arm looped around Diana's shoulders, their voices drifting indistinctly through the night air. They looked nice together, Shelley thought, suffering an unexpected pang of jealousy. She wished she were a few years older, having college guys like Mark falling in love with her. "So,'' Kip broke into her thoughts. "Given how exciting this is turning out to be, would you rather go back downstairs and play backgammon?''

Shelley considered. Backgammon was okay, but what they had now—the cupola, the night, the pleasantly cool breezes and the lulling sound of Mark's and Diana's voices floating up from below... She didn't want to leave this. She wanted to stay up here with Kip, thinking about how wonderful it would be to fall in love.

Not with him, of course. Even though he was tall and well built and intensely handsome, even though this summer he smelled less often of suntan lotion and more often of aftershave lotion, and his voice had settled into a husky baritone, and his arms and legs had developed muscular contours...

Kip was her friend, and she would never risk destroying their friendship by falling in love with him. She wanted to share this tranquil evening with him, though.

"Let's just talk," she said. "Guess who I got a letter from today?"

"Who?"

"My father."

"Oh, yeah?" Kip pulled a face. "What did he have to say for himself?"

"He said he was sorry he couldn't come to the island so often this year." Sighing, she meditated for a moment. "You know, he never talked to me about his job before. He'd go to work, he'd come home, and when I asked him what he did he'd say, 'I made money.' This letter—it was like the first time he actually said anything to me about how hard he worked. He *confided* in me, Kip."

Kip continued to gaze at her, measuring her response. Gradually his lips curved in a smile. "It was nice of him to write. My dad never writes to me."

Because he always comes to the island and sees you, Shelley thought. In all the years her family had summered on Block Island, this was the first time her father had ever sent her a letter from home—and the first summer he hadn't come every weekend.

Maybe the letter didn't bode well. Maybe he'd keep writing letters and never come. Maybe she and her mother ought to go home and help him.

No. Shelley refused to let pessimism ruin what was left of her summer. She would interpret her father's letter in the most favorable light. He thought she was smart and mature, and he loved her. He wanted her forgiveness.

She forgave him and loved him back, and that was that.

Below her, Diana and Mark had stopped talking. Mark nuzzled Diana's neck, and she leaned closer into his arms.

"Do you date a lot?" Kip asked abruptly.

Shelley flinched. Given that he hadn't even noticed her string bikini, she figured he didn't pay much attention to that sort of stuff yet.

She herself was on the slow side when it came to dating—compared to some of her classmates, anyway. Rumors had run rampant through the school last April that Kim Shearson had had an abortion over spring vacation, and once in the gym locker room Carrie Billington's purse had overturned and among the scattered contents Shelley had noticed a plastic case of birth control pills. She knew some girls—girls her own age—were sexually active, while all she herself had done was a little kissing and touching and a lot of resisting and arguing, none of which she had found particularly satisfying.

Still, she had to be more advanced than Kip, who seemed to think his sister was some sort of freak for wanting to make out with Mark. He read *Playboy,* for heaven's sake. What could be more immature?

She gave herself a moment to consider possible answers to his question. "What's 'a lot'?" she equivocated.

Kip narrowed his eyes on her. "Do you date at all?"

"Sure. Do you?"

"Yeah."

It was her turn to narrow her eyes, to regard him skeptically. If he were aware of the opposite sex enough to go out on dates, he should have been aware of her bikini. Then again, maybe he *had* been aware of it, but it had looked so awful on her he'd tactfully refrained from commenting on it.

"Have you ever gone steady with anyone?" she asked.

"No," he said.

"How many girls have you dated?"

"I don't know, a few. Parties and movies and stuff. I took this girl to a school dance, that kind of thing. How about you?"

She knew he was being honest with her, which meant she would have to be honest with him. "Pretty much the same," she conceded.

"Do you make out with guys?" Kip asked in so casual a tone Shelley almost forgot to be offended.

Almost. She gave him such a hard shove he lost his balance and fell against the side wall of the cupola. "Hey," he protested, "it was just a question."

"And that was my answer," she snapped.

"I was only wondering."

"Why?"

He shrugged. "We're friends. Friends ask each other stuff. I'm sorry," he concluded, sounding less apologetic than peeved as he pulled himself back up onto his knees beside her.

Chastened, she turned away. What he'd said was true. She and her friends in Connecticut asked each other how far they let a guy go on a date, and Shelley saw nothing wrong with it. In his own way, Kip—his gender notwithstanding—was as close a friend as any of her girlfriends at home.

"Well . . . okay," she mumbled. "I've made out a couple of times."

"You don't sound real thrilled about it."

"I'm not. It wasn't much fun."

"No?" He eyed her curiously, his lips twitching into a bashful smile. "Geez. It bothers me that I might kiss some girl and then she'll say good-night and go inside and say, 'That wasn't much fun.' I mean, do girls really do that?"

Shelley's heart swelled in her chest. How rare it was for a boy to express his self-doubt so openly. The boys she knew back home all behaved cocky and arrogant and overwhelmingly sure of themselves. Whenever she wrestled with one at the end of a date, his attitude was always that there was something wrong with *her,* not that *he'd* been any part of the problem.

This was why she loved Kip—because he hid nothing from her. Because he didn't put on an act with her, or pretend to be some creepy macho dude.

"I suppose it depends on whether the guy is a good kisser or not," she said.

"How do you get to be a good kisser?"

"Practice, I guess."

As if on cue, both of them rose and peered over the windowsill. Judging by the evidence, Shelley had to conclude that Mark was a good kisser. Diana didn't seem to have any intention of breaking away from him, let alone going inside and issuing a negative critique of his performance.

"He's using his tongue," Kip noted, observing Mark's technique with scholarly intensity.

"That's gross."

"It's supposed to be exciting."

"It isn't," Shelley said.

"You've tried it, huh," Kip easily deduced.

She felt a faint flush warm her cheeks. It faded as quickly as it came, though. She had no reason to be ashamed with Kip. "Yes," she admitted. "I've been kissed that way a few times. It's kind of . . . slimy."

"Maybe the guy needed practice."

"Maybe."

"Or maybe *you* did," Kip contended.

Shelley opened her mouth to refute him, then shut it without speaking. If she could lecture him about male-female equality in literature, he could lecture her about male-female equality in kissing.

Kip continued to gaze at her, his eyes hypnotically dark behind his eyeglasses, his mouth curved in an enigmatic smile. Shelley knew what he was thinking. She was thinking the same thing.

Slowly, without having to explain or ask, Kip leaned toward her and brushed her lips with his. "Was that slimy?" he asked once he'd pulled back.

"No." She swallowed, reconsidered the wisdom of what they were doing, and decided that if she *did* need practice—and there was no question in her mind that she did—she could imagine no one she'd rather practice with than Kip Stroud. He would never laugh at her, never get pushy with her, never force the issue. All he wanted was what she wanted: practice.

"It's the tongue part that's slimy," she explained.

He nodded and glanced out the window again, observing Mark and Diana. "I think," he said, twisting back to Shelley, "we've got to tilt our heads a little—you this way and me that way. So our noses don't collide."

With a shy smile, Shelley tilted her head one way and Kip tilted his head the other. He seemed to be tilting too far—his face was practically perpendicular to hers—and she reached up to readjust the angle of his head. Her hand bumped into the side of his eyeglasses and he winced and jerked away. "Ow! You could break my nose doing that," he groaned.

"Well, take them off then, if they're so dangerous."

He did, setting them carefully in the far corner of the cupola so they wouldn't get crushed. Shelley rarely saw him without his eyeglasses. The bridge of his nose was narrower than she'd expected, with a slight bump in it. It was a really handsome nose. His eyes were handsome, too, larger and more thickly lashed than she'd realized.

He tilted his head again, this time only a few degrees, and covered her mouth with his. His lips were warm and dry. He moved them. She moved hers, too.

"I'm going to try my tongue," he whispered, causing her to giggle from the tickly sensation of his breath against her nose. "Let me know if it's slimy."

"I will," she promised, bracing herself for this new phase by taking a deep breath and tightening her hand on the molding of the windowsill.

His tongue touched her lips and she reflexively pressed them shut.

"Shelley—come on! You've got to help me out a little."

Shelley checked the action below on the veranda. There was no question that Diana was helping Mark out a great deal. "Okay," she mumbled apprehensively, settling down on her haunches and tilting her head again. "Why don't we just, like, touch tongues and see what happens?"

"Okay." He leaned toward her.

"You haven't got a cold or anything, do you?"

"No."

"Because I don't want to get sick from you."

"I don't have a cold," he swore, then closed in on her before she could stall any longer. Tilting his head just a fraction, he molded his mouth to hers.

She forced herself not to react as his tongue slid between her lips. She refused to shrink back as he probed her teeth. And then she acknowledged that it was all right to react, because there was nothing slimy about this at all. It felt— well, strange, but really not bad.

She opened her mouth and rubbed his tongue with the tip of hers. Then they separated and let out their breaths.

"Well?"

"It wasn't gross," she said.

Far from being flattered, he looked disturbed. "Well, like—on a scale of one to ten, how was it?"

"I don't know." She sighed, trying to sort her thoughts. "It wasn't bad, Kip. Maybe we're supposed to do it for a longer time."

"I think you're right." Kip slid his arm around her shoulders, urged her toward him, and fused his mouth with hers again, exploring her lips and then her teeth with his tongue until she opened fully for him.

Once his tongue found hers he moved it from side to side. That made her want to laugh. She started to shake her head, but he stayed where he was, denying her the opportunity to break away. His arm held her close to him, and his fingers coiled through her hair to the nape of her neck, keeping her head at the proper angle. It felt surprisingly pleasant to be caressed on her neck that way.

After a moment the urge to laugh faded and she relaxed in the curve of his arm. He moved his tongue again, this time deep into her mouth and out with a stroking motion that didn't make her want to laugh at all. She felt peculiar all of a sudden, unreasonably warm, as if her heart was pumping blood too rapidly through her body.

He thrust his tongue deep again, and her pulse raced even faster, causing her flesh to tingle with heat. For a fearful moment she couldn't breathe. Her mind went blank, her muscles grew tense. Her breasts felt almost uncomfortably tender, and a fiery sensation gathered between her legs.

"Oh, God," she moaned, twisting away and gulping in a frantic breath of the cool night air.

Kip instinctively tightened his arms around her, drawing her against him. She rested her head on his shoulder and let out a shaky sigh.

"How was that?" he whispered, sounding more than a little breathless himself.

"I don't know," she mumbled. "Okay, I guess." She reconsidered and decided she owed Kip her total honesty. "It was scary, Kip. It felt a little too good, maybe."

"Yeah?" She could almost feel his smile. "On a scale of one to ten—"

"Shut up."

He toyed with her hair again, twirling his fingers through the soft waves in a soothing pattern. His chest rose and fell against her as his breathing slowed. She took comfort in the rhythm, in the solid feel of him. This was Kip. She was safe. Everything was all right.

Gradually her pulse returned to normal and the muscles in her thighs unclenched. It dawned on her that she was as much on the spot as he was. "How about me?" she asked timidly. "Did I do okay?"

"Oh, I think you need more practice," Kip declared in a deliberately pompous tone. She poked him in the ribs and he grunted and slapped her hand away.

"I'm being serious, Kip. Tell me the truth. Was I awful?"

"No, you weren't awful."

"Well... how 'not awful' was I?"

"On a scale of one to ten?"

She considered poking him again, but decided not to. Maybe it was better if they joked about this. If she didn't laugh, she'd dwell on that strange, tantalizing heat that had infused her breasts and hips. "Okay. What's my score?"

"Maybe an eight," he said.

Eight! What an insult! She pushed as far away from him as she could get in the cramped space, and glowered furiously at him. "If I were going to grade you, I would have given you a ten," she said, her voice hushed but bristling with indignation. "And all you can give me is an *eight*?"

"Hey, I'm a tough grader. Like Mr. Goober."

"You're a goob, all right."

His dimpled grin assuaged her anger slightly. "Come on, Shelley, we're both beginners here. If you'd given me a ten I would've called it grade inflation."

"You didn't think it was that good?"

"I thought it was terrific," he said, his eyes solemn despite his smile. "I thought it was better than any kiss I've ever had before."

She eyed him suspiciously, but he looked so earnest she had to believe him. "Then what did I lose two points for?" she asked.

He shifted his legs, bumping hers. She was acutely aware of their lightly haired texture against her smooth skin. After extensive reflection, he said, "You lost two points because you pulled away."

"I was running out of breath."

He shook his head. "I've seen you swim under water for a long, long time before you have to come up for air."

She traced the curves of the sill molding and stared out at the sky, at the nearly full moon blurred behind a layer of fog. "I told you, I was scared," she mumbled, willing to tell him the truth as long as she didn't have to look at him when she did so.

He didn't speak for a while. A breeze rustled through the leaves of the red maple that stood just south of the house. A cricket roiled the air with its persistent chirp. Kip was so still, so silent, that Shelley jumped when she suddenly felt his hand on hers, folding tightly around it. "You know I'd never do anything bad to you," he murmured.

More than before, she couldn't bear to look at him. "I know," she said in a tiny voice.

"I'd never admit to another girl what an amateur I am," he continued, his voice soft and sincere. "But with you . . . Well, you know me. I can't pull a fast one on you. I'm not going to go crazy with you. You know that."

"I know that," she agreed. "That's not why I was scared."

He gave her hand a slight tug, forcing her to look at him. How much did she have to say? How much did he need to know?

Only the truth. "I told you—" she cleared her throat "—it felt too good. I was afraid if I didn't stop right then . . ."

"What?" he coaxed her.

"I don't know. Something might have happened."

"Don't you trust me?"

It's me I don't trust, she almost blurted out. Her cheeks felt warm, her extremities chilly. Closing her eyes, she recalled the sensation of his tongue filling her mouth, retreating and then filling it again in that slow, relentless rhythm...and she experienced the same frightening rush of heat, gathering in two points at her breasts before surging down through her body to her hips, to her womb. She felt heat and dampness and an aching hunger for something. Something more. Something she'd never wanted before. Something she knew instinctively she shouldn't want.

Mortified by the raw emotions rampaging through her, she broke from Kip and fumbled with the trapdoor latch. Before he could stop her, she raced down the ladder to the attic, down again to the small bedroom on the second floor and through the hallway to the bathroom. She locked herself inside.

Gripping the edges of the porcelain pedestal sink, she forced herself to look into the oval mirror above it. She looked feverish, her hair tousled, her eyes watering with tears.

This was too humiliating. Did Kip understand what had happened to her? Did he know about the throbbing, the warmth and dampness, the quivering in her flesh and the inexplicable longing she'd felt when he'd held her against his chest? Did he comprehend what his kiss had done to her? Would he use his knowledge against her?

Would their friendship ever be the same again? Would *she* ever be the same?

She doused her face with cold water, dried it off on one of the towels hanging on a towel ring to the right of the sink, doused her face again and dried it. Digging a comb from the back pocket of her cutoffs, she did her best to straighten out her hair. Then she took a few deep breaths, prayed that Kip wouldn't be waiting for her on the other side of the door, and opened it.

Of course he was waiting—not exactly on the other side of the door but halfway down the hall. He leaned against the railing of the first-floor stairway, looking relatively calm, although his dark eyes glowed with concern. "Hi," he said.

She lowered her gaze to the rug beneath her feet. "Hi."

"Are we still friends?"

She took another breath and realized that her lungs felt better. Whatever Kip did or didn't understand about what had happened to her up in the cupola, he clearly understood her biggest fear—that because of what had happened they couldn't be pals anymore.

But if being pals meant as much to Kip as it did to her, they would survive this. They would be fine.

"Yes," she said, lifting her eyes to him and smiling shyly. "We're still friends."

Relief crashed over his face like a breaking wave. He pushed away from the railing, strode down the hall to her and slung a brotherly, wonderfully unthreatening arm around her shoulders. "Let's get some lemonade," he said. "How about it?"

"Sounds good," she said.

He bowed and kissed the crown of her head. It was a friendly kiss, a kiss that comforted her as much as his earlier kiss had flustered her. It was the kind of kiss that reminded her of what friendship and Kip and the summer's magic were really all about.

With a quiet smile, she slipped her hand into his and walked with him down the stairs.

Chapter Four

That night she didn't dream about Bruce Springsteen, or even Danny Clayburn. She dreamed about Kip.

Maybe it wasn't a dream. She couldn't tell whether she was asleep or awake or somewhere in between. But her eyes remained closed, her mind floating. The air in her bedroom was warm and humid, and the top sheet caressed her body like hands.

Kip's hands.

In her dream he kissed her. His lips danced over hers, and his tongue found hers, and she felt all those dangerous sensations again. Her breasts seemed heavy and overly sensitive, the cotton of her nightgown chafing her swollen nipples, and because this was a dream she could imagine that not her nightgown but Kip was touching her, stroking her skin. She could imagine his long, patrician fingers, light and agile, playing across her flesh, sliding from her breasts lower, to her belly and lower yet, down where she'd never let a boy touch her before.

She shouldn't think these things, but she couldn't seem to stop. What had frightened her in the cupola excited her when she was alone in the sagging single bed, just her and her fantasies of Kip doing things that made her skin burn and her flesh tremble, her hips tense and her breath grow short.

Just her and Kip, exploring each other in her sleep-drugged mind. Here in the darkness of her room beneath the eaves, Shelley was beginning to figure it out.

IT WAS RAINING when she woke up. She'd slept past nine o'clock, but when she dragged herself out of bed she felt tired and achy, as if she'd run a marathon overnight. She got dressed, broke a tooth on her comb trying to unravel the snarls in her hair, and stumbled down the stairs, her head throbbing and her vision blurred.

The bright kitchen light hurt her eyes. Her mother was preparing a shopping list, looking offensively energetic in her denim jumper and Bass sandals. "What kind of cereal do you want me to buy?" she asked. "We're almost out of Cheerios."

The thought of cereal—of any food at all—made Shelley queasy. "I don't care," she said, moving directly to the coffeemaker and filling a mug with hot coffee.

Her mother eyed her with mild disapproval. "You shouldn't have stayed so late at Kip's last night."

Shelley checked herself before embarking on a vehement defense of her virtue. *Nothing* had happened with Kip—and yet everything had happened with him in her mind, in the secret confines of her bed. It was Kip's fault that she was so poorly rested, even if he hadn't actually done anything to her.

"I was home by eleven," she said, recalling not what she'd dreamed but what had happened. "We were playing backgammon and I lost track of time. Anyway, eleven isn't so late."

Her mother shrugged. "It's vacation. I don't care if you sleep late. I just don't want you overstaying your welcome at the Strouds'."

On cue, Shelley heard a tap on the screen door, followed by Kip's voice. "Hello?"

Her mother rolled her eyes. "You two are inseparable," she said with a tolerant chuckle as she left the kitchen to unlatch the door and let him in.

Shelley was grateful to have a moment alone. Simply hearing her mother describe her and Kip as "inseparable" reawakened her memory of Kip's kiss, his mouth inseparable from hers, and then her dreamy mental elaborations on that kiss. Hearing the approach of footsteps, she hid her face behind her mug and took a sip of coffee.

"'Morning," Kip greeted her. His yellow slicker glistened with moisture. He took it off and draped it on the back of a chair.

Shelley peered up at him over the rim of the mug. Despite the slicker's hood, his hair was damp and his eyeglasses were mottled with raindrops. He pulled them off and dried them on the hem of his T-shirt. Shelley remembered how he'd taken them off last night before kissing her. She hastily averted her gaze so she wouldn't have to see the pinpoints of light sparkling in his dark brown irises, the enviable thickness of his lashes and the intriguing bump in his nose.

It wasn't fair that he could look so good so early. She knew she herself must look wretched. At her best she was barely passable; right now, when she was exhausted and in the throes of a sublime headache—to say nothing of totally embarrassed, not only by what she'd felt in Kip's arms but by what she'd felt long afterward in her own bed—she was hardly at her best.

She braced herself for his inevitable ribbing about her ghastly appearance. All he said, however, was, "Can I help myself to some of that coffee? It smells great."

"Go right ahead," Shelley's mother answered for her. "I'm on my way out. If you don't have a preference, Shelley, I'm going to buy shredded wheat."

"I *do* have a preference," Shelley said quickly. "I hate shredded wheat."

"It's good for you," her mother pointed out. "It doesn't have any sugar."

"It doesn't have any taste," Shelley countered.

"All right, I'll get Cheerios," said her mother, lifting her purse from the counter and starting toward the door. "If you go out, leave me a note."

Shelley nodded. She and Kip said goodbye, then listened to her mother's retreating footsteps. The screen door closed with a whoosh and a thump.

Kip turned a chair around and straddled it backward, setting his mug on the table. He leaned his folded arms on the back of the chair and stared across the table at Shelley. She focused on the swirls of steam rising from her mug.

"It isn't much of a beach day," he remarked.

She sighed. Sooner or later he was likely to say something about last night. *She* certainly wasn't going to raise the subject, but if he intended to, she'd rather he did it now, so they could get the conversation over with as quickly as possible.

"I was thinking," he went on, "we could go to the library and you could find me some girl coming-of-age books to read."

Shelley glanced up. Her eyes met his, and she saw in their beautiful brown depths only friendship. Nothing more complicated than that. "Okay," she said with a relieved smile.

Ten minutes later, the coffee mugs rinsed and her rain jacket snapped on, she left the house with Kip. Biking in the rain was sloppy, but they had no alternative. They rode slowly, trying to avoid the puddles and, when that was impossible, lifting their feet off the pedals so the muddy water wouldn't splash up against their legs.

The library was located in Old Harbor. Shelley wasn't surprised to see the shop-lined sidewalks packed with browsers and strollers. On rainy days there wasn't much for the tourists to do besides shop.

She and Kip parked their bikes in the rack outside the library and entered. Shelley adored libraries, and although the Island Free Library was much smaller than the library at home in Westport, Shelley liked it for the simple reason that she was allowed to use it. Tourists didn't have borrowing privileges on the island, but because they paid property taxes the owners of summer homes did. Whenever she used the Island Free Library she felt like a native, a genuine citizen of Block Island.

Not bothering with the card catalogue, she headed straight for the fiction shelves, Kip at her heels. "Don't forget, it's vacation," he whispered. "I don't want to read anything boring."

"These are good books," Shelley assured him, scanning the racks in search of the *L*'s. "Here, Harper Lee, *To Kill a Mockingbird*. You're going to love this." She handed him the novel, then continued to scour the shelves, moving into the *M*'s. "Oh, this is a great book. *The Member of the Wedding,* Carson McCullers."

"What's it about?" Kip asked as he took the book from her.

"A girl coming of age," Shelley told him.

"Great," he grunted, though he was smiling.

"And here—" she handed him a third book "—*The Bell Jar* by Sylvia Plath. It's about—"

"A girl coming of age," he completed.

"A girl having a nervous breakdown," Shelley corrected him, then grinned. "Which is probably the same thing."

Kip shared her smile. Then he touched his hand to her elbow and directed her down the aisle. "Come on, I want to choose a book for you."

He had never taken her arm like that before. It was a curiously chivalrous gesture, not exactly romantic but not quite friendly, either. It was...protective. Possessive. She liked it.

He stopped in the *H*'s. "Here," he said, pulling *The Sun Also Rises* from a shelf. "There's a good, manly book for you."

"I've read it already," she told him.

"Okay. How about…" He scanned the shelves and pulled out Hesse's *Steppenwolf*.

"I've read it."

"Robert Heinlein, *Stranger in a Strange Land*."

"I've read it," she said.

He scowled. "Is there anything you *haven't* read?"

"Not in the *H*'s."

He glared at her, then dissolved in quiet laughter. "I bet you're going to be an English teacher when you grow up."

"I'd love to be an English teacher," she admitted. "Or better yet, a professor of literature at some college. I'd love to get paid to read novels and talk about them."

"I can just imagine the reading lists you'd come up with," Kip muttered, although his smile didn't flag. "All books by women, right? All books about girls coming of age."

"Why not?" She skimmed the shelves in search of another book for Kip.

"No more books for me," he halted her. "These things have to be returned in two weeks—I'll be lucky if I can finish three by then. Here." He pulled a slender volume from a shelf and presented it to her. "Kafka. If you want to become a literature professor, you've got to get into this stuff."

She tilted her head to read the spine. "Metamorphosis."

"It's about a man who turns into a bug."

"Yuck!"

"*Real* macho stuff," he joked.

"All right," she said, "I'll read it." She didn't know whether he was pulling her leg about the book's subject matter. She wasn't going to let Kip think he could gross her out, though.

They carried their books to the checkout desk, where they both presented their cards to the librarian. She smiled and took Kip's pile first. "Samuel," she said, reading the name on Kip's card before she inserted it into the dating machine.

Kip wrinkled his nose. His legal name was Samuel Brockett Stroud III, but nobody ever called him Samuel—or even Sam—except when he was in trouble and his mother would intone, "Sam-you-well, I'd like to talk to you," in a foreboding voice. His grandfather had been called Samuel and his father—Samuel Brockett Stroud II—was called Brock. According to Kip, credit for his nickname went to Diana. When he was born people had referred to him as a "chip off the old block," but three-year-old Diana had misunderstood half of it and mispronounced the rest and called him a "Kip off the old Brock."

Once their books had been checked out, Shelley and Kip left the library. The rain had lightened to a drizzle, but they both rode their bikes one-handed so they could use their left hands to hold their books under the flaps of their raincoats. They steered straight for Kip's house.

As soon as they'd shed their wet outerwear and shoes, they ascended to the cupola. Kip adjusted the windows so no rain would come in, and there, in the cramped, gloomily lit room, they read. They occupied diagonal corners, their legs stretched out between them. Whenever one of them shifted, their knees touched.

The first time Kip's knee bumped Shelley's she flinched and glanced up. Kip was immersed in the opening chapter of *To Kill a Mockingbird,* poring intently over the page, his brow furrowed in concentration. He appeared unaware that their legs had brushed.

It took Shelley only a second to recover from the contact. This wasn't last night; they weren't kissing, or practicing kissing, or grading each other's performance, or any of it. They were merely friends, reading away a rainy morning.

With a contented sigh that was almost a laugh, Shelley lowered her eyes back to the first page of *Metamorphosis*, which, she had discovered with some horror, truly was about a man who turned into a bug. Nothing—neither squeamishness nor skittishness—could persuade her to leave the cupola right now. Nothing—not even the possibility that her legs and Kip's were going to bang each other black and blue in the crowded space—could convince her that there was anything she'd rather be doing right now.

Kissing Kip had been a revelation. Reading with him as the rain drummed soothingly on the roof above them and his legs stretched alongside hers, warm and strong, was just as gratifying.

With another sigh, she relaxed into the corner and read about how Gregor Samsa, a normal human being, woke up one morning and found himself trapped inside the body of a cockroach.

SHE WAS HAVING THEM every night, now—sensual dreams, erotic dreams. Dreams of Kip.

One night she dreamed they were dancing. They were at a school dance, one of those dorky Friday night events in the gymnasium, with tacky crepe paper streamers dangling from the basketball hoops and a half dozen teachers standing around the perimeter of the gym, looking bored as they chaperoned the students. In the dream Kip materialized out of a crowd of boys. He was dressed in his Harvard T-shirt, jeans and mocs—she'd never seen him in anything other than summer apparel, and she couldn't picture him in a jacket and tie. She was wearing the forest-green wraparound dress she'd bought at Ann Taylor last Christmas, and the high-heel black sandals that always killed her ankles—except, of course, in the dream her ankles felt wonderful—and the gold choker her father had given her for her birthday. Kip walked directly to her and suddenly they were drifting across the dance floor, not really dancing so much as hugging, holding each other. The flared skirt of her dress swirled around her knees, and Kip's arms tightened around her waist, and his eyeglasses vanished as he bowed to kiss her....

In another dream they were lying on a blanket at their favorite secluded beach near Dorie's Cove. Shelley had on her string bikini, and as Kip kissed her he plucked open the bows that held the swimsuit together. She dreamed of him touching her breasts—not groping and mauling her, the way the guys who had tried to touch her back in "America" would do it, but gently, sweetly, so that it didn't seem like an assault or an act of conquest, but rather like something he was doing only to please her.

She woke up from that dream gasping and overheated, so embarrassed she almost refused to see Kip the next day. But it was a gloriously sunny Friday morning, and she knew her father wasn't coming that weekend. If she vetoed Kip's suggestion that they go to the beach she would wind up hanging out at the cottage with her mother, being depressed.

So she biked down to the beach near Dorie's Cove with Kip. She wore one of her one-piece suits, however, and when she went into the water with him she gave him a stern look and said, "Please don't dunk me today."

He didn't ask any questions. He didn't grill her on her prickly disposition or inquire as to whether she had her period. All he said was "Okay."

They swam together, not racing, not splashing, just swimming, floating, enjoying the water until she stepped on a broken shell. Its sharp edge sliced open her toe, and she let out a scream.

Kip gathered her into his arms, carried her out of the water, laid her down on the towel and swabbed her bleeding toe with a towel. "I haven't got any bandages," he said, pressing the towel tightly against the cut. "I'll ride up to the house and get a first-aid kit."

Pushing herself up into a sitting position, she eased the towel away and examined her wound. It was a small cut, very clean. "Don't bother," she said. "It'll clot soon."

Instead of returning to the water, Kip remained on the blanket beside her. He donned his sunglasses, rolled onto his back, and talked about how good he considered *To Kill a Mockingbird*. "I'd like to see the movie, now that I've read the book."

"It's a great flick. Gregory Peck starred in it. And you know who had played Boo Radley? Robert Duvall."

"No kidding?" Kip digested that fact, then leaned across the blanket and pulled the towel away from her toe. "Still bleeding," he reported.

"Just slightly. I'll live."

Lying back down, he chuckled. "You know what I like about you, Shell? You're not a prima donna."

"As compared to...?"

"Oh, Diana, for instance." He rolled onto his side and propped his head up with his hand. "You wouldn't believe the fight she had with Mark last night. We're talking radioactive. She used words I didn't think she knew."

"What did they fight about?" Shelley asked.

"Mark told her he couldn't afford to take her out for dinner at Harborside Inn. Diana said if he really loved her he'd take her out to fancy restaurants sometimes, instead of always to Aldo's for pizza. He works there, so I think he gets a discount."

"Well... after a while a person could get sick of pizza," Shelley pointed out, trying to be fair.

"The issue isn't cuisine. It's how much money Mark's spending on her. She thinks he's not spending enough. She can be a real shrew sometimes."

Shelley lifted the towel away from her toe. The gash had stopped oozing and was beginning to scab. Tossing the towel aside, she stretched out next to Kip. She was glad they never fought about stuff like that.

If they were dating, maybe they would. Once you started dating, you had to obey all sorts of unwritten rules and contracts: if the guy spent X amount of money on you, you had to let him go a certain distance sexually. And vice versa—if you let a guy go a certain distance, he was obligated to spend X amount of money on you.

She wondered why it had to be that way. Feminists were always saying it was all right for girls to ask guys out and pay for the date—and sure, that sounded great in theory. But if the girl spent all that money, was she supposed to paw the guy afterward? What if she didn't want to paw the guy?

It was so much simpler being friends. Sometimes Kip paid for things and sometimes Shelley did, and they were equals. When Kip touched her, he touched her as a friend. As far as Shelley's desires... She kept them to herself and saved them for her dreams, where they wouldn't get her into trouble.

"Your father's not coming this weekend, is he," Kip remarked.

Shelley sighed. Her toe had stopped stinging and started throbbing. She rolled onto her stomach and rested her chin on her folded arms. "Nope."

"If you'd like to spend Saturday at my house—"

"Thanks, but no." While she was disappointed by her father's inability to come to the island, she was no longer devastated by it.

"Really, it's no problem," Kip insisted. "I don't think we've got any plans—although I'm sure my father will think of some horrible chore for me, like painting the porch railings or something."

"And you want me there to help you," Shelley joked.

"Of course not. I'm just saying—"

"I'll be fine this weekend," Shelley told him. "I don't want to impose on your family."

"I wasn't thinking about my family," Kip said, his light tone failing to disguise the seriousness of his words. "I was thinking about me. *I'd* like you to come."

She twisted her head to look at him. He was staring at her; she could feel the force of his gaze right through the dark lenses of his sunglasses. For a charged moment she thought he was going to kiss her.

What he did was reach out and tuck a damp strand of her hair behind her ear. It was something he'd done a million times before, but this time... this time his touch was different. This time it seemed very personal.

"Maybe," she murmured. "Maybe I could stop by for a little while."

He smiled. "Good."

That night the dream was about his hand on her cheek, lifting a lock of her hair and brushing it behind her ear. She dreamed of him molding his palm to the back of her head and pulling her toward him on the blanket, taking her by the shoulders and pulling her... pulling her...

Her eyes flew open. In the vague twilight that filtered through her curtains she made out the shadowy figure of her mother looming over her, pulling her into a sitting position. "Wake up," her mother demanded. "Wake up, Shelley."

"What?" Shelley mumbled, furious with her mother for having interrupted such a delicious dream.

"You have to wake up."

She considered reminding her mother of what she'd said the other day—that it was vacation and Shelley could sleep late if she wanted to—but she was too groggy to string together so many words. "Why?" was all she could manage.

Her mother let go of her shoulders and turned away. Slowly, much too slowly, Shelley realized that something was wrong.

"Mom?"

Her mother walked to the door and reached into the hallway. When she turned back she was holding a suitcase. "We're going home," she said.

Shelley stared. Her eyes focused on the shadowy shape of her mother, on the large tweed suitcase. The murky light seeping through her curtains began to intensify, washing over her mother's face. Shelley noticed that her mother's hair was uncharacteristically messy, her lips pinched, her cheeks wet.

"Mom?"

"Just do as I say."

"But—"

"Don't ask," her mother said rapidly. "I don't know what the hell is going on. I got a phone call. There's trouble at home. We've got to go."

"Is it Dad?"

"Yes. Pack your stuff—as much as you can, everything you can fit in. And get dressed. I'll be in to help you in a while."

Dazed, Shelley remained on the bed for several minutes after her mother departed. They had to go. There was trouble at home, trouble with Dad.

Oh, God. This was it. Life as she knew it was about to end.

She picked up her watch from the night table, tilted its face until the weak light from the window fell upon it, and squinted at the numerals: 5:38. She shivered uncontrollably, her teeth chattering. Her father was in trouble. He was leaving the family. He was sick. He had a lover. He'd hurt himself.

I don't know what the hell is going on. Don't ask.

Shelley experienced a brutal insight into what the hero of *Metamorphosis* must have felt like when he woke up and found out he'd turned into a cockroach. Shelley might as well have turned into an insect herself. Her universe had transformed. Nothing would ever be the same again. She didn't know how she knew this, but she knew.

She had to phone Kip. She had to see him.

With a sudden burst of energy, she shoved back the top sheet and sprang out of bed. Without bothering to turn on the light, she yanked off her nightgown and rummaged in her dresser for something to wear: long pants, because the early mornings on the island could be chilly, and her Yale shirt. She felt through the drawer and heard the rustle of paper. Between two shirts she located the letter her father had written. She pulled it out, slid the stationery from the envelope and unfolded it. Disjointed words and phrases leaped out at her: "I think you can handle it... I know you're mad at me... You're a smart, mature young lady... I hope you can find it in your heart to forgive me... I love you, Shelley."

She stifled the urge to cry. If Kip were with her she could fall apart, but he wasn't.

She had to talk to him.

She dressed quickly, then left her bedroom for her parents room across the hall. "I need to make a call," she said, ignoring the open suitcases on her mother's bed, the piles of clothing, linens and toiletries scattered about.

"Don't be silly. It's too early to call anyone."

"I've got to talk to Kip."

"Absolutely not," her mother said, grabbing her wrist for emphasis. "His whole family is sleeping right now, Shelley. You can't call people at this hour."

"Someone called you."

"Dad called me. He's my husband. It's different."

"I want to talk to Kip!"

"Not now," her mother asserted gruffly, forcing her back toward the door. "Go pack. Maybe there'll be time to call him later." Her mother didn't release her arm until she was in the hall.

Shelley took a deep breath. Her wrist hurt. Her toe hurt where she'd cut it yesterday. Her head hurt, her heart, her soul.

She packed chaotically, tossing articles into the suitcase in no particular order. Her shorts. Her box of earrings. Her beach towel. Her suntan lotion. Her dresses. Her pillowcase. Her mascara. Her sandals—and then she pulled them out and slipped them onto her feet. Her string bikini. Her barrettes. The letter from her father.

She pulled that out, too, and stuffed it into her purse.

There was still plenty of room in the suitcase. She threw in blouses, slacks, her raincoat, her paperbacks. She set aside the Kafka book from the library. "Mom?" she called into the other room. "What about my library book?"

"Forget it."

"I can't forget it. They'll fine me if I don't return it on time."

"Shelley." Her mother sounded so tense, so frantic, Shelley felt guilty for bothering her about something as trivial as a library book. "We'll stick it in the book drop on our way to the ferry," her mother said.

Shelley folded her sheets, tossed them into the suitcase and shuddered. Seeing the naked mattress forced her to acknowledge that she was truly leaving the island, that this wasn't just a jaunt to "America," that she might not be coming back.

She concentrated on the mechanics of packing to prevent herself from thinking about the implications of it. Her hand mirror. Her framed seashell collection. Her wraparound Indian-print skirt. The nail enamel she'd never used because her nails never grew long enough to polish. Her address book. Her sweatshirts. The hinged velvet box containing her gold choker...

She lifted the box back out of the suitcase, opened it, removed the necklace and fastened it around her throat.

Glimpsing her reflection in the mirror, she smothered another sob. She didn't want to leave. She wanted everything to stay the same—even if her father didn't come to the island every weekend. She wanted her life the way it had been before this morning. She wanted to go back to yesterday, to the day she'd spent on the beach with Kip, when he'd pressed the towel against her injured toe, when he'd curled a lock of her hair behind her ear.

It was nearly six o'clock. She could call him now.

Her mother had left the master bedroom, and Shelley noticed that the upstairs telephone had already been unplugged and packed. She raced down the stairs and found her mother in the kitchen, yanking canned foods and utensils out of the cabinets and throwing them willy-nilly into cartons.

"I'm calling Kip," Shelley said, moving to the wall phone.

"You can call him later. There's too much to do right now. See those cartons? They're full. Fold down the flaps and carry them out to the car, okay?"

"You packed the coffee-maker," Shelley noticed with a dismay that seemed wildly out of proportion. "I wanted a cup."

"I'll buy you some coffee in Old Harbor if we've got time before the first ferry. Please start loading the cartons."

Shelley hoisted one of the cartons off the table and staggered outside with it. The air in the front yard was dense with mist, the grass slick with dew. Pale pink blades of light cut through the trees from the east, heralding the dawn of a perfect beach day.

No. No day would ever be perfect again. Not after this.

Setting the heavy carton down in the back of her mother's Volvo wagon, Shelley pressed her fisted hands to her eyes. She didn't want to see a gorgeous sunrise. She didn't want to think about the islanders asleep in their beds as the morning fog burned away. Everyone else in the world would be awakening into a day filled with promise. Everyone else but Shelley and her parents.

For the next twenty minutes she lugged cartons back and forth from the kitchen to the car. She demanded that her mother leave room for her bicycle, and they spent ten more minutes shifting the cartons around to open a narrow space for the bike. Then they went back upstairs for their suitcases. Her mother tossed some extra linens into Shelley's suitcase, and they stormed through the bathroom like looters on a spree, grabbing everything that wasn't nailed down.

By seven-fifteen, the car was packed. Shelley wondered whether her mother was going to close the house completely, the way she usually did on Labor Day, draping cloths over the furniture and latching the shutters against the island's winter storms. She didn't do more than lock the front and back doors, and Shelley wished she could interpret that to mean they would be coming back before the end of the summer.

But she couldn't convince herself.

They drove down the quiet, winding lane toward Old Harbor. At Shelley's insistence her mother veered in at the library driveway so Shelley could drop her book into the overnight slot, and then they traveled the final blocks to the ferry dock.

Her mother purchased tickets, paid the transport fee for the car and handed the ignition key to one of the ferry workers. She and Shelley stood aside as he turned the car around and backed it onto the ferry. Viewing the mass of cartons and bags and her bike crammed inside the car caused Shelley's eyes to fill.

She wanted to scream, curse, hit things, demand that someone prove to her that this was just a creepy nightmare, her punishment for having enjoyed so many sinfully passionate dreams during the last several nights.

But she was awake. This was real. And when she turned, teary-eyed, to her mother, she saw that her mother had cupped her hands to her face and was crying.

"It's going to be all right," Shelley said, her voice sounding distant and totally unpersuasive to herself.

"Of course it is," her mother responded, sounding just as false.

Shelley glanced at the pay phone near the ferry office. Maybe she could call Kip now.

But she couldn't leave her mother. The woman was falling apart, weeping shamelessly, right there in front of the ferry workers and the other passengers standing in line to board the boat.

"You're growing up," her father had written to Shelley. And suddenly she felt terribly old.

She put her arm around her mother's quaking shoulders. Pulling the ferry tickets from her mother's clenched hand, Shelley handed them to the ticket-taker and led her mother across the paved dock to the boat. She guided her mother upstairs to the passenger deck and they took seats on a bench. Her mother hid her face against Shelley's shoulder and sobbed.

Shelley remained composed. Someone had to be an adult, and clearly it wasn't going to be her mother. *You're growing up,* she told herself. *You're coming of age.*

Sunlight spread across the surface of the water in the harbor, splintering on the tips of the waves. Below her the ferry's engine rumbled and churned. The boat slid slowly, inexorably out of its slip, and the island receded, retreated, vanished from sight.

Her mother fell still, her head heavy on Shelley's shoulder. Shelley continued to stare at the water, ignoring the mews of the sea gulls circling overhead, the chatter of passengers sharing the bench with them, the lulling motions of the ferry as it moved through the calm waters of the sound, the shouted greetings of the crew of a trawler passing them in its journey south.

She simply stared, seeing nothing, refusing to think about the fate that awaited her on the mainland. Except for one thing: she would call Kip. The minute they got home, the very instant they entered the house, she would call him.

That was the only part of her future she cared about, the only part she could look forward to, the only part still within her control. She promised herself that she would call him. She clung to that promise, embraced it, depended on it to keep her sane and steady through the long trip home.

It was a promise she would not keep.

Part Two
Kip

Chapter Five

Kip leaned against the railing, watching the slate-gray water churn and foam below him as the ferry cut across the wind-whipped sound to the island. The sky was the same malevolent gray color as the sea, the clouds low and oppressive. Although it was only the second week in September, the wind was wintry, slicing through his sweater and shirt and sending a chill deep into him.

He wondered when he had last closed his eyes.

He supposed he must have blinked once in a while during the past thirteen months. If he hadn't he would have gone blind. Probably he closed his eyes while he slept, too, although sleep had been his nemesis for a long time. He fought it, resisted it, wrestled with it; only after a furious nightly battle did he surrender to it, at which point his eyelids slid shut and he saw Amanda.

She was permanently imprinted on the insides of his lids, permanently branded into the blackest part of his soul. If he focused only on what existed outside himself, on the cold metal railing around which his hands were curled, on the persistent rocking of the ferry, on the thrumming of the engine, the uniform gray of water and sky, the gulls hovering and swooping for fish just a few feet from the boat, he could fend her off. For a while, at least.

When he closed his eyes and saw her, she invariably appeared in one of three incarnations. In the first she was alive and beautiful, her skin creamy, her light brown eyes shining with laughter, her Cupid's-bow lips curving naturally into a smile. Her cheekbones were delicate, angling up and outward, and her hair was a luscious cascade of black curls. She was waving at him, stepping into the crosswalk to join him in Union Square, where he had been waiting for her that warm evening.

It agonized him to see her so dynamic and spirited and happy. The second vision was worse, however. In it she was lying on Geary Street, her head resting against the curb, her body extended into the road.

The worst vision was the third one, in which she stood in the middle of the crosswalk, frozen in place as she gaped at the Toyota Supra racing heedlessly down Geary Street, not slowing for the red light. Not stopping for the twenty-six-year-old woman in the tailored white suit and green shell blouse, the nylons and black pumps, the earrings Kip had given her for Christmas and the ring he had given her when he'd given her his heart. Not stopping for the woman with the wild black curls.

If only she had been heedless, as well, perhaps Kip might have been able to endure it. If only she hadn't known, in that split second before the bumper of the car lifted her off her feet, flung her into the air like a rag doll and sent her flying halfway down the block, where she landed against the curb, suddenly motionless, suddenly silent... If only she hadn't known that what she was witnessing when she saw the Toyota was her own death bearing down on her...

The cold wind stung his face, but he resolutely kept his eyes open. If he didn't, he might see her the third way, the way she'd looked an instant before the impact, when she'd realized what was about to happen to her.

Coming to the island was a stupid idea. He should have thought it through, but he'd been so numb for so long he'd forgotten how to think rationally. Now here he was, an hour out of Pt. Judith, without a clue as to why he'd agreed to come or what the hell he would do when he arrived or how in God's name spending some time on the island was going to change anything in his crazy, meaningless life.

When his mother had flown out to San Francisco four months ago and realized what a zombie he'd become, she'd packed him up and brought him back to Boston. He hadn't had the will to argue with her, so he'd let her take charge of his life. He could be a zombie as easily in his parents' house in Chestnut Hill as he could in his own San Francisco co-op.

His father had arranged a job for him with an associate in Boston, and that was fine, too. One thing Kip could do was work. In the months preceding his move back east he had been putting in ten and twelve hour days at his office in the financial district, functioning with astonishing efficiency and earning his company loads of money. He had been meeting with clients and advising them on investment strategies, running their figures through his computer, devising new financial plans for them and taking them out for expensive lunches at elegant restaurants, although he couldn't recall tasting anything he'd eaten during those gourmet luncheons. He had been expert at matching his shirts to his suits, knotting his ties and pairing his socks. None of this took any real thought, and he'd been conducting his days and his career with an eerie normality.

Then, when he ran out of excuses to stay at the office, he had been returning to the co-op in Pacific Heights—*their* co-op, the co-op he and Amanda had bought together once they were both out of graduate school and could afford their first real home—and turning back into a zombie.

He discovered he could perform his act of superficial sanity as well in Boston as in San Francisco: the professional look, the professional attitude, the productivity. After a few weeks in Chestnut Hill, he was able to make reasonably civilized talk with his parents over dinner, al-

though he still couldn't taste the food. When Diana flew up
from Baltimore with the baby, he indulged in the simple
pleasures of bouncing Victoria on his knee and tickling her
round little belly. After a while, he could almost pass for a
human being.

"He's getting better," the family whispered among
themselves. "He's beginning to snap out of it."

Aunt Martha hosted a barbecue on Labor Day. Kip actually thought he could cope with a family gathering. He
looked forward to seeing his cousin Becky—who was now
a sophomore at Williams College, his alma mater—and his
other cousins, and Diana's husband Glenn, who had pulled
strings and traded vacation days in order to accompany his
wife and daughter to the party. Kip went to his aunt and
uncle's house determined to have fun, something he hadn't
done in too long a time.

"Kip!" Aunt Martha charged into the driveway and
smothered him in an effusive bear hug the minute he
climbed out of his car. "Kip! It's so good to see you! You're
looking wonderful!"

That was a lie; he looked like hell. He hugged her anyway.

"Uncle Ned'll get you something to drink," she said,
arching an arm around his waist and ushering him around
the house to the backyard. "You come with me. I've got
someone I want you to meet."

On the patio beside the pool, she presented him to the
daughter of one of her neighbors. The woman was a bright,
attractive architect in her late twenties, currently living near
Harvard Square. She was single. Kip understood at once
why this charming young woman had been invited.

No. He couldn't cope. He closed his eyes and the visions
flashed through his brain, all three of them, Amanda alive,
Amanda dead, Amanda staring down her own death.

He couldn't deal with this.

His aunt had barely finished making the introductions when he mumbled "Excuse me" and stalked away. He hurried around the house to the driveway, climbed into his car, drove back to Chestnut Hill and shut himself up inside his room.

"It isn't healthy, Kip," his mother shouted through the door a while later, when she and his father arrived home from the party.

"Tell me something I don't know."

"It's been over a year."

"Thanks for keeping track."

"Diana thinks you should see a therapist—"

"I saw a therapist in San Francisco. He said everyone heals at his own pace. Well, my pace happens to be real slow, Mom. I don't think I need to have some therapist in Boston tell me that."

"I don't think you need that, either," his mother said, opening the door a crack and peeking in. "I also think maybe you don't need your well-meaning relatives meddling in your life."

He gazed at her, surprised and grateful.

"There's always the house on Block Island," she said.

He studied her as she stood in the doorway. In her mid-fifties, she was still a hearty, youthful woman, her hair more gray than brown but her face relatively unlined and her eyes astute. "I thought you hadn't been there for years," he said.

"We haven't, except for a weekend now and then. We've rented it out summers. But this summer's lease ran from Memorial Day to Labor Day. The tenants will have cleared out by tomorrow if not today. I can call the agent on the island just to make sure, but certainly by the end of the week the house should be empty. Why don't you go there for a while?"

He considered it.

"You'd have the place to yourself, Kip. Some time alone, but within shouting distance if you needed us. Take a leave of absence from work—Harrison will survive without you. I'm worried that if you stick around here you may not survive at all."

The island. The house. Why not? He couldn't possibly feel worse there than he did here.

"You were always so happy on Block Island," his mother reminded him. "Maybe if you went you'd be able to clear your head and unwind a little."

"Okay." He rose, crossed the room and gave his mother a hug. "Thanks."

"We love you, Kip," his mother whispered. "Maybe this is what you need."

What I need I can't have, he thought as the ferry carried him closer and closer to a destination he wasn't sure he wanted to reach. *What I need is gone. What I need is Amanda.*

The fog streaked his eyeglasses with water, and he removed them. Pulling a handkerchief from the hip pocket of his khaki trousers, he wiped the round lenses clean, then dried the gold frame and slid the glasses back on.

The island loomed ahead. The ferry droned its horn as it passed the first of the stone breakwaters into Old Harbor. Kip gazed at the shopfronts and Victorian hotels lining Water Street, their outlines gradually clarifying through the swirling fog. As the boat drew closer to shore he was able to make out the people strolling along the street and swarming around the pier. They moved so slowly, he thought. Much more slowly than the hustling business people he encountered in Boston every day.

This was a good idea, after all. Coming here was the right thing to do.

If he told himself that enough times, he might start to believe it.

The ferry sounded one final, mournful blast of its horn as it inched up to the dock. Kip pushed away from the railing and merged with the other passengers as they filed down from the narrow stairway to the bottom deck. His Saab was positioned to be the first car off the boat. He climbed in, started the engine, and shifted into gear as soon as one of the ferry workers signaled him that it was safe to disembark.

A decade had passed since he'd last been on the island, yet little had changed. A few stores had new names, a few building facades wore a fresh coat of paint, but the ambiance was the same: shops, boutiques, ice-cream parlors, everything tidy and unpretentious. The bookstore, the art gallery, the brick-inlaid sidewalks. The flower boxes. The Surf Hotel, the National, the alley leading to Aldo's. The Seaside Market.

Kip maneuvered into a parking space near the market, shut off the engine and got out of the car. He had been breathing in the briny sea air ever since he'd boarded the ferry at Pt. Judith over an hour ago, but now, for the first time, it struck him that he was truly on Block Island, separated from his family not only by sixty miles of highway but by twelve miles of sea. He felt more removed from them now than he had when he'd been three thousand miles away in San Francisco.

He entered the Seaside Market. He wasn't consciously expecting to recognize any of its customers or clerks, but he still found it jarring that every face in the store was unknown to him.

Not that it mattered. He hadn't come here to socialize, to renew old acquaintances. He lifted a basket from the stack near the cashier and wandered up and down the aisles, pulling items at random from the crowded shelves: cornflakes, a bag of apples, a bottle of orange juice, coffee, a loaf of bread, milk, peanut butter. It didn't really matter what he tossed into the basket; he wouldn't taste any of it when he ate it.

At the rear of the store were shelves of liquor, and there Kip paused. He could slap together a sandwich for dinner and munch on cornflakes for breakfast, but a whole lot of hours stretched between dinner and breakfast, hours he would spend alternately trying to ward off sleep and yielding to its torments. He needed something to get through those hours, ammunition to fight off the demons.

He chose a bottle of Jack Daniel's. A big one, the largest one the store had in stock.

He paid for his purchases and carried the bags out to the Saab. Tomorrow, he promised himself, he would go to the bigger grocery store over on Ocean Avenue and buy some real food. For tonight, peanut butter, apples and bourbon would do just fine.

He started the car, pulled out of the space and cruised toward High Street. The last couple of summers he'd spent on the island he'd had his driver's license, but driving on the narrow island roads still felt peculiar to him, almost sacrilegious.

He wondered if he would find his ten-speed bicycle in the basement of his parents' house. If he did, it would undoubtedly need an overhaul—a complete cleaning, a lube job, air in the tires, the works.

Great therapy, he thought sardonically. And after he was done overhauling his bike, he could weave some baskets.

Spotting an unfamiliar store up the road, he slowed the car. He'd left the shopping area when he'd turned off Water Street. But here, amid bungalows and cottages, a pharmacy had sprung up.

Block Island had never had a pharmacy before. At long last, on the brink of the twenty-first century, someone had finally realized that people on the island sometimes needed medicine.

Especially if they spent the night guzzling bourbon.

He steered into the small lot beside the shingled building and yanked on the parking brake. As enthusiastic as he was about drinking himself into a stupor tonight, he had enough foresight to want to have a hangover remedy on hand when he woke up tomorrow.

He climbed onto the porch of the shingled building. Inside he was confronted by the usual drug-store merchandise: racks of paperbacks, beach toys, a vast array of videos for rent. He roamed up and down the aisles until he located the aspirin.

There was no cashier posted near the door, so he wandered back to the rear of the store, where an elevated counter marked the pharmacy section. Behind it was a glassed-in area of metal shelves lined with mysterious medical-looking boxes and vials. One end of the counter held a computerized cash register.

"Hello?" he called out.

"Be right out," a woman's voice responded. After a moment he spotted a white-coated figure emerging from behind one of the metal shelves, carrying a clipboard and a pen. She stopped and jotted something onto the clipboard, then scanned the shelf in front of her and jotted another note.

Kip glanced over his shoulder at the rack behind him, checking to see if there was anything else he ought to buy while he was there. He heard the woman's footsteps as she strode around the glass barrier to the counter. Reaching for his wallet, he turned back to make his purchase.

Shelley.

No, of course not. He must be mistaken. The woman nearing the counter couldn't possibly be...

Yet the hair that gently brushed past her shoulders was the same dark blond as Shelley Ballard's had been. Her eyes were the same expressive gray. Her lips were as full and soft, her height as statuesque. Her forehead was as high as Shelley's had been, her fingers as long and graceful. He could almost see those fingers tossing a Frisbee with brutal accuracy.

She couldn't be Shelley. Shelley had vanished without a trace—was it twelve years ago? This pharmacist might be tall and athletically built, her body trim in a skirt and blouse beneath her open white lab coat, her eyes clear and direct as she scrutinized him—but she couldn't be Shelley.

She frowned slightly. "Kip?" she murmured.

In Shelley's voice.

"Oh, my God."

"It's you?"

"Oh, God. Shelley."

The bottle of aspirin slipped unnoticed from his hand and dropped onto the counter. His attention was riveted to the woman darting around the counter, her arms outstretched, her face radiating a delight so contagious Kip felt a strange, wholly unexpected surge of joy. He extended his arms and she threw herself into them.

"Shelley," he whispered, hugging her hard.

She hugged him with equal force. "This is incredible. Kip, I can't believe it's you! I can't believe it."

"Believe it. It's me," he said.

She stepped back and beamed at him. For a pregnant minute they simply stared at each other, absorbed each other.

"You look good," she said.

"I look lousy," he argued.

She chuckled. "Okay. You look a little haggard. But—I mean, God, Kip, you've grown up."

"So have you."

"On you it looks good."

"On you, too," he said, giving her a sweeping assessment. Her legs were still long, her calves sleek below the hem of her skirt. Her hips were still compact, her waist slender, her bosom nicely proportioned. Her face had matured in a remarkable way. There was nothing specific he could identify as a sign of aging—no crow's feet or frown lines—but he sensed a wisdom about her he'd never discerned when they were kids. Her eyes were older, somehow. They'd seen more of life, and they intrigued him as they never had before.

"I like your new eyeglasses," she said.

"New?" He let out a laugh. The glasses he had on were four years old.

"You've turned into a yuppie," she added, appraising his hand-knit sweater and tailored slacks.

"I'm afraid so." He continued to study her eyes, wondering what exactly they had seen, where she had been for the past dozen years, why she had left him without saying goodbye so many summers ago. Wondering whether it was Shelley herself or merely the shock of seeing her that sent his mood soaring.

What made her look good to him had less to do with her inherent beauty than with his memory of everything she'd once been—his companion, his critic, his sounding board and sparring partner, his ally. His friend. Gazing into her bright eyes he saw not only their intelligence but the trust he'd once had in her, the affinity they'd shared, the honesty that had never, never abandoned them in their friendship.

"What are you doing here?" he asked, realizing at once that that was an inane thing to say.

"I work here."

"On the island?"

"Yes. Here in the pharmacy. I'm the pharmacist." As if to prove it, she pointed to the name tag pinned to the breast pocket of her jacket: Shelley Ballard, Pharmacist.

He shook his head. "Never in my wildest dreams would I have predicted that you'd wind up a pharmacist. You were supposed to be...an English teacher, right?" Just before she'd dropped out of his life she had loaded him up with all those novels from the library, he recalled. Excellent novels. She'd known what she was doing when she'd recommended them.

"Well..." Her smile took on a certain poignancy. "Things worked out differently. But tell me, are you staying long? I guess your folks' house is empty now, isn't it?

Jean Sanderson usually closes things up right after Labor Day.''

Kip frowned. ''Who?''

''Jean Sanderson. She's a realtor here. She oversees a lot of summer rentals, including your parents' house.'' Shelley grinned. ''I'm a year-rounder now, Kip, I don't know the summer people anymore, but I know the islanders.''

''How long have you been living here?''

''Three years,'' she told him. ''Jean says your folks have been to the house a few times in the past several years, but I've never seen them. Since I'm working and all... *You* haven't been on the island recently, have you? If you were here and I missed you I'd die.''

A quiet laugh filled his throat. In her youth she had always been threatening to die over some minor embarrassment or mishap. ''No,'' he assured her, the urge to laugh fading as his heart filled with an aching nostalgia for those simple days when all he knew of death was Shelley's melodramatic declarations. ''I was living out in California until a few months ago.''

''California! Oh, how exciting! I've never been to California.''

Lord. This was really Shelley. He was actually standing two feet from her, talking to her, gazing at her, inhaling her faint honey-sweet fragrance. ''Why are you here?'' he asked, regretting at once the accusing undertone in his voice. More gently he said, ''I mean *here,* on Block Island? Back then, Shelley, you just—one day you just disappeared, and...'' He realized he was stammering and shut up.

Her smile expanded and at the same time grew pensive. ''It's a long story,'' she said.

''I'd like to hear it.''

She glanced away. ''I've got to work. I'm taking inventory. When you've got to order everything from the mainland it can get tense if the stocks dwindle.''

''Maybe we could have dinner tonight,'' he suggested.

She brightened. "That would be great. Where should we go?"

"Anywhere. You decide."

"I close up here around five-thirty. We could meet at a restaurant at six, or...do you want me to pick you up? Or you can pick me up. Whatever is easiest for you."

"I'll pick you up. Where do you live?"

"A few blocks from here, on Spring Street. I've got an apartment in a two-family house. Let me write down the address." She pulled a blank receipt from a pad on the counter and scribbled her address and telephone number. Then she tore the sheet from the pad and pressed it into Kip's hand. "This is fantastic, Kip. I'm so glad you're here."

"I'm glad you're here, too," he said.

She clasped his hands in hers. "Six o'clock, then," she confirmed. Her hands felt slim in his, cool and smooth. Abruptly she arched her eyebrows and looked down at his left hand. Her thumb rested against his ring finger—against the plain gold band circling it. "You're married!" she exclaimed, clapping her hands together in jubilation. "Oh, Kip, how wonderful! You're married! Why didn't you say something? Is your wife here with you? Oh, please—bring her along for dinner. I want to meet her..." She tapered off, her exuberance draining away as she gazed into his face and saw the stark sorrow he knew he couldn't hide.

He hadn't gotten around to removing his wedding ring yet. He couldn't bring himself to take it off. He should, he had to, but he couldn't. Taking it off would be like an amputation.

"I'm not married," he told her, his voice low and strained.

Shelley's arms dropped to her sides. "Oh," she said uncertainly, her gaze lingering on his left hand.

He struggled to reclaim the happiness he'd experienced at finding her here, but it seemed permanently gone. "I'm sorry," he mumbled, looking away. "I—I don't think—I'm not quite up to going out to a restaurant for dinner," he said. "I'm sorry."

"That's all right," she said, obviously bewildered. "Some other time, maybe."

"No." Suddenly it was imperative that he make things clear to her. He wanted her company; he wanted to learn why she'd left so long ago, what had happened to her, what had brought her back to Block Island. He wanted her friendship once more.

But he didn't think he could survive a fancy dinner at a restaurant, where he would have to dress smartly and act suavely and contend with the presence of other suave, smartly dressed diners seated at tables all around him. "Look, I—" He took a deep breath. "I haven't got much, but if you'd like to come up to the house, we could throw together some sandwiches."

She gazed into his eyes. "If you don't want to—"

"I *do* want to."

"Are you sure?"

"Very sure."

She smiled slightly. "How about if I come up to the house and bring a pizza?"

"Even better," he said.

She stared at him for a minute longer. Then, with a swift glance at his wedding band, she moved back around the counter to the cash register. "I'll ring this up for you," she said, righting the bottle of aspirin and entering its price into the computerized machine.

He noticed the concentration in her face, the confusion that haunted her eyes for a moment and then vanished behind a carefully wrought mask of brisk competence. She was pulling back from him, withdrawing, interpreting his reticence as a lack of candor on his part.

She slid the bottle into a paper bag and handed it to him. Her eyes met his and he saw in them doubt, distrust and something else he couldn't interpret. "Eight dollars and forty-seven cents," she said.

He gave her a ten dollar bill and she gave him his change. "I really want you to come to the house," he said.

Her gaze held his. "I'll be there," she promised.

"You remember where it is, don't you?"

"I could find it with my eyes closed."

He studied her face, reveling in its blessed familiarity. Something had happened to her twelve summers ago, something significant, something that had altered her existence forever. Something just as traumatic had happened to him. If anyone would understand what he'd been through, Shelley would.

"I've missed you," he said.

Her eyes shimmered with tears, but she didn't look away. "I've missed you, too."

"I'll see you tonight," he murmured, then turned and walked down the aisle to the front door. He didn't want to watch her cry, not here, not in this public place, surrounded by jars of acne cream and boxes of gauze.

"I'll see you," she echoed, her voice softer than a whisper.

He barely heard her words, but he felt them deep in his heart. And for the first time in ages he found himself looking forward to dinner.

Chapter Six

He was in the cupola when she showed up. The glass in his hand was full; he'd already polished off one dose of bourbon and was starting on his second. For better or worse, the liquor had had no effect on him so far.

He'd arrived at the house besieged by conflicting emotions. The place looked well-maintained, the lawn trimmed, the trees pruned and the rose and honeysuckle bushes trailing decoratively over the stone walls. The house's exterior must have been painted within the previous year; salty sea breezes could destroy a paint job with ruthless dispatch, but the clapboard siding and gingerbread trim looked clean and fresh. He'd cruised up the driveway past the house to the detached garage, left the engine running while he opened the padlock that held the doors shut, and drove in.

He told himself, again and again, that coming here was a good idea. He chanted the words like a mantra, waiting for the moment when he would start to believe them. As soon as he crossed the threshold into the front hall, though, apprehension clutched him by the throat.

Coming here was *not* a good idea. This was a place of happiness, not mourning. It was a place of joyful memories. He felt like a trespasser, polluting the atmosphere with his grief.

Setting down his suitcase and the bag of groceries in the entry, he wandered into the living room. His gaze traveled from the fireplace to the framed print of a Winslow Homer seascape above it, from the overstuffed sofa where his mother used to stretch out, listening to her beloved Handel and Bach on the stereo, to the ancient rocking chair where his grandmother used to doze.

His grandmother had passed away three and a half years ago. Although she'd been eighty-eight years old her death had pained Kip. He'd consoled himself with the knowledge that she'd lived a rich life bursting with experience and surrounded by love.

Amanda had been surrounded by love, too. But she hadn't gotten her full allotment of experience. She had only just begun to live her life.

He hurried out of the room, stopped to retrieve the groceries and went into the kitchen. Again his vision drank in not just the scene itself but the memories that haunted it. He surveyed the windowed cabinets, the deep double-basin sink, the door to the pantry, the marble-topped counters. He remembered sitting on one of those counters, munching on an apple and swinging his feet until his mother yelled at him for scuffing the cabinet with his shoes. He remembered sneaking up on Diana when she was seated at the circular table in the walk-out bay and shoving an ice cube down the back of her shirt. He remembered gobbling his breakfast and then tearing out the back door, eager to join Shelley for a day of adventure.

Amanda would have loved this room. She would have loved the high ceilings, the scent of cinnamon that hung in the air, the spring latches that held the cabinets shut, the black-and-white checkerboard tiles covering the floor. She would have loved spreading out her cooking paraphernalia on the spacious counters, cluttering every available surface as she made stuffed chicken breasts or Creole shrimp. She had always complained about the cramped size of the kitchen in their Pacific Heights apartment.

He issued a pungent curse. Blasphemy couldn't scare away his thoughts of her, though. She remained stubbornly with him; he couldn't stop seeing his surroundings through her eyes.

Crossing the room, he turned on the refrigerator and unloaded the groceries.

After filling a highball glass with bourbon, he carried his suitcase up to the second floor, to the bedroom that had been his. Summer people had been using the room for the last decade, but he still thought of it as his. The rugs were where they'd always been, the framed map of Block Island, the maple dresser. He placed the suitcase on the mattress and his drink on the night table, then opened both the windows to ventilate the room. In the closet he found clean linens. He unpacked and made up the bed, punctuating each task with a sip of bourbon.

Yet when he was done he remained obsessed with Amanda. He thought about how she would have loved the window seat... how she would have loved sharing the bed with him.

Abruptly he left the room, refilled his glass and then headed back upstairs, into the smallest bedroom, up the ladder stairs.

Compared to the chilly air outdoors, the cupola was stifling. Kip opened the windows and gazed out. It was too foggy to see much, but he resolutely faced north, knowing that on a clear day the view would be of New Harbor and the Great Salt Pond. Looking east toward Old Harbor would mean looking at where he'd come from. He'd journeyed to the island to turn his back on where he'd come from, to escape from it. As if such a thing were possible.

The bourbon slipped smoothly down his throat. He rested his forearms against the window ledge and watched white curls of mist skirt the ground. It reminded him of the fog in San Francisco.

He cursed again.

The sound of an automobile rattling along the gravel driveway jolted him. He had been so deeply submerged in gloomy thoughts he had all but forgotten about Shelley. Rotating, he glanced out the southern window in time to see a Chevy Blazer coasting to a halt near the front walk. The driver's door swung open and Shelley emerged, dressed in blue jeans and a colorful sweater. She reached back into the Blazer and pulled out a pizza box and a paper bag.

Her arrival couldn't dispel the plumes of fog blanketing the island, but it dispelled the fog in Kip's mind. He looked at the glass in his hand and frowned, as if not quite sure how it had gotten there.

Less than a minute later he was opening the front door to her. "Hi," she said.

He held open the screen door and she stepped inside. Her eyes were wide, flitting around the entry. "It feels so strange to be here," she said.

"It feels pretty strange to me, too," he admitted, taking the pizza box from her. It was hot, the bottom beginning to wilt from its steamy contents, and he hurried down the hall to the kitchen with it. Turning, he discovered that Shelley hadn't followed him.

He found her in the living room, hugging the paper bag and gazing about her. He had a pretty good idea what she was going through—the shock of recollection, the blunt impact of realizing how much time had gone by since she'd last stood in that room, how much had happened in that time, how much she'd changed. He understood because he was going through the same thing.

Unlike him, though, she didn't seem upset. When she rotated to face him her eyes were glowing, her lips spread in a smile. "I've lived on Block Island for three years," she said, "but I haven't felt I was truly here until this minute. Your

house was so much a part of the island for me. And now..."
She sighed happily. "I feel like I'm really back."

Tentatively he returned her smile. If being inside his house
could make her so happy, he was glad to have been able to
open the door and let her in.

She extended the bag toward him. "I brought some beer,
too," she said. "I considered bringing lemonade, but..."
She shrugged.

Lemonade. How many times had he drunk lemonade with
Shelley? He relaxed, his smile widening. "We'd better eat
the pizza before it gets cold," he suggested.

They walked together into the kitchen. He supposed they
could use the dining room, but he felt more comfortable in
the kitchen. Shelley had never been one for formality; he
assumed she wouldn't object.

While he set the table she opened the box and loosened a
couple of slices. He pulled the beer out of the bag, removed
two bottles and slid the other four onto a shelf in the refrigerator. "Would you like a glass?" he asked as he twisted off
the caps.

Shelley shook her head. She was looking at the bottle of
Jack Daniel's and the filled glass on the counter.

He wondered whether he should assure her that he'd pre-
fer a beer to bourbon right now, whether he should explain
to her that while bourbon was a good drink to consume in
the company of bleak memories, in the company of an old
friend beer was more appropriate. He decided to say nothing.

She sat, and he took the chair across the table from her.
After she'd placed two slices of pizza on their plates, he
closed the lid of the box, giving himself an unobstructed
view of her face. Her eyes were still shining, lucid and
cheerful, more silver than gray.

He raised his bottle and clinked it against hers. "Here's
to you," he toasted.

"To you," she said simultaneously, then laughed. "To both of us."

"To friendship," he said, then drank. It was all he could do to keep from toasting her laughter. The mere sound of it brought back so many memories—*good* memories of romping at the beach and racing each other on their bikes, engaging in cutthroat competition over backgammon, showing off their knowledge and goofing around. Shelley Ballard was a woman now, but her laughter was young and musical and infectious.

She bit off the narrow point of her slice of pizza, chewed and swallowed. Her eyes never straying from him, she grinned. "I feel very self-conscious," she declared.

"Why?"

"You're staring at me. Why don't you eat?"

He dutifully took a bite. He didn't stop staring, though. "So, you actually live here on the island."

"I actually do. I've got a B.I. zip code, a four-six-six telephone exchange and a Rhode Island driver's license."

"And you're here year-round. What's it like in the winter?" In all the years his parents had owned this house, he had never been on the island during the winter.

"Empty," she told him. "Cold and blissfully empty. There are only about seven hundred and fifty people here in the winter. Everyone knows everyone. We look out for each other, but everyone respects everyone else's privacy. It's very quiet."

Why an attractive young woman like Shelley would want that sort of quiet existence puzzled him. He had come to the island to heal in solitude. What if Shelley had come for the same reason?

"How did you wind up a pharmacist?" he asked.

"God knows," she said, then laughed again, a shimmering laugh that warmed the room. "I don't think it was a conscious decision. It was subliminal."

"Come on," he argued with a smile. "Nobody becomes a pharmacist *subliminally*. You've got to take all those chemistry and biology courses."

She sipped her beer, her lips curved in a grin even as she tipped the bottle against her mouth. "Once I decided to major in pharmacology, I took the courses I needed. I can assure you I was very conscious of the curriculum. Amazingly enough, I discovered I had a knack for applied science." She took another bite of her pizza. "How about you? What sort of work do you do?"

"Financial consulting," he answered. "You were right—I'm a yuppie."

"Wasn't your father in finance?"

"Real estate and urban development," Kip corrected her. "My specialty is helping small companies organize their financial strategies."

"Did you do that in California, too?"

He nodded, refusing to acknowledge the reflexive twinge any mention of California invariably caused. "I took an M.B.A. at Stanford. It's really disgustingly yuppie-ish," he summarized with a smile. When was the last time he'd been able to joke about his illustrious education and his fast-track career? Only Shelley could get him to laugh at himself. "For a while I was in danger of taking up golf, but the urge seems to have faded."

"Thank heavens," Shelley said with pretended solemnity. "You don't wear plaid slacks, do you?"

"I avoid them like the plague," he swore, holding his hand up.

"Suspenders?"

"Never."

"I guess you aren't too far gone, then."

He chuckled. "And meanwhile, you're running around in a white coat, drugging people. You've got some nerve making fun of me."

"Kip, if anyone has the nerve to make fun of you, it's me."

"Only because you know I'll retaliate. So tell me more about this white-coat job of yours. I still can't imagine you reading prescription slips and counting tablets."

"Sometimes I can't imagine it, either," she confessed, toying with a strand of mozzarella, her gaze distant as she chased her thoughts. "I think I became a pharmacist because I knew, deep in my heart, that I wanted to live here. I wanted to come back to the island and settle down. And the island didn't have a pharmacist. If I got the training, I could provide a needed service and support myself, too. It took a while to work it out. I held a job in 'America' for a couple of years after graduation, and waited until the pieces fell into place."

"Do you own the pharmacy?"

She let out a snort. "I'm in debt up to my ears, Kip. Even if I'd wanted to take out a business loan I wouldn't have qualified for one."

That surprised him. He had never thought of the Ballards as super-rich, but surely they'd been comfortably well off. Shelley had never been strapped for funds when he'd known her. He couldn't believe her parents would refuse to lend her some money if there was no other way to finance her dream.

Unless, of course, they couldn't afford to help her out. Perhaps that was what had happened to her the summer she'd disappeared: a reversal in her family's finances. "Was that it?" he guessed. "Your family went broke?"

She had been reaching for a second slice of pizza, but as soon as he'd verbalized his hunch she stopped. Her hands fell to her lap and her gaze darted about the room, as if searching for something to focus on.

"You don't have to answer that," he said contritely.

"I think I do," she responded. "That's why I came for dinner, isn't it?"

"You came because we're friends," he said, astonished at how right that sounded, how true it was. After so many years without a word from her, she could reenter his life and he could still think of her as a friend.

He watched as she curved her fingers around her beer bottle and lifted it. Her hand trembled slightly as she brought the bottle to her lips and sipped. Then she lowered it and met his probing gaze. "Yes, Kip, my family went broke. In every sense of the word."

The confession seemed to exhaust her. She returned her hand to her lap and leaned back in her chair, fixing her eyes on something behind Kip, something just above his right shoulder.

He waited for her to elaborate, but she didn't. "I hated you for a while," he said, then cringed at how reproachful he sounded.

She accepted his rudeness without blinking. "Because I never called you?" she asked.

"Never called, never wrote... I wrote to you, but my letter was returned, stamped Addressee Unknown. In all the time we were friends, Shelley, we'd never had secrets—and then you left without any explanation, without a single word."

She seemed to be struggling to resurrect her smile, but her eyes brimmed with sadness as they narrowed on his face. "I had planned to call you," she confessed. "I should have. But... things didn't work out the way I had hoped."

"How did they work out?" he asked gently.

She toyed with the label on her beer bottle, tracing its edge with her fingernail. "It was my father," she said, her voice taking on a harsh quality. "You remember my father, don't you?"

Kip nodded. "You were angry with him that summer because he wouldn't visit every weekend."

"That's right. He kept spending his weekends back in Connecticut." All the humor was gone from her voice now, all the warmth. She sounded taut, almost brittle, on the verge of cracking.

"You thought he might be having an affair or something." How had Kip remembered that? After so many years, why had Shelley's adolescent fears remained with him?

A grim laugh escaped her. "Well, that wasn't quite the problem. He *had* been having an affair, but by that summer it was winding down. He'd established certain precedents with his sweetheart, though..."

It hurt Kip to hear the hostility in her voice. Shelley had never been a bitter person. She'd been sweet and ingenuous, principled yet sentimental.

He considered changing the subject. But he wanted to know the truth. He wanted to know what had happened to her.

"My father was embezzling from the bank where he was an officer," she finally said. Her fingernail caught the corner of the bottle label and tore off a shred. With obvious effort, she forced her hand to lie motionless on the table. "He was arrested. He had been skimming for years—first to buy his sweetie nice things without my mother finding out about it, and then to keep his sweetie satisfied so she wouldn't break up his marriage. As if she was the one who broke up the marriage. It was my father. *He* was the one who was married; *he* was the one who should have known better."

Her rage was apparently aimed at her father's infidelity. But embezzlement seemed a much greater transgression to Kip. "Was he convicted?" he asked.

Shelley's eyes were so icy they sent a shiver up his spine. "Yes. He was convicted on a federal charge of tax evasion. Apparently you're supposed to declare your embezzlement income on your 1040, and he failed to do that. He got hit with a heavy fine and served time in the federal prison in Danbury."

"He went to jail?"

She nodded. "Only on the federal charge. The bank dropped its prosecution in favor of a negotiated settlement. We had to sell everything to pay them back. *Everything,*" she stressed, spitting out the syllables. "Our house in Westport—and the house here on the island, of course. The cars. The furniture. My mother's jewelry. Even my gold necklace—the one my father gave me for my birthday. The bank and the feds took it all. Every last penny."

Kip realized he was gaping at her and deliberately looked away. He could scarcely comprehend what she was telling him. Then again, he supposed the situation would have been just as incomprehensible to Shelley if she hadn't lived through it.

"The ultimate irony," she went on in a tone low and tense with fury, "was that my father's girlfriend didn't have to give back anything. She kept her condo and her jewelry and everything else my father gave her. My mother and I lost everything because we were legally connected to him. We were his family, so we had to pay the price."

For a while Kip could think of nothing to say. He listened to the purr of the refrigerator's motor, the slap of a curtain cord against the wall as a breeze fluttered through the open bay windows, the slow, steady whisper of Shelley breathing in and out, her eyes now blank as she moved beyond anger to that numbness Kip was all too familiar with. Finally he asked, "How is your mother?"

Shelley made a face and drank some beer. "She's remarried. She lives in Houston. She's not very happy, but she has three meals a day and a roof over her head, so she doesn't complain."

Kip remembered Mary Ballard. She'd been an attractive woman, blond and stylish and somewhat aloof—but he'd suspected that was a result of bashfulness, not arrogance. The time she'd come with Shelley to a barbecue at his house, she'd seemed overwhelmed by the bustle and noise and the effusiveness of his family. But she'd been a nice woman.

Evidently she'd gotten as raw a deal as Shelley. He wondered why Shelley sounded so cynical when she talked about her.

Shelley apparently read his mind. "My mother," she explained, "doesn't know how to function without a man. She's never had a paying job in her life. There we were, absolutely broke, with my father up on criminal charges. My mother divorced him—you can't blame her for that. But there was no alimony. There was no *anything*—except debts. She and I moved in with her sister in Houston. I got an after-school job flipping burgers and my mother worked on commission as a salesclerk in a clothing boutique—where she earned zilch. The woman doesn't know how to sell. All she knows is how to be a wife. So she grabbed the first man who came along and hung on for dear life." She grimaced and shook her head.

"You don't like him?"

"No, I don't like him. He's cold and uncommunicative. He has no sense of humor. He's an emotional miser. But he and my mother have... an understanding."

Shelley reached for her beer bottle, then changed her mind and nudged it away. "I go to Houston to visit them every year at Christmas. While I'm there I count the days until I can leave and come back here. I can't stand my mother's husband. I can't stand my father, either. My father took everything I valued in life—family and trust and love and security—and he trashed it. He ruined it. At least my mother's new husband isn't deceitful. He supports her financially and she's there for him in bed every night. He gives her money and she gives him sex. The whole business stinks. I will never let myself become dependent on a man. Never."

The words emerged flat and chilly, in a slow, practiced tempo. Kip sensed that Shelley had thought more about this resolution than about her decision to become a pharmacist. He tried to link the hurt, frightened woman across the table from him to the bubbly, carefree girl he'd known twelve years ago. Tried but failed.

He considered pointing out to her that not all marriages were like her mother's, that not all men were either philandering embezzlers or emotional abusers. He considered reminding her of the trust and affection his parents shared, proof that some men and women were honest and loving with each other. But what good would it do to remind Shelley of everything she didn't have?

He couldn't blame her for the conclusions she'd reached or the scars she'd been left with. He couldn't cure her. He knew all too well that some wounds never healed.

He reached across the table and covered her hand with his. He felt her tension in the cold stiffness of her fingers. "I forgive you for not calling me," he murmured.

She glanced at him. Able to read the sympathy in his expression, she offered a shy smile. "Thank you," she said. He knew she was thanking him not for his forgiveness but for listening and not judging, for being someone she could trust even though she hadn't seen him in years, even though he was a man and she no longer trusted men.

They sat at the table for a long while, neither of them speaking. The sky outside the windows gradually darkened, making the kitchen seem brighter and cozier in contrast. Shelley gazed at the uneaten pizza, the scratched pine surface of the table, the intricate pattern of stitches across the front of Kip's sweater. She gazed at his hand covering hers.

She gazed at his ring.

"DO YOU MIND COMING UP here?" he asked.

"No, not at all." Two short steps took her to the windowsill where she knelt, exactly as she and Kip used to kneel, with her arms resting on the sill and the vista of the front yard spread below. Tonight that vista was blurred by the fog, but Kip didn't care.

He wanted to answer the questions she was too polite to ask. He supposed she would have been more comfortable on the veranda—he could have dragged a couple of Adirondack chairs out of the garage—or the living room, or in the den, with the television turned on, offering a distraction if it turned out they needed one. But he couldn't imagine baring his soul to her anywhere else but in the cupola.

They'd brought two fresh beers with them. Because he'd left the windows open earlier the air was noticeably fresher in the tiny room. Moonlight filtered through thick layers of mist to illuminate the cupola with a smudgy silver glow.

"She died a year ago August," he said.

Shelley turned from the window and sat—in the corner where she'd always sat. Kip took the corner diagonally opposite her—*his* corner. They stretched their legs out, as they'd done so many times before.

This felt right. He was glad she'd agreed to come upstairs with him. Here in their special place, he could tell Shelley why he wore a wedding band.

Shelley's face reflected compassion. "Had she been ill?"

He shook his head. "No. She was hit by a car."

Shelley winced.

"I—" He stared down into the narrow-bore opening of the beer bottle balanced on his thighs. "I saw the accident. I watched it. I watched her die, Shelley." He had never actually spoken those words before. His parents had learned, in bits and pieces, from reading the accident report and talking to the police officer who had been the first on the scene, that Kip had been standing on the corner and had witnessed the accident. But he himself had never told them. He'd never told them what horrible visions assailed him whenever he closed his eyes.

"What was her name?"

"Amanda."

"Tell me everything about her, Kip."

Everything? He lifted his eyes and frowned. Shelley nodded, informing him that she honestly wanted him to tell her.

So he did. He told her about how he'd met Amanda at Mt. Holyoke College when he'd driven down to the school with a friend of his who was dating a friend of hers. He told Shelley about how they'd spent every weekend together from then on, even in the summers, about how they'd coordinated their professional school applications, deciding to move to California when she got into the law school at U.C. Berkeley and he got into Stanford. He told her about the first time he'd brought her to Chestnut Hill to meet his parents, about how everyone had adored her, about how she'd taught his mother how to braid bread dough and debated politics with his father.

He told Shelley about the curly black hair that had so disgruntled Amanda—until frizzy hair had suddenly become the height of fashion. He told Shelley about her crystal-clear soprano voice, the solos she performed in her college choir.

He told Shelley about their wedding, the flowers Amanda had worn in her hair and the rose she'd pinned to his lapel. He'd told her about their "honeymoon"—an exhausting cross-country drive to California—and the ugly, poorly lit apartment they'd found in Hayward, halfway between their two campuses. He told her about how hard they'd both worked, studying and holding down part-time jobs, somehow finding something romantic in eating spaghetti five nights a week.

Kip had finished business school and gotten a job in San Francisco. They'd moved up to Berkeley for Amanda's final year of law school, and then she'd been hired as an associate at a prestigious firm. They'd purchased their co-op, given up spaghetti for shellfish and sun-dried tomatoes, learned about wines, bought the Saab. They'd met every evening after work, sometimes only to ride the bus home together, sometimes to walk to Chinatown for dinner, sometimes to shop.

Kip hadn't really liked shopping that much, he told Shelley. But Amanda had. One evening, a little more than a year after they'd moved to San Francisco, she'd asked if he would mind her stopping at Macy's in Union Square; the store had advertised a sale on belts, and she'd wanted to find a new leather belt for her jungle-print jumpsuit.

Kip had told her he'd wait for her in the park across the street. It had been a beautiful, balmy evening, and he'd thought people-watching in the park would be more fun than debating the merits of various belts in a crowded department store.

He'd ambled about the park for twenty minutes, and then he'd spotted Amanda emerging from the store. He'd strolled to the corner to meet her, and she'd waved at him, checked the traffic light, stepped out into the street and died.

"I haven't handled it very well," he said.

Shelley's legs rested against his. She had listened, saying nothing, only nodding and sipping her beer and nodding again as his story poured out of him. "Is there a good way to handle something like that?" she asked.

He smiled. "I've missed you," he whispered. When he'd said it at the pharmacy earlier that day he'd meant it, but not until this minute, when she had made the kindest, most sensible remark anyone had said to him since the accident, had he realized how very much he missed having her in his life.

She was in his life now. And he knew that, although he would never get over losing Amanda, never feel whole again and never stop grieving, things *would* get better. Life would start to become bearable once more.

He had Shelley—his pal, his buddy, his soul mate. His friend. Things would get better.

Chapter Seven

He rose early, feeling unusually well rested, without any aftereffects—no hangover, no recollection of nightmares tormenting him throughout the night. With a vigor he hadn't experienced in ages, he showered and shaved, slugged down a cup of coffee and gave the house a close, objective inspection.

By the end of an hour he'd compiled an impressive list of projects. The banisters needed refinishing. The faucet in the family bathroom sink dripped. The upstairs veranda had some loose planks. Most of the windows required caulking. His bicycle, stored in the cellar along with the barbecue grill, the lawn furniture, the picnic table and a couple of beach umbrellas, cried out for an overhaul, just as he'd predicted.

Maybe such projects were nothing more than busywork, therapy, petty exercises in the art of staying sane. He didn't care. He was here and he was going to do things.

The first thing he was going to do was drive to the supermarket on Ocean Avenue and buy some food. The pizza he'd eaten last night hadn't been on a par with what one could buy in Boston's North End, but at least he'd perceived a degree of flavor in his dinner. He would hardly call that proof that he was cured, but it was a positive sign.

At the supermarket he stocked up on staples, meat and fish, vegetables and junk food. From there he went to the hardware store. The proprietor looked vaguely familiar, but Kip didn't bother to introduce himself. He drove home, put the groceries away and carried the hardware supplies down to the cellar. The rest of the morning he devoted to the resuscitation of his bicycle.

By lunchtime he was ready for another shower. Most of the cobwebs he'd cleaned off the tire spokes had stuck to him; his forearms were covered with grime and his chin was smeared with grease. He welcomed the dirt, though. Not once in the hours he'd spent laboring on the bike had he envisioned Amanda. Not once had he seen her immobilized in the crosswalk on Geary, waiting for death to steal her away.

What he'd thought about while he worked was Block Island, the sunny morning that had greeted him, the distinctive blend of aromas filling the air—late-blooming marigolds, apples, salt and sand—the tranquillity of the empty house. In San Francisco he had awakened to the cacophony of automobile traffic along Pacific Avenue. In Chestnut Hill he'd arisen to the sounds of his mother bustling about the house, yammering on the telephone, soliciting volunteers for the Special Olympics or organizing a fund-raiser for the Dana Farber Institute, planning a League of Women Voters meeting and blasting Vivaldi through the stereo speakers.

Here—nothing. Nothing but the low sweet moan of the wind arching over the stone walls and spinning through the leaves of the red maple near his bedroom windows. Nothing but the friendly creaking of the house's timbers and the high-pitched caws of sea gulls wheeling overhead.

Once he'd filled the tires with the air pump he found on a shelf in a corner of the cellar, he lugged the bicycle up the stairs and out onto the front porch, then went back indoors to wash up and change his clothes. After downing a peanut butter sandwich, he took off on a bike ride.

Instinct navigated him along the twisting lanes he remembered so well, around the corner, over a hill to the tiny Cape Cod-style cottage that used to belong to the Ballards. It was pale yellow—when Shelley had lived there it had been brown—and a shingle hung from the porch railing with The Hansens engraved into it. It hurt him to see that proud label announcing to the world that the Ballards had been dispossessed of their summer house.

Probably it hurt Shelley even more.

He steered away from the cottage, following the sinuous curves of the island roads until he reached the pharmacy on High Street. He swung off his bike, chained it to the bike rack, and entered.

Shelley's voice reached him from the rear of the store. Striding down an aisle to the counter, he slowed when he saw that she was conferring with an elderly man. "I can refill this prescription only one more time, Ed," she said as she slid a brown plastic bottle of pills into a paper bag and presented it to him.

"And then what am I supposed to do?" the customer asked.

"Go back to the doctor. He has to monitor your blood pressure. If it's improved he may want to change your prescription."

"What if it hasn't improved?" the man inquired, pulling the bottle from the bag and squinting at the printed instructions on the label.

"Then the doctor may renew this prescription—or he may try something else. Now, if you have any problems—dizziness, drowsiness, blurred vision, anything like that—you call the doctor right away. Don't stop taking the pills, but let him know."

"Okay."

"And give my regards to Lucille."

"Okay. You take care of yourself, Shelley." He turned and headed for the door, nodding at Kip as he edged past him in the narrow aisle.

Shelley smiled at Kip. The moment his eyes met hers he experienced a jolt of delight. She wore a lavender blouse, a floral-patterned skirt and her white pharmacist jacket. Her hair was brushed back from her face, which was devoid of makeup. She looked fresh and full of energy, not like someone who had already put in a good four or five hours of work.

Talking to her in the cupola last night had been cathartic. After he'd run out of words they'd remained up there, their legs spanning the room, their backs nestled into opposite corners. They'd spoken little. Her nearness alone had been enough to buoy him.

After awhile she'd announced that it was time for her to leave. "Some of us have to go to work in the morning," she'd reminded him. He'd walked her down the stairs and outside to her Blazer. Beside the driver's side door he'd kissed her cheek and then gathered her into his arms, savoring her strength, her comforting warmth.

He had male friends—one or two holdovers from his youth still living in the Boston area, a few classmates from Williams with whom he kept in sporadic touch, a couple of buddies back in San Francisco. But what he felt for Shelley transcended any other friendship he'd ever known. He treasured her ability to listen, her refusal to judge him, her unwillingness to lay out a timetable for his recovery.

If he had admitted to his other friends that he wasn't handling Amanda's death well, they would likely have said "Buck up, old boy. Let's sweat it out on the squash court." What Shelley had said last night was a confirmation, an affirmation. What she'd said assured him that she understood, that she accepted him as he was, without attaching conditions or pressuring him with expectations. He'd told her he was a mess and she'd told him it was all right to be a mess. Having her back in his life was a miracle.

Returning her smile, he sauntered down the aisle to the counter.

"How's it going?" she asked.

"Great. I've decided to fix up the house."

"Does it need fixing?"

He nodded. "Here and there. It's time for me to add some calluses to these yuppie hands of mine."

She chuckled. "We've got a wide variety of skin creams in stock if you decide you don't like dry skin."

"Do you take a personal interest in all your customers?" he asked, thinking not of himself but of the elderly man who'd just left the pharmacy.

Shelley's chuckle evolved into a laugh. "You mean, like Ed Burkholtz? He's not just my customer—he's my neighbor. I told you, everybody knows everybody on the island. The year-rounders are one big happy family."

For a brief, irrational moment Kip felt like an outsider. He had no right to be resentful; he *was* an outsider. He should be glad a member of the big happy family was willing to treat him as a welcome visitor.

Footsteps on the plank floor alerted him to the arrival of another customer. Glancing over his shoulder, Kip observed a clean-scrubbed young man, clad in the crisp shirt and starched trousers of a Coast Guard uniform, entering the pharmacy and moving directly to the rear of the store. The man's auburn hair was neatly combed above an open, square-jawed face; he removed his sunglasses to reveal sparkling green eyes. "How's my favorite drug dealer?" he greeted Shelley as he approached the counter.

She acknowledged him with a wary smile. "Hello, Jack," she said, then noticed the amiable curiosity with which the man was eyeing Kip. "Jack, this is Kip Stroud, an old friend of mine. Kip, Jack MacRae."

Jack extended his right hand and Kip shook it. "An old friend, eh? Did you boat over from the mainland?"

"Yes."

"Say," Jack said, turning back to Shelley with a hopeful grin, "could I earn some points with you by risking my life to rescue him?"

"He took the ferry," Shelley told Jack. "He isn't a boater."

"Darn. Those ferries are so safe. I'll have to find some other way to become your hero."

Shelley's smile relaxed slightly. "I'd rather you never had to be a hero, Jack. The only time you Coast Guard guys get to be heroes is when someone is in trouble."

"Yeah. Life sure is boring when everybody's safe." His grin conveyed that he was joking. He acknowledged Kip with a nod and said, "Nice meeting you." Then he pivoted back to Shelley, effectively shouldering Kip out of the way.

Realizing that Jack wanted to talk privately with Shelley, Kip wandered over to the videotape section of the store and spun one of the cylindrical racks. Behind him he heard a muffled exchange of voices, Jack's deep and warm and Shelley's muted and laconic. Peeking discreetly around the rack, Kip saw Jack leaning on his elbows on the counter and gazing intently at Shelley, who stood perfectly straight. She neither bowed toward him nor shrank from him. Her smile seemed frosty to Kip, her gaze restrained.

Kip spun another circular rack and then glanced toward Shelley again. Her smile had become gentle; she was shaking her head no. Jack spread his hands palm up and murmured something. Shelley's smile widened, and she shook her head again.

Jack pushed away from the counter. He was smiling, too, but his shoulders appeared stiff to Kip. "Well," he said, "I'll count the minutes till my next shore leave."

"Shore leave!" Shelley guffawed.

"Ah, you hard-hearted wench. Have a nice visit," he called toward Kip as he strolled down an aisle to the front of the store and exited the building.

Kip watched Jack's departure, then gravitated back to Shelley's post at the rear of the store. "Is he your boyfriend?" he asked.

Shelley's smile faded and she rolled her eyes. "Only in his dreams."

"He seems like a nice guy."

"Yes, he does."

Kip frowned slightly. The normal response would have been, "He *is*." Shelley's words implied that what Jack *seemed* and what he *was* were two different things. "What's wrong with him?" Kip asked.

Shelley let her gaze meet his for a second, then marched to her computer and began tapping on its keys. "Nothing he can help," she answered dryly. "I'm just not interested."

Now it was Kip's turn to lean on the counter. Like Jack, he rested his elbows against it and propped his chin in his hands, not to be closer to Shelley but simply to see her, since she was half hidden behind the computer. "I've got to admit, I wondered how a single woman managed to have a social life on an island like this," he said. "I guess there must be guys back on the mainland."

"I guess there must be," Shelley agreed, her gaze riveted to the computer monitor and her mouth shaping a grim line.

Kip scrutinized her thoughtfully, taking in her wistful gray eyes, the determined set of her chin, her proud posture and the nimble speed of her fingers as they skimmed the computer keyboard. While far from model-perfect or glamorous, she was a remarkably appealing woman. Her face had an intriguing complexity to it and her body was lithe and leggy, not fragile in a fine-boned way but strong and healthy and capable.

In another frame of mind—in another lifetime—Kip would pursue her. He'd court her and seduce her and fall in love with her. Such passion was out of the question for him now, of course, and given his history with Shelley, a seduction attempt would be way out of line.

But if he were just a man, not an old friend or a new widower but simply a man, he would have gotten in line right behind Jack MacRae, eagerly awaiting his chance to become Shelley's hero.

"Are you dating someone else?" he asked, still curious as to why she was "just not interested" in a good-looking, good-natured, obviously smitten fellow like Jack.

Shelley pressed her lips together and stared obdurately at the screen. "No," she said after a long minute.

"Maybe you think it's none of my business," he persevered. "But . . . we got together for dinner last night, and I was going to ask if you were free for dinner tonight—" The sharp look she gave him silenced him for a moment. Belatedly he concluded, "If you're seeing someone else I shouldn't be monopolizing your evenings."

Her expression softened slightly. "Don't worry about it," she said.

"Meaning . . . you're free for dinner?"

"Meaning . . ." She sighed. "I told you last night, Kip."

She had told him a great many things last night. But she hadn't told him she wasn't dating anyone.

Once again, the thump of footsteps behind him signaled the arrival of customers. If he wanted to interrogate Shelley further, now was not the time. "So," he ventured cautiously, "can we have dinner tonight?"

She shut off the computer and turned to him. Her eyes were hard and sharp, cutting deep into him. But he couldn't interpret the emotion in them. "As friends," she said.

Was that it? Did she think he was trying to romance her? He'd stripped his emotions bare last night, and let her feast her eyes on his scars. He'd exposed his damaged heart and his tattered soul. She ought to know better than to think he was a wolf on the prowl, coming on to her in search of a few casual thrills.

"Of course, as friends," he snapped.

"Fine. Six o'clock?"

"I'll pick you up," he said brusquely, then rotated on his heel and stalked out of the store.

Not until he reached his bicycle did his anger begin to dissipate. He unlocked the chain and rode away. He pedaled hard, his eyes monitoring the treacherous curves in the road while his mind journeyed in its own directions, sorting out his emotions.

He had been alone over a year. Many people seemed to believe that a year was long enough, that he ought to be ready to jump back into the world of mature adult relationships. That he ought to be horny.

Maybe he was. But he couldn't separate sex from Amanda in his mind. He couldn't separate sex from love. He couldn't just think of it as a physical release, no strings attached, no feelings involved.

He didn't blame people for assuming the monkish life he was leading was somehow unnatural. Shelley should have known better, though. She should have known better than to think he was putting the moves on her, for God's sake. She shouldn't have had to demand a guarantee that if he took her out for dinner tonight he would be doing so as her friend and nothing more. She should have known.

She *did* know, he refuted himself. Her cryptic response to him in the pharmacy had nothing to do with where he was coming from or what he was going through.

It had to do with what *she* was going through. He wasn't sure how or why, but it had to do with her.

HE ARRIVED AT HER ADDRESS at a little past six. He'd left his house in plenty of time, stopped in the front yard to cut a few late-blooming roses from the front hedge for her, and driven over to Spring Street. The house bearing her number wasn't clearly marked, though, and he'd driven past it twice before he spotted the faded, paint-flecked numbers on the shingles above the front door.

It was a squat charcoal-gray house, much too small to contain apartments. Yet there were two mailboxes beside the door, and two doorbells. He parked on the unpaved shoulder, got out, walked up the overgrown path to the porch and rang the bell with Ballard printed beneath it.

In less than a minute Shelley opened the door to him. She was dressed in a simple white dress that set off her summer tan, and white leather flats. Her smile at seeing Kip was so sincere he all but forgot about the unresolved tension that had stretched between them that afternoon.

"Hi," he said, extending the roses. "These are for you."

"Oh, Kip, they're beautiful!" She took them carefully and dipped her nose to the blossoms to inhale their fragrance. "Come on in," she said. "I'll put them in some water."

He entered and followed Shelley up a narrow flight of stairs. Her apartment occupied the entire second floor, but given how small the house was, her home was microscopic. She'd done the best she could to decorate the living room, though, adorning the window with feathery lace curtains, hanging bright landscape prints on the dreary dun-colored walls, arranging what furniture she had to look cozy rather than crowded.

She exited into the kitchen. Through the doorway Kip saw her arrange the roses in a glass vase. She carried the vase back into the living room and set it on the scratched coffee table in front of the love seat. "There," she said brightly. "They really liven up the room, don't they?"

"I'm not sure how long they'll last," he warned. "It's the end of the season."

She fussed with one of the roses. "I'll enjoy them anyway. Thank you, Kip."

Her gratitude seemed a bit profuse for a few cut flowers. It dawned on Kip that maybe this was her way of apologizing for having acted suspiciously toward him earlier—just as, perhaps, bringing the flowers had been his way of apologizing for whatever he'd done to arouse her suspicion.

He wasn't used to playing games with her, trying to outguess her or read her mind. He and Shelley had always been frank with each other in the past. "Are we okay?" he asked, shoving his hands in his pockets and eyeing her dubiously.

She lifted her eyes from the roses and bravely met his gaze. "We're fine."

"I said something wrong this afternoon."

"And I overreacted. I'm sorry."

He laughed uncertainly. "The trouble is, I don't know what I said that was wrong."

She offered a crooked smile. "I'll answer any question you want, Kip, but maybe we should head for the restaurant first."

He nodded, handed her the white envelope purse that was lying on the end table beside him, and ushered her out of the gloomy little apartment. "Any question, huh," he murmured as they descended the stairs to the front door.

"Within reason."

"Like . . . how come a single professional woman lives in such a tiny place?"

"Because she's trying to save money," Shelley answered without hesitation. "Because she's paying off loans and trying to save up to buy a house, and because from June through August even that tiny place has an astronomical rent. On September first it dropped fifty percent, but during peak season my landlady can get top dollar for that hellhole."

"It isn't a hellhole," Kip argued, suddenly ashamed of himself for having denigrated it. "It's just small."

"It's ridiculous. I can't even open the bedroom closet door all the way. My bed blocks it."

He helped her into the Saab, closed her door and then climbed in behind the wheel. "I made reservations at Winfield's," he told her, and smiled when she nodded her approval. He started the engine and cruised down the road before asking, "Are you still in debt from your father?"

He almost expected her to retract her offer to answer any question he asked, but she didn't. She shot him a cryptic look, then faced forward. "No. Not directly," she said. "It's a college loan. I went to the University of Texas, which wasn't too expensive since I was a state resident at the time. But it still cost real money."

"Were you able to get any aid?"

She issued a bitter laugh. "I probably would have qualified for some, but I couldn't bring myself to fill out forms that asked how come your parents couldn't pay your schooling costs. I couldn't bring myself to write, 'My father's in jail and my stepfather's a jerk.' So I took out some loans and flipped hamburgers and pieced together an education as best I could."

She fidgeted with her purse. "I won't ask any more," he promised.

"I don't mind talking about it," she said. "But if you mind listening—"

"No." That wasn't quite true, he admitted silently. He did mind hearing the corrosive undertone in her voice when she talked about her father. He did mind thinking about what the demolition of her family cost her, not so much in money as in spirit.

By the time they reached the restaurant she seemed more relaxed. The hostess led them to a table with a view of the setting sun. They occupied themselves with the business of ordering, and when Kip finally found himself able to concentrate solely on Shelley she appeared mellow.

"My mother says hello," he told her.

"Oh?"

"I phoned her this afternoon. I told her you were on the island. She was happy—for me even more than for you."

"She's worried about you, isn't she?"

"Yes." He paused when the waiter arrived with the Bordeaux they'd ordered. After Kip tasted it, the waiter filled their glasses and vanished. "I think," Kip said, "my mother believes you're going to cure me."

"I hope you explained that I'm a pharmacist, not a doctor," Shelley quipped.

He acknowledged Shelley's joke with a slight smile, then grew solemn again. "My mother might know what she's talking about this time," he said. "I want to drink to you, Shelley, so don't interrupt and drink to me. This is for you." He touched his glass to hers and sipped.

Her eyes shimmered above the rim of her goblet, a glittering silvery gray as she met his unwavering gaze. After a slight hesitation she sipped her wine. A tiny drop remained on her lip when she lowered her glass, and she caught it with the tip of her tongue.

It was an astonishingly sexy gesture.

Perhaps what startled Kip most was that he noticed, that he could look at a woman flicking her tongue against her upper lip and think it was sexy.

Especially when that woman was Shelley Ballard. "We *are* good friends," he said as much to himself as to her.

At last she broke her gaze from him. The corners of her mouth twitched upward in a shy smile, and she brushed a tendril of gold-tinged hair back from her cheek. "I know, Kip." She took another sip of wine, then sighed. "I'm sorry I acted like a maniac in the pharmacy today."

"Not a maniac," he argued mildly. "Just temperamental."

Her grin expanded. "I know Jack is a nice guy, and he's been trying to get me to go out with him for months. But...I don't date, Kip. I mean—this, right now—it isn't a date."

"Of course not," he teased. "I was planning to split the bill with you."

"Like hell," she shot back. "Who paid for the pizza and beer yesterday?"

He laughed briefly, then grew solemn. "We're agreed that this isn't a date. I don't date, either, Shelley. I'm not—I'm not ready for it."

She nodded.

"Everyone else in the world seems to think I should be, but I'm not," he explained, feeling the need to justify his own touchiness that afternoon. "When you acted as if you believed I was asking you out, I thought, damn, even Shelley thinks I should be dating by now. Sometimes..." He drifted off for a moment. "Sometimes I think I'll never be ready."

She looked sympathetic, and he braced himself for the possibility that she would say something awful, some platitude about how he shouldn't give up hope, he should never say never. Her pity, however, was aimed elsewhere. "It must be ghastly having everyone in the world telling you what you should or shouldn't do. Particularly when you know they're only trying to help."

"You must get lots of 'helpful' advice, too."

"No," Shelley told him. "My mother wouldn't dare to advise me. Maybe in private she wrings her hands, and every now and then she makes some remark about how isolated I must be, living all alone on the island. But she knows what happens to women who put too much trust in men. She's been there. And I guess she loves me enough not to want me to follow in her footsteps."

Kip scrutinized her thoughtfully. It bothered him that she was so willing to condemn all men for the actions of a few bad ones. But given how he despised the well-meaning interference of his loved ones, he would spare Shelley any well-meaning interference from him—except to say, "You can trust me, Shelley. I hope you know that."

"I do," she said. "I think it's when you combine trust with love that you get into trouble. Love robs you of perspective. It makes you ignore the things you don't want to see. My mother loved my father—and so did I. There were so many signs, Kip, so many things I should have noticed. But I didn't, because I loved him and trusted him." She gazed out the window for a moment, her mouth curved in a poignant smile as the sinking sun painted the sky with streaks of fire. Not until the sun had slipped completely below the horizon did she turn back to Kip. "I'm not in love with you, Kip. So I suppose it's safe to trust you."

The smile she gave him was curiously diffident. She let her eyes reach to his again, brave, beautiful silver-gray eyes, and took another sip of wine. He gazed at her defiantly raised chin, her smooth cheeks, the fullness of her lips, and thought for an insane moment how sad it was that they would never be in love with each other.

Sad but safe. He was as safe with Shelley as she was with him. And right now, they both seemed to need that more than anything else.

Chapter Eight

"How do you know all this stuff?" Shelley asked.

He bent the brush bristles against his palm to test their softness, then swirled the brush around in the jar of solvent and rinsed it beneath the spout of the kitchen sink. "How do I know all what stuff?" he shot back.

"How to refinish the banisters."

Glancing over his shoulder at her, he laughed. "There really isn't much to know."

"You knew what grades of sandpaper to use, and which brushes, and... I don't know," she said with a shrug. "I'm impressed. You don't seem like a Mr. Fix-It kind of guy."

"Casting aspersions on my manhood, are you? I'm insulted," he said, feigning indignation. He shook the excess water from the brush, laid it on the counter with the others he'd already cleaned and dried his hands on a towel. "You seem to forget, Shelley, that I spent many a summer weekend helping my father fix things around this house."

"That's right," she recalled. "You worked your fingers to the bone while Diana lounged around rhapsodizing about her latest heartthrob."

"Exactly."

Afternoon sunshine streamed through the bay windows, filling the kitchen with golden light. Kip had argued with Shelley over her decision to spend her day off helping him refinish the staircase railings, but she had claimed that there was nothing else she'd rather do. "Besides," she'd informed him, "it isn't really my day off. As long as the pharmacy is open, I'm on call." The electronic pager hooked onto her belt proved that.

The pager hadn't beeped since Shelley had arrived at the house at ten o'clock that morning. Except for a half-hour break for lunch and another break at around two-thirty to split a bottle of beer on the front veranda, they'd been working straight through.

It was nearly four o'clock now, still bright and balmy outside. "Let's take a ride," Kip said.

"Let's," she agreed with a grin.

He tossed the towel onto the counter, adjusted his glasses more comfortably on his nose, and studied the woman perched on the kitchen table in her faded blue jeans and oversized T-shirt. For a crazed moment he imagined Shelley and himself slipping through a crack in time, tumbling backward until they were fifteen again. Shelley's hair would be longer, her fingernails shorter, her feet shod in sandals rather than white leather sneakers. But basically she would have looked just as she looked today, her cheeks arching as she smiled, her eyes glowing, her long legs swinging freely, her attitude easy and amiable and amazingly open.

In the nine days since he'd landed at Old Harbor he'd done a lot of work on the house. He'd insulated the windows, put new washers in the bathroom faucets, mopped all the hardwood floors with a water-vinegar solution, swept the cellar, given the lawn its autumn dose of fertilizer, repaired some roof shingles on the garage, sanded the stairway railings and slapped on a fresh coat of varnish.

And he'd seen Shelley. Occasionally he dropped in at the pharmacy to say hello, and every evening was reserved for her. Sometimes they ate dinner at a restaurant, sometimes at his house. One evening she'd insisted that he come to her apartment for supper. The two of them had barely fit into the kitchen, and Kip had suggested that they coordinate their respiration so they wouldn't both try to inhale at the same time and cause the walls to implode. By the time dessert was served he had developed new insights into the meaning of claustrophobia.

It didn't matter, though. He'd enjoyed eating in her cramped little flat as much as he enjoyed eating in his roomy kitchen or at any of the restaurants around the island. A miracle cure: he was actually starting to enjoy eating again.

It wasn't simply that Shelley's presence conquered his loneliness. In truth, the loneliness he suffered couldn't be conquered. It was with him and always would be. Like a chronic illness, it might subside for a while, lying dormant deep within him, and then without any warning or apparent provocation it would flare up again. He was coming to understand the nature of it, to adapt to it, to treasure those moments when the symptoms weren't pronounced and to withstand those moments when the pain rose up against him.

Unlike his parents, Shelley didn't expect him ever to be completely free of his affliction. She recognized the way he experienced it—sometimes it was obvious and sometimes it was buried, but it was always present, something he would live with for the rest of his life. She didn't view it as a weakness, a flaw he could overcome if only he put his mind to it.

He could be himself with her. He didn't have to try hard, to force anything, to worry about earning her approval or fending off her pity. He could relax with the confidence that she accepted him as he was.

Just like when they were kids.

She sprang off the table and headed outside with him. Her bicycle, a spiffy black ten-speed which, she'd boasted, she had bought brand new shortly after she'd moved to the island, was parked beside the front veranda. She waited patiently while Kip wheeled his rejuvenated bike out of the garage and met up with her in front of the house. They coasted down the driveway and turned onto the street.

In the olden days Kip would have challenged her to a race, but he'd outgrown that childish competitiveness long ago. It was much nicer to ride side by side with her, to glance to the left and see her strong profile, her hair glittering in the sunshine as the wind lifted it back from her face.

"So," she called to him over the wind, "what's Diana doing these days, anyway?"

"Well, she's settled on one heartthrob," Kip told her. "She married a guy named Glenn Hobart. He's an endocrinologist at Johns Hopkins in Baltimore, and she's a special education teacher."

Shelley seemed delighted. "That's wonderful."

"Actually, she's on a leave of absence right now. She had a baby back in January. A daughter, Victoria. The most beautiful girl in the world—says her unbiased uncle," he added with a self-mocking grin. "Diana was going to go back to work this September, but she decided to take another year off. She's really into motherhood."

"And you're really into uncle-hood," Shelley guessed, shooting him a quick look and then concentrating on steering around a sharp curve in the road. "I wish I had a sister. You always used to fight with Diana, but still . . . it's nice having a sibling."

"Yes," he conceded. For all the squabbling, for all the taunting and raging and threats of retribution, he loved Diana and she loved him. Within days of his returning to Boston with his mother last spring, Diana had rearranged her life and carted her baby up to Chestnut Hill just to be with him, to offer him whatever support she could.

He thought about how much Shelley would have benefited from having a sibling with whom she could share the burden of her family's debacle. Obviously she couldn't lean on her mother.

Kip wished he could have helped her in some way. He wished he could have been the brother she didn't have.

Without thinking consciously about where they were going, they found themselves veering off West Side Road toward Dorie's Cove. They bypassed the main beach and bounced along a rutted dirt path to the edge of a grass-covered cliff. At the end of the path they braked. Shelley looked at Kip, her eyes bright.

In no time, Kip stashed the bicycles behind the familiar old boulder where they'd always hidden them in the past. Then he and Shelley picked their way carefully over the tumbled rocks and stones, down the cliff to their special beach.

The sand was a shimmering salmon color, reflecting the blushing light of the late afternoon sun. Shelley yanked off her sneakers and socks, rolled up the hems of her pants and jogged to the water's edge. Kip lagged behind, gazing about him at the cliff, the sand, the wind spiraling against the walls of their hidden cove, leaving the unkempt dune grass to whisper in its wake.

How many afternoons had he spent here? How many dreams had he dreamed in this hideaway? Why couldn't life be as painless now as it was then?

Keeping on his sneakers, he crossed the sand to stand near Shelley, just a few feet behind her where the incoming tide hadn't yet reached. She gazed out at the blue-gray water of the sound, at the stripe of light the sun painted across the still water, narrow in the distance and spreading as it neared them. He filled his lungs with the clean, salty air, then let it out in a long, wistful sigh.

"Amanda would have loved this place," he murmured.

Shelley didn't turn. She didn't say anything. Her hands on her hips, she stared resolutely out toward the horizon. If he hadn't noticed the barely perceptible stiffening in her shoulders, he would have thought she hadn't heard him.

She *had* heard him, though—and abruptly it occurred to him that he shouldn't have said what he'd said. This place belonged to him and Shelley and their childhood. Amanda had never been a part of it.

"I'm sorry."

Shelley raked her wind-tossed locks of hair out of her eyes, but she didn't turn. "No need to be."

"If she'd stumbled onto this beach when we were kids, we would have harassed her until she'd left."

At last Shelley turned, smiling wryly. "Yeah. We were an obnoxious pair."

"I don't know why I even thought of her just now," he said, still feeling a compulsion to explain, to apologize.

Shelley's smile grew tender. "You thought of her because you loved her and you loved this place. If she'd intruded on us today, we wouldn't have chased her away. We would have invited her to join us. We would have shared it with her."

Yes. They would have. Not just Kip but Shelley. She cared so much about him, she could welcome his wife into their memories.

"You would have liked Amanda," he said.

"Probably better than I like you," Shelley teased.

He reached out and took her hand. She moved to him, her wet feet caked with sand, her hair tangled. When she stood toe to toe with him he released her hand and wrapped his arms tightly around her waist. "She would have liked you, too," he said. "You're an incredible woman, Shelley."

She opened her mouth to speak, then reconsidered and said nothing. Closing her arms around him, she let her head come to rest against his shoulder. He ran his fingertips up her spine and into her hair, unraveling the snarled waves. He longed to tell her how much these days had meant to him, how much this one day meant, this one moment alone with her in their secret cove, standing in the warmth of the setting sun while the wind curled gently around them. He hoped his embrace conveyed what he couldn't express in words.

Holding her filled him with the harmony of those days gone by, the peace and confidence and optimism that had once defined his existence. With Shelley he could remember what it was like to know that quiet joy.

With Shelley he could believe that someday he might experience it again.

THURSDAY MORNING he got a call from Harrison Shaw, the friend of his father's who had hired him when he'd moved back from San Francisco to Chestnut Hill. "I just thought I'd check in and see how you were making out," Harrison said jovially.

Kip owed Harrison a great deal. The man had hired Kip for no other reason than that he was Brock Stroud's son, and as a result Kip had done everything within his power to make sure Harrison never regretted granting that favor. Kip had thrown himself into his first project, a loser that all the other consultants at Harrison's firm had declined. To everyone's surprise, Kip had come up with a good strategy for the hemorrhaging high-tech firm, divesting it of its least productive subsidiary and using the money from the sale to facilitate more extensive research on its fiber-optic products.

Harrison had found a place for Kip in his firm as an act of charity. But Kip had had every intention of earning the right to stay there, and with one project, he'd done that.

"I'm doing well," Kip told Harrison over the telephone. "How are things back in 'America'?"

"I beg your pardon?"

Kip laughed. "Sorry, that's what people on Block Island call the mainland."

"Maybe you've been there too long, if you're starting to speak the native tongue," Harrison joked. "Your father mentioned that you've been in touch with him and your

mother every few days. He said you told them you were
getting some rest and exercise.''

''Exercise,'' Kip groaned. ''I've been doing repairs on his
house. What he calls exercise I call cheap labor.''

''Well, speaking of cheap labor... I've got a new client I
think you could do a repair on. I don't want to rush you,
Kip—I know your situation and I want to accommodate you
any way I can. But we've got another of those teeter-totter
little high-tech companies peering anxiously into the abyss.
Just your kind of thing.''

''I don't know if it's my kind of thing, Harrison. I did it
once, but it's nothing like what I was doing back in San
Francisco.''

''You aren't in San Francisco now, Kip. You're working
for me. If you can't handle it, fine, but if you can, I could
really use you back in the office.''

Kip turned to gaze out the window. It was already nine-
thirty. Since the mist hadn't yet burned away, it was likely
to linger all day. It swirled above the grass in a vague, mysterious pattern, one of Mother Nature's glorious special ef-
fects.

Even on gray days like this, Kip loved being on the island. The stretch of days he'd spent here had done him
good. But maybe he'd been here long enough. Maybe the
time had come to face real life once more.

He could try, anyway. He could return to Boston and do
another wham-bang consultation for Harrison. If the walls
started to close in on him again, if his ability to laugh stalled
out, if he closed his eyes and saw Amanda's face twisted into
a silent scream of dread ... he would jump on the next ferry
out of Pt. Judith.

The island would always be here for him when he needed
it. He had no doubt he would need it again—merely thinking about going back to Boston cast a nebulous shadow over
his mood. But there was a limit to how long he could hide.

He felt stronger now than he had a week ago, or even a day ago.

He would try. He would go back to "America" and try to function.

"I could be there on Monday," he said.

"I'M UNDERDRESSED," Shelley groaned as she stepped into the house and glimpsed the dining room.

Kip had telephoned her at the pharmacy and informed her that he would make dinner at his house that night. He'd wanted to do something special to celebrate their reunion and to thank her for her friendship over the past two weeks. It would be a festive occasion; whatever goodbyes he exchanged with Shelley wouldn't be permanent. He would be coming back, visiting the island again, staying in touch.

He'd spent hours scouring the island's shops for candles, fresh scallops, an assortment of produce and wine. Amanda had been the gourmet cook in their marriage, but Kip had been her willing assistant, and he'd picked up a few skills along the way.

Given the ambitions of his menu, he decided the dining room would be the appropriate setting. He covered the ancient mahogany table with a lace cloth he'd located in one of the breakfront drawers, and set two places with matching cloth napkins. A pair of candlesticks flanked a vase that held the last scraggly rose he'd found clinging to one of the bushes near the stone wall.

Outside, the cool, humid air held the scent of the ocean. Inside the house the air smelled of wine and butter and herbs.

Shelley stood in the entry, her hands shoved into the pockets of her corduroy skirt, and inspected the elegant dining-room table. "I came straight from work," she told him. "It was getting late, so I didn't bother to go home and change. Which is just as well, I suppose—if I *had* gone home, I probably would have changed into jeans." Grinning she tore her gaze from the dining room to study him. He had on his khakis and a crisp, fresh shirt.

She followed him into the kitchen, where he engaged in a flurry of final preparations. After making the appropriate oohs and ahhs over the feast he'd prepared, she offered to toss the salad, but he refused. "I'm the chef," he told her. "I'll toss my own creations, thank you."

She held up her hands in surrender. "Toss away."

He carried the salad and vinaigrette dressing to the dining room, returned for the scallops and rice, the bottle of Moselle and the French bread. Then, with playful gallantry, he came back to the kitchen, bowed, and offered her his arm. She dutifully slipped her hand around the bend in his elbow and let him escort her to her seat.

"What's this all about?" she asked, suspicion filtering through her obvious delight at the elegant meal.

"What it's all about," he said, "is..." Smiling, he settled himself in the chair across from her and considered various replies. As he did, he watched the twin flames of the candles flicker in the breeze from the open window, shedding their dancing golden light across her face. She returned his smile, her eyes unwavering on him, her smile mesmerizing.

He would tell her about his plans to return to Boston, but not yet. "I felt like showing off."

"Showing off is right. When you came to my house for dinner I made broiled chicken."

"It was very good broiled chicken," he assured her. He couldn't resist adding, with a patronizing smirk, "Not as good as this is going to be, but I'm sure you did your best."

She wadded up her napkin, threatening to hurl it across the table at him, then laughed and tasted a scallop. "You're right," she conceded after swallowing. "You win the Block Island cook-off. This is outstanding. When did you learn to cook?"

"Amanda taught me."

"She was a good teacher. This is fantastic," Shelley said before spearing another scallop and popping it into her mouth.

They talked about inconsequential things during dinner. Kip told Shelley about his continuing attempts to educate himself about wine and Shelley confessed she still wasn't quite clear on the difference between Burgundy and Beaujolais. She told him that at the University of Texas, long-neck beer was the drink of choice and wine was considered a beverage for sissies and Yankees. "Which is redundant, since they think all Yankees are sissies," she explained. "The best thing about Texas, as far as I'm concerned, is that everyone is tall there. I never feel like a freak when I'm there."

"You don't feel like a freak here, do you?"

"I used to, back at the high school in Westport. I was taller than half the boys in my class."

"Ah. How reassuring it must be for you to find yourself surrounded by all those brawny beer-swigging cowboys," he teased.

"Believe it," she teased right back. "You wouldn't catch any of those manly men of the Lone Star State tossing their own salads."

"The only reason I'm so liberated is because you made me read all those girl coming-of-age novels during my formative years."

"For which you should thank me," she said with phony piety.

"For which I *do* thank you," he murmured, growing solemn. Dinner was winding down. Their refilled wineglasses were already half-empty, and the candles had melted down to stubs. The time had come for Kip to tell her he was leaving the island—and to tell her how much her friendship meant to him. He didn't want to put a damper on the evening or wax overly sentimental, but these things had to be said.

Shelley gazed at him, her eyebrows arched with expectation.

He returned her gaze and felt himself relax. With Shelley he didn't have to panic about choosing the right words, expressing himself with precision, making the proper impression. He could say anything, and if she misunderstood he'd say it again differently, and yet again if need be, knowing she'd stick with him until he got his message across.

"I'm going back to Boston this weekend," he said.

She gave herself a moment to digest his announcement. Then she nodded.

"My boss wants me back at the office. He's been generous about letting me take off from work for a while. I don't want to take advantage of him."

She smiled slightly. "You didn't exactly take off from work," she reminded him. "You've knocked yourself out working on the house here."

"Busy work," he said, remembering that when he'd first taken inventory of the maintenance projects that needed doing around the house, he'd considered them little more than an attempt to distract himself from his grief. They'd helped.

Shelley had helped more. "I'm not going to make a speech, Shelley. I'm not going to say goodbye. I plan to come back to the island when I can. I like it here."

Her smile expanded. "So do I."

He traced the rim of his wineglass with his index finger, searching for a way to convey his feelings without sounding corny—and then giving up. If he sounded corny he sounded corny. "Your friendship means a lot to me," he said. "Without you I don't know if I could have pulled myself together. I would still be a mass of exposed nerves, fighting off the nightmares. You've done so much for me, Shelley— I can't begin to thank you. I never want us to lose track of each other. I want you to promise you'll never disappear on me again. Okay?"

Shelley's smile changed once more, becoming softer, quieter, more profoundly felt. "I'm afraid to make a promise like that," she admitted, continuing before he could protest. "But for you I will." She sipped her wine, then cradled her glass in her hands, her eyes steady on him. "I don't want your thanks, Kip. Friendship works both ways. You've done a lot for me, too."

Her words pleased and surprised him. "What have I done for you—other than teach you the correct way to varnish a stairway railing?"

"You cooked me this incredible meal," she joked, then became serious once more. "You taught me that I'm capable of trusting a man. You reminded me of how nice it can be to trust someone."

His eyes drank her in. She looked serene, satisfied, stunningly honest. Nothing was hidden in her face, nothing held back. Her smile was genuine, sweet and affectionate.

He hadn't been aware of teaching her anything. Then again, she probably hadn't been aware of doing anything deliberate to help him. Their relationship wasn't a product of conscious effort. What they did for each other—what they had always done for each other, even as eight-year-old playmates so many years ago—was natural and instinctive. They talked—and they listened. They felt each other's pain and shared each other's wonder. Their friendship was built on loyalty, humor and trust—an immeasurable degree of trust.

"So," he said with a wink, "thanks to me, you're going to give old Jack MacRae of the U.S. Coast Guard another chance?"

Shelley wrinkled her nose. "I trust *you*, Kip. That doesn't mean I trust everyone."

"I'm sure I'm not the only trustworthy man in the world."

She snorted. "Oh, maybe there are three or four others. But don't tell me you haven't noticed that the vast majority of men in this world are creeps."

"We're not talking about your father, Shelley. We're talking about guys like me."

"Guys like you are rare," she informed him in a calm, matter-of-fact tone. "Believe me, I've looked. I've done my share of dating, Kip. I've given it the old college try, and I've gotten pressured and hoodwinked and made a fool of. I've never met a man I could love and trust at the same time. If I had…" She sent him a rueful smile. "I'd probably be with him right now."

Her candor touched him. He had sensed bitterness in her that first time they'd talked, nibbling pizza in the kitchen. But now he comprehended her sorrow from a new perspective. The old saw about loving and losing hit home; he realized that in spite of his agony over losing Amanda, he had been lucky to experience such a marvelous love once in his life. Shelley had never known a love like that. It didn't seem fair.

Yet she didn't deserve his sympathy. She'd made her peace with the world. She'd found a solution that worked for her. Kip couldn't bring himself to pity her.

"For a long time," she said, her voice low and velvety in the candlelit room, "all I wanted was to be in control of my life. I wanted to be self-reliant, to make my own decisions, to prove to myself that I didn't need anyone. My mother used to say she was afraid to travel solo. Well, that was what I wanted to do—travel solo."

"Do you still want that?" he asked.

"It's a part of me now," she explained. "It's not something I have to want anymore. It's a part of my life." Lapsing into thought, she gazed at the reflection of the candlelight on the surface of her wine. After a moment she lifted her eyes back to Kip. "Until you came to the island, I was so afraid of losing that control that I didn't dare to make room in my life for anyone else. I'm not afraid anymore. You've proven that I can like a man without losing my autonomy, that I can be friends with a man and still travel solo."

"And that's what you want?"

"More than anything." She set down her glass, reached across the table and clasped his hand. "And so...I thank you."

A great deal passed between them in that embrace of hands, more than they'd communicated with words. When, at long last, Shelley pulled her hand away and rose from her chair, Kip felt as if he had absorbed the essence of her touch, as if it would always be inside him.

He stood and blew out the candles. Without speaking—without having to say anything—they gathered the dishes and brought them to the kitchen. They worked smoothly together, neither having to tell the other what to do. Kip wrapped the leftovers and placed them in the refrigerator; Shelley scraped the dishes and stacked them in the sink; Kip washed, Shelley dried. Every now and then his eyes would meet hers and they would smile.

He couldn't remember the last time he'd felt this content. Amanda wasn't with him but he still felt good, without guilt or grief gnawing at the edges of his happiness, without an aching void in his soul.

When the dishes were all put away, Shelley glanced at her watch and sighed. "I really should be going," she said.

Nodding, he took her hand and strolled with her out of the kitchen, down the hall and through the front door. The fog had thickened with nightfall; the air was cool and damp, dulling the outlines of the porch railing, the red maple and the Chevy Blazer in the driveway.

He continued to hold her hand as they ambled through the dense mist to the truck. Kip wanted to speak, but he wasn't sure what to say. So much had already been said, so many emotions revealed. A bond had been created between them, a promise sealed.

Maybe he didn't have to say anything, other than goodbye. He could say that without qualms now, because no matter whether he sailed across the sound or flew across the continent, Shelley would remain in his life in some vital way.

At her truck she stopped and turned to face him. "I'll try to stop by the pharmacy tomorrow," he said.

"If you can. You're going to be pretty busy packing."

"I'll make the time." He lifted his hands to her shoulders and pulled her toward him for a farewell kiss.

She looped her arms around his waist and touched her mouth to his. He was startled by the unexpected stirring in his body, the sudden flash of sensation along his nerve endings as her lips brushed innocently over his. She had such soft lips.

He wasn't certain if what he heard was a gust of wind or the catch of her breath. Her limpid eyes peered into his, questioning.

The only answer he could think of was *yes*. He wanted this. He wanted to kiss her again.

He bowed and pressed his mouth cautiously to hers. His pulse drummed in his temples as her lips moved against his with equal caution.

They were friends. He hadn't desired a woman in so long. Shelley trusted him.

He angled his head just enough to fuse his mouth to hers. The sound he heard was definitely her breath, a tiny gasp followed by a hushed, lyrical sigh as her mouth opened beneath his. Their tongues found each other, first shy and then eager, tangling and tempting, mating with wild abandon.

He groaned. It had been so long since he had wanted this, so long since he'd been with a woman he could want this way. His body hummed with yearning. His muscles flexed and strained; his skin begged for the feel of a woman's hands on it. Shelley's hands.

Shelley.

With great reluctance he broke the kiss. He mustn't do this to her. They'd just established that they were true, trusting friends. No matter how much he wanted her at this moment, he would never do anything to undermine their friendship.

That was what he meant to say. Only one word emerged, though. "Stay."

She looked up at him. Her eyes glittered enigmatically; her lips looked as alluring as they'd felt. It took all his willpower not to crush her mouth with his and deny her the chance to speak.

She appeared on the verge of shaking her head. She withdrew her hands from his waist, then lifted them to his chest. He waited for her to push him away.

After an endless moment she let her fingers drift up to his shoulders. They molded to him, trailed toward his arms and back again, exploring, curious, undecided. Her gaze held his; her lips remained gently parted, air passing between them in shallow breaths.

Moonlight fought its way through the heavy fog. The light in her eyes was much brighter, illuminating her face. A smile whispered over her lips.

She guided his mouth back to hers.

Chapter Nine

He led her through the moonlit room to his bed. After folding down the covers, he beckoned her to sit on the edge of the mattress. He knelt on the floor in front of her and gazed up into her face. It seemed both familiar and strange to him, her eyes bright in a way he'd never seen them before, her lips curved in a knowing smile. This had not been an impulsive decision on her part. She understood what she was doing in Kip's room. She had willingly chosen to come here.

He turned his attention to her feet, easing off her loafers and setting them aside. He skimmed his hands up her legs, beneath her skirt, along the outer edges of her thighs. Her breath grew short but she didn't object, didn't recoil.

He raised his eyes to hers. She lifted her hips so he could remove her stockings. Her skin felt warm against his fingertips, silky. His hands shook slightly as he peeled down her hose and panties.

He prayed she knew how much this meant to him, how important she was to him. He prayed that after so many months of self-imposed abstinence—in thought as well as deed—he would be able to contain himself, to please her, to make this as special for her as it was for him.

The temptation to run his fingers back up her naked legs was too great. He forced himself to pull his hands away, then rose and sat on the bed beside her. As he unfastened the top button of her blouse she plucked his eyeglasses off and placed them on the night table. "I don't want to break your nose," she said with a smile.

Remembering, he grinned. They had been so earnest that night in the cupola twelve years ago, practicing their kisses and assessing the results, two solemn students trying to get it right. Two intimate friends.

He kissed her chin, her nose, the lid of each eye, the corners of her smile. His body remained tense with anticipation, but his mind and his heart relaxed. His soul vibrated with laughter as well as passion. If any woman could see him through his first attempt to throw off the past and become a complete man once more, it was Shelley. He trusted no other woman the way he trusted her.

They attacked each other's clothes, pulling and tugging, unbuttoning and unbuckling until they were both naked. Kip guided Shelley down to the mattress. Her tall, beautiful body extended nearly the length of the bed.

He caressed her skin—not silk, he decided, but satin, smooth and supple, a tactile delight spread out before him, awaiting the pleasure of his touch. He traced her collarbone, her firm, round breasts. He circled one nipple, then rubbed it with his thumb and felt it stiffen, felt threads of arousal tightening below the surface. Once he'd teased the other nipple into the same exquisite condition, he let his hand journey lower, over her ribs, her stomach, over the sharp point of her hipbone, over the sleek contour of her thigh.

She touched him, too, probing the strong arch of his back, twining her fingers through the wiry hair of his chest, strumming along his ribs, down over the muscles of his abdomen and lower yet, making a brief but daring foray into the thick, dark hair at his groin. Her glancing caress caused him to suck in a shaky breath.

The trembling inside his soul grew fiercer, less laughter than need now, but he did his best to ignore it, to take his time. He'd waited more than a year for this; he could wait a few minutes longer. He had to be sure Shelley was with him, the moment right for her.

His mouth sought hers, capturing it in a devouring kiss as his hands continued to roam over her. She bent her leg, offering him her knee; he took more than she offered, abandoning the knee for her thigh, massaging the smooth, warm flesh and savoring her hushed moan as he moved his hand upward.

Her hips arched in silent beseechment. He obeyed her unspoken demand, cupping his hand between her legs and sinking his fingers into her. She cried out, her smile gone, her eyes half-closed as he circled and dipped, steeping her in her own sweet arousal. One of her hands dug into his shoulder and the other darted down between their bodies, seeking, finding him, stroking until his need for her became unbearable.

He rose onto her, pulled her legs around him, and slid into the pulsing heat of her. So good, he thought as she arched again, drawing him deeper. She felt so good, so perfect, as if she had been shaped just for him, as if the tight, damp darkness of her had been waiting for this instant, this union. As if his body had been waiting for no one but her.

They moved together, finding their rhythm, letting their instincts take over. As strong and brave as Shelley had always been, now she was tender, delicate, unabashedly feminine. Her skin felt incredibly soft against his, her breasts soft beneath the firm muscles of his chest, her lips soft as his tongue plundered her mouth, her gasps of rapture so soft, so heavenly. Her enveloping warmth so unspeakably soft as he surged within her.

He leaned back to gaze down at her. Her eyes were still half-closed, glazed but steady, watching him as he watched her. Her teeth were clamped on her lower lip and her hips rose to meet his thrusts. Her body grew taut beneath him, striving, reaching. She molded her hands to his hips and held him motionless inside her.

He caught his breath and went still as he felt the contractions seize her, the exquisite bliss of her climax overtaking her, pounding through her flesh, culminating in a tremulous groan torn from the depths of her soul. And then he let go.

He was all sensation, all energy, exploding with ecstasy. He'd forgotten what this was like; he hadn't let himself remember. He'd forgotten, until this moment with this woman, the freedom, the relief, the stunning pleasure of it.

This was what it meant to be alive—and now, after so many long months, he was alive again. Shelley had brought him back to life.

Exhausted, he collapsed into her arms. His body felt weak; his mind drifted. Not until he felt her stirring languidly under his smothering weight did he regain full consciousness. He began to lift himself off her, but she wouldn't release him; she ringed her arms around his waist and held him to her, nestled between her legs, allowing him only to brace himself with his arms so she could breathe more easily.

Her hair was splayed across the pillow, her lower lip still bearing the imprint of her teeth. Her eyes searched his face, luminous yet unreadable.

"Was that all right?" he asked in a hushed, hoarse voice.

Her eyes widened, and an astounded laugh escaped her. "Should I grade you on a scale of one to ten?"

He opened his mouth to explain that what he needed to know was whether *they* were all right, whether after what they'd just shared they could still be friends. Yet her joke was all the answer he needed. It reminded him that their relationship was strong and enduring, that this was not the first time they had strayed beyond the boundaries of friendship, and that no matter what they'd done she could still laugh with him and tease him.

He mirrored her smile. "Okay. On a scale of one to ten . . . ?"

She frowned in spurious concentration, then announced her verdict. "Eight."

Eight? Good God. If he'd been the scorekeeper he would have given this a ten. A ten thousand.

Her laughter cut through his insecurity, and he relaxed and eased out of her arms, settling next to her on his side so he could continue to gaze at her. "All right," he said patiently. "What did I lose two points for?"

She grinned at him. "You lost two points for deducting two points from my kiss that time in the cupola."

"Ah. A lady with a long memory."

"A long memory and a big grudge."

"What can I do to earn back those points?"

"Hmm." She pretended to give the question a great deal of thought. As she contemplated various possibilities she draped her hand over his side, running it down toward his waist and then forward to weave through the sweat-damp curls of hair matting his chest.

His body reacted all over, in a deliciously uncomfortable way. He cupped his hand over hers and held it. Together they felt his heartbeat, slower than it had been a minute ago but still fierce and strong. "Keep touching me like that," he whispered, "and you're going to have another opportunity to grade me real soon."

"Is that a warning?"

"A statement of fact." He leaned forward to kiss her. "You're dangerously sexy."

"Oh, right," she scoffed.

"You are."

"How much wine was in that scallop dish you made?"

He frowned. "Don't you know how attractive you are?"

Her smile lost its sardonic edge. "What I know is, the last time you were on Block Island you didn't notice anything the least bit sexy about me."

"You mean, when we were kids?"

"When we were fifteen."

He let out a laugh. "When we were fifteen..." He stroked his thumb over her hand, exploring the slender ridge of her knuckles, the smoothness of her skin. "I thought you were the sexiest girl I'd ever laid eyes on."

"Like hell. You thought I was just a guy, someone to pal around with."

"If I thought you were just a guy, do you think I would have made out with you in the cupola?"

"That wasn't making out," she argued. "That was just practice."

"Sure," he humored her. "That was the most exciting practice I ever had. Didn't you have any idea what you were doing to me that summer?"

She appeared genuinely perplexed. "No. What was I doing to you?"

"Making me crazy."

"Really?"

"Constantly. I was in a continuous state of insanity from you, Shelley. I remember one day..." He reminisced, a nostalgic warmth wrapping around him. "We biked down to our special beach near Dorie's Cove, and you had on this bathing suit—if you could call it that. It was really just three microscopic triangles held together by a thread. One triangle was here—" he bowed and kissed one of her breasts "—one was here—" he kissed her other breast "—and one larger triangle down here." He stroked his hand through the thatch of blond hair curling between her legs. "It was blue, I think—"

Her hips moved reflexively against his hand, and when she spoke her voice sounded unusually husky. "It was turquoise. And you didn't even notice it."

"Didn't notice it? Are you kidding?"

She pouted slightly. "Well, you didn't say anything when I wore it."

He laughed again. "Cripes, Shelley—I was speechless. As I recall, I had to flee into the water so you wouldn't see what that bathing suit was doing to me."

Her eyes grew round. "Really?"

"For months afterward, whenever I saw a triangle I got a hard-on."

She gave him a shove. "I'll bet."

He stroked his fingers down between her legs again, a teasingly light brush against her. It was an unfair tactic, but it kept her from trying to shove him away. "I was a kid," he reminded her. "Embarrassingly inexperienced. Heavy on the fantasies, but lean when it came to action." He deepened his caress, savoring the restless motions of her body, the uneven rasp of her breath as she responded to his touch. "You were my friend, Shelley. It scared me to think of you in sexual terms."

She forced her eyes open. "I'm still your friend," she whispered.

"Maybe it still scares me," he confessed before sliding his free hand around her waist and drawing her to him. Their mouths met, and the fear he'd just confessed to burned away in the heat of her kiss.

Rolling onto his back, he pulled her on top of him, down around him, sliding his hands forward from the pliant curves of her bottom to her thighs, to the place where their bodies met most intimately. He touched her as she rocked against him, and kissed her, and arched deep into her, filling her, binding himself to her in flesh and sensation, in friendship and love.

If he'd stopped to think, he might have been scared again. But he wasn't thinking right now. He was only feeling, glorying in the splendor of being alive, a man making love to a woman.

For this one magnificent night he didn't need to think, and he had nothing to fear.

WHEN HE WOKE UP he was alone.

The room was awash in the pearlescent light of early morning. The bed was warm, the sheets tangled around his naked body. Through an open window he heard the distant honks of a gaggle of geese migrating south. Everything appeared in a myopic blur to him, except for one thing, one thing he saw with excruciating vividness: Shelley was gone.

Panic slammed into his chest, knocking the wind out of his lungs. Where was she? How could she have left? Had he lost her again? Forever this time?

Frantic, he vaulted out of bed and grabbed his slacks from the floor, where they'd spent the night crumbled in a heap. He yanked them on, lifted his equally wrinkled shirt from the rug and punched his arms through the sleeves. He shuffled his bare feet into his loafers, figuring he'd need to be wearing shoes if he had to chase her down in his car. Not bothering to button his shirt, he reached for his glasses and surveyed the room.

Her purse was on the dresser. He let out a long breath as relief flowed through him. She wouldn't have left without taking her purse. She had to be here—somewhere.

Abandoning his bedroom, he glanced down the hall to the small bedroom containing the stairs up to the cupola. She might have gone up there if she'd needed time to think, to reflect on the night they'd spent together. He supposed he needed time to think and reflect, as well, but first he had to find her.

He started toward the small bedroom, then inhaled the aroma of brewing coffee and halted. She must be in the kitchen.

Reversing direction, he headed downstairs. His pulse gradually slowed to normal, and his eyes adjusted to the delicate shafts of dawn light streaming through the windows. At the bottom of the stairs he strode down the hall to the kitchen.

The room was empty. He saw the coffeemaker on the counter, its decanter full of coffee. A clean mug stood on the counter beside it, waiting for him.

Where the hell was she?

He filled the mug and carried it into the dining room. Through the window he spotted her outside on the front veranda. Fully dressed, she leaned against the railing and gazed out at the mist rising off the dew-drenched grass. A mug was balanced on the railing beside her elbow.

She had her back to him, and he took a minute to study her. Her hair glinted with streaks of blond, her shoulders were gracefully broad, her spine straight, her waist narrow, her hips lean and her legs, her long legs . . .

His groin tensed, a detached appreciation of her figure combining with his still-fresh memories of what her body had felt like, what it had done to him, what miraculous things it had made him feel. Last night had been incredible.

But it wasn't last night anymore.

He hesitated. Now that he'd found Shelley he had no idea what to do or say.

At fifteen he'd had pathetically little sexual experience with girls; at twenty-seven he had little experience in how to survive the awkwardness of a morning after. He'd sown his wild oats in college—but only until his junior year, when he'd met Amanda and fallen madly in love. She was the last woman with whom he'd ever awakened after a night of sex.

Until now.

This wasn't a typical situation. Shelley wasn't some woman he'd met and become infatuated with. Nor was she someone he'd picked up for a carefree night of fun. She was his friend, for God's sake. His friend.

He adored her; he thought she was the greatest. He wanted to be able to come to Block Island and visit her, to talk with her as they'd always talked, to feel comfortable with her. But he didn't *love* her.

Had last night changed everything they were to each other? Was he going to have to regard her not as a friend but as a lover now? Would she demand that they renegotiate their relationship?

He cursed.

He didn't want anything to change. He wanted Shelley to be the woman he trusted, the woman who had helped him to recover, who had given him the support and compassion he'd needed to become human and whole.

He didn't love her, though—not in the way last night might have implied. Not even after a moonlit interlude of glorious sex, of passion and humor and astonishing intimacy.

Not the way he'd loved Amanda.

As understanding as Shelley was, he doubted she would be able to understand that. She was a woman, and when a man slept with a woman... it changed things.

Their relationship had always been grounded in honesty, and if Kip had anything to say about it, that aspect would never change. He would simply have to be honest with her, reassure her that she was special but explain, if there was any question, any confusion—if, after all these years, Shelley had somehow failed to understand what was going on between him and herself...

He would just have to be honest, that was all.

He took a quick sip of coffee for fortitude, then left the dining room. He pushed the front door open and stepped out onto the porch. "Good morning," he said.

She turned from the railing and saw him. The smile she gave him was one of pure, distilled pleasure. Her eyes were gentle, her posture relaxed, her expression profoundly tranquil. "I made some coffee—" she began, then noticed the mug in his hand and grinned. "Oh. I see you've found it."

He glanced down into his mug. Steam rose from it in translucent wisps. He searched for inspiration in the vapor as it curled into the air and evaporated. His thoughts were just as ephemeral. They rose up, seeming almost tangible, and then evanesced into the cool morning air.

He had to say something. He had to meet Shelley's courageous, open gaze and say something. "Shelley—"

"No, Kip," she said, her voice low and certain. She crossed the veranda to him, her nearness compelling him to lift his eyes to her. She brushed her fingertips lightly over his lips and smiled. "No explanations. No regrets. It happened, that's all. It happened."

His heart seemed to swell inside him, growing heavy, aching beneath the overwhelming burden of his emotions. She *did* understand, everything, completely.

He stared into her silver-gray eyes, absorbing their depth and beauty, the boundless faith illuminating them. "I have no explanations," he murmured, curving his hand over her cheek, using his thumb to tuck an errant strand of golden hair behind her ear, as he'd done innumerable times before. "I also have no regrets."

"We're still friends?" she half asked.

"Always, Shelley." He set his mug on the railing and gathered her into his arms. "Always," he whispered, and prayed for it to be the truth.

He had lost Amanda, and the pain of losing her had been almost beyond bearing. Losing Shelley would hurt just as much.

She was not his lover, but she was his friend, and she understood the difference. She understood.

SIX WEEKS LATER, he moved into his new apartment in Back Bay. It was a charming one-bedroom place with a terrific view of the Charles River, and while the rent was outrageously high he could afford it.

His parents had donated a few essential pieces of furniture, but most of his belongings were still inside moving cartons. He had no shelves for his books, and only one three-drawer chest for his clothes. He had left all his furniture in San Francisco, but now that he was finally of reasonably sound mind, he could begin to cope with the idea of selling the co-op and transporting the rest of his belongings east.

The day he'd signed the lease he joined a health club in the neighborhood; one of his old high-school buddies, now an attorney on Beacon Hill, was also a member. An art dealer who lived in his building had sold him a couple of framed Georgia O'Keeffe prints at discount for his barren walls. Another neighbor, noticing the fresh-paint smell of his apartment, had given him several spice pomanders. Harrison Shaw and his wife had presented him with a set of towels as a housewarming gift.

Last night Kip had gone out to dinner with a friend of a friend of his old high-school classmate. A buyer for Jordan Marsh, Eileen was a bubbly woman, devoted to Chinese food and Sixties rock music. She had coppery red hair, pretty green eyes and a full, almost plump figure that had tempted Kip in a supremely healthy way. He hadn't acted on that temptation, but the fact that he could respond to her pleased him. He'd asked her to have dinner with him again on Saturday night, and she'd accepted the invitation.

He was ready to start his new life. He was ready to take care of himself. He was ready to be a fully functioning adult once more.

He still had black moments, flashes of Amanda tearing across his brain, nightmares and episodes of sheer anguish. Occasionally he found himself eating at a counter in the kitchen, standing up, not because he lacked a dining table but because he was lonely, because he had no one with whom to share his coffee and bicker over the sections of the newspaper. Sometimes when he was walking down a busy street he'd see a petite, well-dressed woman with curly black hair and sorrow would squeeze his heart until he was staggered by the pain.

But those times were fewer and farther between. He had his life back. He was all right. Better than all right—he was happy.

The night the call came, he was particularly happy because he'd beaten the pants off Dave Alvord on the squash court after work. Even after a year away from the game his skills hadn't atrophied. He'd played aggressively, enthusiastically, burning off the tensions of a day at work as well as other tensions, undefined and unexamined, latent but always there. By the time he'd aced his final serve he'd been too fatigued to be tense. Dave had cheerfully called him something unprintable, and Kip had salved Dave's wounded pride by treating him to an iced tea in the club's lounge once they'd both showered and donned their street clothes. They'd made a date for a rematch, then went their separate ways home.

Kip bounded into his apartment, carrying his athletic bag and racket along with his briefcase and the letters he'd found in his mailbox downstairs. He flipped through the envelopes—nothing worthy of his immediate attention—and got a cold beer. He removed his suit jacket, loosened his tie, rolled up his shirt sleeves and strode into the bedroom, where he kicked off his loafers.

The telephone rang. Making a mental note to buy a phone extension for the bedroom, he returned to the living room, lifted the telephone off the floor, flopped into the easy chair—the only piece of furniture in the room—and answered. "Hello?"

"Kip? It's Shelley."

"Shelley!" A broad grin spread across his face. God, he missed her. He missed their daily visits, their casual conversations, their easy camaraderie. He'd intended to give her a call, but things had been hectic since he'd returned from

Block Island. The first few weeks he'd spent every day at work and every evening looking at apartments for rent; the past ten days he'd spent every day at work and every evening trying to turn his new residence into something resembling a home.

He should have been in touch with Shelley, though. If not for her—if not for Block Island, the brisk sea air, the house-maintenance projects, the long bicycle rides, but mostly Shelley herself, her company, her gentle presence and unflagging loyalty—he wouldn't have made it this far. He would have still been a basket case, drowning in self-pity, haunted by the past.

He suffered a twinge of guilt for having neglected her, but that didn't diminish his delight at hearing her voice. "Hi!" he said. "I moved."

"Yes, I know. I called your parents' house, and your mother gave me this number."

"Right." He took a quick sip of beer, then set the bottle down on the floor beside the chair and gazed about the Spartan room. "I've been meaning to phone you, but it's been crazy. It took me awhile to find this apartment, and to get settled in . . . Slowly but surely it's coming together."

"Congratulations."

"The place is a disaster. No—I mean it's really nice, but it's empty. I've barely begun to unpack. Right now I'm sitting in the only chair I own and staring at six unpacked cartons lined up along the opposite wall. I think one of them contains my record collection, but since I haven't got a stereo . . ." He settled more comfortably into the overstuffed cushions, kicking one leg over one of the chair's arms and swinging his foot. Simply hearing Shelley's voice made his apartment seem brighter, more like home. "I felt the time had come for me to move out of my parents' place," he said. "They're wonderful—well, I don't have to tell you that—but when I got back from Block Island I just felt...ready.'' He sighed. ''I should have called, Shelley.''

''You've been busy.''

''Even so, I should have called.''

She offered no argument. Evidently she agreed with him.

''So you're back at work?'' she asked.

''Yes, and loving it. Harrison—my boss—stuck me with a really screwy client. The challenge is unbelievable, but I love it. I can walk to work from my new apartment, which is great. I'm getting myself back into shape, Shell. As a matter of fact, I just got home from a killer squash game with a friend of mine. I'm eating better, too.''

''Scallops in wine?'' she asked.

He heard the humorous lilt in her voice; he could picture her smile. ''I wish,'' he muttered with pretended dismay. ''I need some equipment for the kitchen. All I've got is a skillet and two pots. But if you visit, I promise I'll go out and invest in some cookware. How about it?'' he said, his smile widening. The invitation had popped out unexpectedly, but as soon as he verbalized it he was thrilled. He took a sip of beer and said, ''Why don't you come visit me in Boston? We can go to a museum, take in a show... You can give me some advice on what kind of furniture I should buy, and in return I'll stuff you with gourmet food. How about it?''

A long silence, and then, ''I don't think so, Kip.''

Belatedly it dawned on him that perhaps she hadn't called just to shoot the breeze with him. ''What's up?'' he asked, unconsciously sitting straighter.

''Well...'' He heard the crackle of long-distance static on the line. ''I'm pregnant.''

''Kip?''

He heard her voice but somehow he couldn't respond. He simply stared at the Georgia O'Keeffe print on the wall opposite him, a sensuous symmetrical rendering of an orchid. He concentrated on the smooth plastic of the receiver in one hand, the cold beer bottle in the other, the weight of the telephone base in his lap. And he listened to the silence Shelley's statement left in its wake.

Unable to digest what she'd said, he closed his eyes. He expected to see Amanda, but all he saw was blackness, a bit frightening yet at the same time curiously restful. The emotion that jolted might have been horror or dread, or something quite different. It was dark, elusive, portentous.

"Kip?" she said again after a minute.

"Are you sure?" he asked, his voice a faint rasp.

"I haven't seen Dr. Hodge yet. I used a home pregnancy test—we carry them at the pharmacy. It tested positive." She paused, giving him the opportunity to say something. He didn't know what to say, though. "When I go to Dr. Hodge, everyone on the island is going to know. I thought...I thought you should know first."

Should he thank her for that courtesy? Should he feel honored that she told him before everybody on Block Island knew?

God help him, what was he going to do? He'd only just gotten back on his feet again. He'd only just started to feel his life taking shape, falling back within his control, resembling normality. He'd only just begun to master his destiny, to set new goals and look toward the future with something other than anguish or apathy.

He'd only moved into his apartment. He hadn't even unpacked, for crying out loud!

Why couldn't he get a handle on what he was feeling? Why couldn't he clear his head? Damn it to hell, why couldn't he *think?*

"I assumed you'd want to know," Shelley said, sounding keenly disappointed.

"I do," he insisted. "I do want to know. It's just..." He set down the beer, leaned forward and planted his feet firmly on the hardwood floor in front of him, as if a more stringent posture would clarify the situation and tell him what he was supposed to do. "Why didn't you say anything? That night, I mean—before we made love. You should have told me you weren't using anything. You should have stopped me."

"I couldn't have stopped you, Kip. I couldn't have stopped myself." There was no accusation in her voice, no blame. She sounded lucid, thoughtful. "I couldn't leave you that night. Maybe I should have. Maybe I should have gotten in my car and driven away. But I couldn't." She mulled over her words. "I said no regrets, Kip. And I meant it."

"Not even now?"

"Not even now." She paused again. "I want to have the baby."

"Okay," he said at once. The ramifications of her decision circled infuriatingly around his brain. He wished they would slow down so he could grab hold of them. They were amorphous, intangible, too fast, too fleeting. His struggle to think caused his breath to grow short, his pulse to quicken, his head to pound.

"I want you to understand, Kip—that's *my* choice. You have a choice, too."

"No. I mean, if you want to have the baby—"

"No one has to know you're the father. I can lie. I can tell them I don't know who the father is."

A weak laugh escaped him. "Anyone who knows you would never believe that."

"It doesn't matter whether or not anyone believes me. What matters is, if you want me to, I'll keep you out of it. No one would have to know. It would be my secret." She was calm, blessedly calm. Obviously she'd had more time to accustom herself to the situation than he had, but he envied her her steadiness, her resolve. "I don't want you to feel an obligation, Kip. I've made my choice, but you have the right to make your choice, too."

"No," he said again, and hearing himself speak the word so forcefully filled him with an odd, totally unjustified satisfaction. "If you want the baby, Shelley, we'll have the baby. I'm the father. I'm not going to run away from that."

"Okay."

"We could even get married if you'd like." Why not? They were friends. She was so considerate of him she would willingly protect him from the consequences of his own recklessness. She was a good person, kind and intelligent. They trusted each other. She would never leave him in the lurch. "How about it? Would you like to get married?"

"No," she said with such quiet fervor he was insulted. Marrying him wasn't such a vile idea, was it? Her swift rejection made it seem as if she thought he'd suggested swallowing poison.

When she spoke again she used her calm, rational tone. "I don't believe in marriage, Kip. You know that. I would never want to get married, not even because of this. *Definitely* not because of this."

"Shelley."

"Marriage guarantees nothing. It would be hypocritical to get married just to make things look proper. I'm not going to become dependent on a man who doesn't love me. That's not for me."

"Shelley—"

"And anyway, you're not ready for marriage. That's not what you want, or what you need. I know you're doing well, you're feeling better. But you're still in mourning for Amanda. You're still in love with her. You know that."

Yes. He knew that. He wished he could swear to Shelley that he *was* ready for marriage, that he *did* love her, that he was over Amanda and never thought about her anymore, never missed her, never wished to have her in his arms again.

But he couldn't lie, not to Shelley. Her relentless honesty compelled the same from him.

"If you won't marry me," he conceded, "at least let me help out financially."

"All right."

"I'm the father. I want to do whatever I can."

"Fine."

I'm the father. Why didn't enunciating those three words shock him? Why didn't they shake him to his soul? *I'm the father.*

God. He was going to be a father. Shelley was carrying his child inside her. His baby. A piece of him, living inside her, a piece of his life.

"Shelley?"

"Yes?"

"I want to do more than help out financially," he heard himself say, and the words sounded right to him, hopeful, as honest as everything that had ever passed between them. "I want to *be* its father. I'm not sure what that's going to entail, but . . . I want to be a father to my child."

Her silence implied that she wasn't sure what it was going to entail, either. "We'll work it out," she said after a moment. "If that's what you want, Kip, we'll work it out."

They talked for a few minutes more, their words measured and cautious. Kip promised to call Shelley the following evening after she'd seen Dr. Hodge, and they wished each other a good night and hung up.

He fingered the phone in his lap and stared at nothing in particular. Then he lowered the phone to the floor, lifted his beer and sank back into his chair.

A baby. Shelley was going to have a baby. *His* baby. *Theirs.*

He tried to picture her pregnant, her belly swollen, her breasts enlarged, her face radiant. As incomprehensible as that image was, even more incomprehensible was the thought of an actual infant emerging from her, a creature smaller even than his niece, Victoria. Kip tried to imagine himself holding his newborn child, lifting it into his arms, talking to it and teaching it, initiating it into the magnificence of life.

He ought to be chastising himself for his carelessness, worrying about his future, scrambling to figure out how in hell he was going to be a father to a baby whose mother lived on an island two and a half hours away. He ought to be wondering how, when his own mental health was such a fragile thing, he was ever going to find the strength to take on a responsibility like this. He ought to be tearing himself up.

But all he could think about was that a new life had staked its claim on his world. He had spent a long time grappling with death and all its crushing pain. Now there was something more significant for him to contend with than death.

There was this: a baby. His baby.

Part Three
The Cupola

Chapter Ten

Hearing the crunch of tires on gravel, Shelley set down the weeding claw and tossed her garden gloves onto the ground beside it. Then she rose to her feet, dusted off the knees of her jeans and smoothed out her shirt. Her hair was pinned back in a loose ponytail, but a few strands had escaped the barrette and drizzled forward, tickling her cheeks as she wandered around from the side of the house. The sight of Kip's Saab rolling to a halt at the top of the driveway brought a frown to her face.

Kip frequently spent his weekends on the island. He didn't have to; Shelley was willing to accommodate him if he wanted to have Jamie spend the weekend with him in "America." But Kip insisted he preferred to come to the island, not only because it was easier on Shelley and Jamie but because he liked being there, getting away from Providence and unwinding in the island's restful atmosphere.

On those occasions when he did want to spend the weekend on the mainland, Shelley usually delivered Jamie to Kip in Pt. Judith Friday night or Saturday morning, and Kip brought Jamie back on the five o'clock ferry into Old Harbor. Shelley would meet them at the boat landing and the three of them would go out to dinner at one of the restaurants on Water Street. Then Jamie and Shelley would wave

Kip off on the 8:00 p.m. ferry back to Pt. Judith, where he would have left his car.

It was only a little past one o'clock now, however—and Kip had brought his car onto the island. Shielding her eyes in the glaring midday sun, Shelley spotted Jamie in the bucket seat next to Kip. The back seat was folded down and the rear of the car was filled with cartons.

Her frown deepened momentarily, then dissolved as she heard Jamie's sweet, chirping voice through the open window. "Mommy! Mommy!" he sang out as Kip unfastened the harness of his child safety seat. Sliding down from the seat, Jamie opened the door and bolted out of the car, shouting, "Soo-pri! Soo-pri! Mommy! Soo-pri!"

He raced to her on his pudgy toddler legs, and she raced to him. He all but flew into her outstretched arms, and she swooped him into the air and swung him around before peppering his fine blond curls with kisses. "Hello, Jamie! Hello! Did you have a good time with Daddy?"

"Daddy say we drive home an' soo-pri you," Jamie babbled. At two years old, he had a limited vocabulary, and he mispronounced at least eighty percent of the words he knew.

"I *am* surprised," she admitted, half to Jamie and half to Kip, who had emerged from behind the wheel. Clad in jeans, a loose-fitting cotton shirt, sneakers and sunglasses, he approached shyly, as if not wishing to intrude on the exuberant reunion of mother and child.

Reaching her, he planted a chaste kiss on her cheek. "Hi," he said.

"Hi." She searched his face for an explanation as to why he'd brought Jamie home early and spent over twenty dollars to transport his car to the island. But his eyes were hidden behind the dark sunglasses and his mouth curved in a cryptic smile.

Before she could question him, Jamie declared, "I see Gramma Grampa! I go see Gramma Grampa!"

"I know you saw them," Shelley confirmed, smiling and nuzzling Jamie's soft round chin. "You went to a barbecue to celebrate your birthday, didn't you? You went all the way up to Chestnut Hill."

"I see Gramma Grampa an' they gimme stuff."

"What stuff?" Shelley asked, eyeing Kip with amused concern.

He groaned. "You can imagine. A Nerf football, a set of construction trucks for the beach, a ridiculous outfit that looks expensive but doesn't have a snap crotch, a Paddington Bear, a gingerbread cookie that's almost as big as he is, an inflatable bowling set and a space shuttle."

"A whole space shuttle. I hope we have room for it in the back yard," Shelley joked.

Kip smiled, then turned back toward the car. "I'll go get his things."

"What are all those boxes you've got in the back?" she asked.

He headed toward the car, calling over his shoulder, "We'll talk later."

She watched as he opened the hatchback and pulled Jamie's overnight bag and a half-used package of diapers out, leaving the cartons untouched. Perhaps they contained pieces of an unassembled space shuttle, she thought wryly. Jamie was squirming in her arms, and she set him down. He skipped across the lawn to Kip. "I hep Daddy," he said, yanking the diaper package out of Kip's hand.

Shelley grinned. When Jamie decided he wanted to "hep," one was wise not to disagree.

Her smile grew gentle as she watched Jamie and Kip stroll across the lawn to the front veranda. Jamie might have inherited Shelley's blond hair, but his square chin, high forehead and chocolate-brown eyes were very much his father's. Seeing the way he gazed up at his father, with such reverence and love in his little face, spread a tremulous warmth deep into Shelley's chest.

Kip was a good father, better than she had dared to imagine he would be. When she thought about the enormous changes Jamie had wrought in her own life, they seemed paltry compared to the changes Kip had undergone. He had set up a satellite office for Harrison Shaw's consulting firm in Providence so he could live nearer his son, and he'd abandoned his alleged dream apartment in Back Bay for a bland, boxy apartment no more than a half hour's drive from the ferry terminal in Pt. Judith. He had used the proceeds from the sale of his co-op in San Francisco to buy the house on Block Island from his parents, and he had insisted that Shelley move there. He wouldn't have her living with a baby in that intolerably small flat on Spring Street, he'd sworn. His child needed space, a yard to run around in and a nursery to sleep in, trees to climb and a cupola for spying on neighbors and dreaming dreams.

Shelley hadn't argued. She had always adored the Stroud house, and it seemed like the perfect place to raise a child. Alice McCormick lived just down the road, and Shelley could bicycle Jamie over each morning and pick him up each afternoon without going out of her way. In her late forties, Alice had raised two children of her own and was thus far proving to be a wonderful baby-sitter for Jamie.

Another advantage of the Stroud house was that it offered Kip a convenient place to stay during his weekends on the island. He'd insisted that Shelley take the master bedroom for herself, and Diana's old bedroom had been converted into a nursery for Jamie. Kip used his own bedroom during his visits.

That was as it should be, Shelley told herself again and again. She and Kip were united by their love for Jamie, but they weren't lovers. One night two years and nine months ago something extraordinary had happened, something irrational and inexplicable and probably wrong—except that it had led to Jamie.

But it would never happen again. She and Kip were too sensible now. They were on top of things, in control.

"How are your parents?" she asked, accompanying Kip and Jamie into the house.

Before Kip could answer, Jamie dropped his diaper bag in the hall and darted into the kitchen, shouting, "Deuce! Deuce!"

Shifting gears, Kip and Shelley chased after him. While Kip got the lidded toddler cup from Jamie's suitcase Shelley got the apple juice, their movements perfectly coordinated.

Once Jamie was belted into his high chair with his juice, Kip got around to answering Shelley. "My parents are fine," he said. "They sent their regards." He pulled off his sunglasses and rubbed the small red marks they left on the bridge of his nose. "You should have come," he remarked, sounding not so much reproving as wistful.

Shelley had given a great deal of thought to joining Kip and Jamie for their jaunt up to Chestnut Hill. She'd always been fond of the Strouds, and they'd generously extended an invitation to her for this barbecue—a birthday celebration for Jamie. Surely no one would claim that a child's own mother didn't belong at his birthday party.

Yet Shelley would have felt out of place there. Not because of anything the Strouds might do—they always treated her with affection—but because of Kip, because Jamie's birth had made things different between them. Because she wasn't married to Kip and never would be, and she didn't want to get used to being a part of his family.

They'd done well together, puzzling out the complications of raising Jamie as two separate parents living on two separate land masses. It wasn't that hard, actually. They shared the same priorities and based their decisions on the same criterion: what would be best for Jamie.

Their methods of discipline and their levels of tolerance meshed. They were in basic agreement on Jamie's diet, his sleep schedule, his selection of toys and his wardrobe. When Shelley had asked Kip if he wanted to name his son Samuel Brockett Stroud IV, Kip had said "Absolutely not!" and Shelley had been secretly pleased. They'd named him after Kip's maternal grandfather, James, instead.

When Kip had reluctantly conceded that Shelley ought to have primary custody, she'd been touched by his confidence in her and by the profound sacrifice he was making in letting Jamie remain with her on the island. In turn, she did everything within her power to make sure Kip got to spend all his weekends with his son, even if that meant that Kip would on occasion wind up sleeping just across the hall from her.

The first time he'd asked if she would mind his staying at the house, she'd laughed at the absurdity of the question. Of course he would stay at the house. He owned the place, for heaven's sake. He'd spent the best days of his youth in the house. He'd made love with Shelley in the house.

"I'll use my old bedroom, of course," he'd said.

Of course.

If only she didn't find him so damnably attractive. If only each year hadn't added an intriguing new layer of complexity to his appearance, a patina of experience and strength. If only he wasn't so good with Jamie and so considerate of her. If only they could feel as easy and natural with each other as they had before that one fateful night.

But they couldn't. Their relationship had metamorphosed. Like the Kafka parable Kip had once urged her to read, Shelley had found her life irrevocably altered after that night when need and desire had won over common sense.

They couldn't go back. It was too late. The friendship they'd once had was gone forever, and the new relationship that had taken its place was more cautious, more civil, more courteous. They could speak their hearts when it came to Jamie; they could open their souls when it came to him.

But for each other, for themselves . . . they'd lost the ability to do it.

"We'll talk later," he had said when she'd asked about the cartons filling the back of his car. And they would. They would talk about what time Jamie had gone to bed yesterday, and what time he'd awakened that morning, what he'd eaten, how he'd behaved, whether he'd sucked his thumb or tried to stuff dead leaves into his mouth or pestered cousin Sally's cat. They would talk about how many outfits he'd soiled and how many kisses he'd received. And maybe, if there was any time left before Kip had to catch the last ferry back to the mainland, they'd talk about the cartons he had brought to the island.

But they wouldn't talk about themselves. They wouldn't talk about each other. They wouldn't talk about the fact that, despite their promise to be friends always and forever, Shelley felt as if she and Kip were lost to each other.

IT WAS THE WAY they hugged, Kip realized, the way Shelley gathered Jamie into her arms and pressed her mouth to the sweet, warm skin of his chubby neck. The way Jamie wrapped his arms around her and squealed and giggled and shouted, as if his love for her was too overwhelming to be expressed in a normal voice. The way her eyes lit up with sparks of silver, and her mouth slipped into a beautiful smile, and the two of them, mother and child, fused in some spiritual way...and he would feel left out, dying to be a part of it.

He wondered how she would react to his proposition. He was apprehensive about asking. He shouldn't be; he should be able to ask her anything, raise any subject, discuss any new development.

But they couldn't talk to each other the way they used to. Ever since Jamie had come along, it seemed as if Kip and Shelley couldn't talk to each other about anything except their son.

"Who wants to go to the beach?" he asked once Jamie was done guzzling his juice.

Shelley shot him a bewildered look. Before she could question him, however, Jamie erupted in a cheer. "Beach! Go beach!"

Shelley set his cup on the dish rack and turned, sending Kip another perplexed look. He could guess what she was thinking: that he wasn't even supposed to be on the island right now, let alone settling in for an afternoon's entertainment. She deserved an explanation, but not now, not when Jamie was running around. Not when Kip needed a little time with the two of them to make sure he'd made the right decision.

She shrugged. "Going to the beach sounds like more fun than weeding the flower beds. Come on upstairs, Jamie, let's get you into a swimsuit."

Twenty minutes later found Shelley maneuvering the Blazer into a parking space near State Beach. She and Kip unloaded an umbrella, a blanket, some towels and a couple of beach chairs from the back. Proudly carrying two of his new toy trucks, Jamie scampered ahead through a break in the dune grass to the white sand beyond. By the time Shelley and Kip caught up to him he had planted his well-diapered bottom on the sand and was using the steam shovel to load the dump truck with tide-smoothed pebbles and shells.

"I guess this is as good a place as any," Kip said, digging the base of the umbrella into the sand and keeping a furtive eye on Shelley. She stepped out of her sandals and pulled the beach shirt over her head.

It wasn't the first time Kip had seen her in a bathing suit. It wasn't even the first time he'd seen her in one since Jamie's birth. Even so, it was the first time he'd seen her in one since he'd reached certain conclusions about where his life was heading, and her appearance affected him more strongly than it should have. He admired her long, slim legs, her remarkably flat tummy, the mature roundness of her breasts. They were the one part of her that hadn't returned to pre-pregnancy dimensions after she'd stopped nursing. They filled the upper portion of her one-piece suit, stretching the dark blue fabric taut, rising in enticing curves above the suit's low-cut neckline.

Shelley had cleavage. This shouldn't have shocked Kip—and it didn't, he swore to himself. It didn't mean anything to him. Even if it did, he couldn't do a damn thing about it.

Lowering herself into one of the beach chairs, she glanced at him and caught him staring at her. Her smile was hesitant, tinged with curiosity.

"You've been working on your tan," he said, feeling compelled to explain himself.

She looked at Jamie and said nothing. He noticed the slight movement in her throat as she swallowed.

He must have been insane to think he could pull this off. With thighs like hers, and those fine, graceful shoulders, that small waist and those firm, full breasts, with all that warmth and love inside her, all that patience and independence...

Two years and nine months had passed since he'd made love with her. Two years and nine months, and he hadn't met a single woman who could make him forget that one incredible night. He had no right to want her. She was his friend—unless he gave in to his baser instincts and tried to seduce her. If he betrayed her trust that way, it would destroy whatever friendship they had.

"So," she said, her eyes still on Jamie as he plowed his toy vehicles through the sand, "how is Becky enjoying law school?"

"Enjoying isn't the word," he replied, stripping down to his swimming trunks and sinking into the other beach chair, a couple of feet to Shelley's left. "She was pretty stressed out. I told her she ought to come down to the island and unwind."

As soon as the words were out he cast Shelley a quick look. He hadn't even told her about his own plans. Would she resent his inviting his cousin to the house?

Apparently not. "I've always liked Becky," she said. "If she wants to come, it's all right with me."

"She just moved into a new apartment with another woman from the law school. She said that between scrounging furniture and doing her summer clerkship she doesn't know if she'll be able to take any time off." Why were they talking about Becky? Why wasn't Kip telling Shelley about the cartons in the Saab and the cartons back in Providence?

Why wasn't he telling her how beautiful she looked?

"Jamie!" she shouted as the little boy pushed his truck toward the water's edge. "Don't go so far!"

"Can I stay tonight?" Kip asked, attempting a casual tone.

Her eyes remained on Jamie until he'd U-turned his dump truck and made his meandering way back along the beach to their umbrella. "Of course," she said, so automatically Kip knew she couldn't have given the request any thought.

"Listen, Shelley, I—"

"Jamie!" she cried out. He had abandoned his truck and was chasing a frisky dog across the sand. Rolling her eyes, Shelley hoisted herself out of the chair and started after him.

Kip watched her jog along the beach, loose-limbed and agile, her taut hips shifting and her breasts rising and falling rhythmically as she ran. Maybe it would be better if he saw her daily. Enough exposure and he might develop a healthy resistance to her.

Either that, or he'd make a pass at her and she'd cut him down. For all he knew, she might have dozens of boyfriends. She might date during the week, or on weekends when Jamie was visiting Kip on the mainland. She didn't want any sort of serious relationship with a man. She didn't trust them. Maybe she just fooled around...

A soft groan escaped him at the thought of her fooling around. He wasn't jealous, though—he didn't want to fool around with Shelley. He wanted to be close to her, that was all. He wanted to be as close as they'd been as children, as close as they'd been as teenagers. As close as they'd been in the days before Jamie was conceived, and that night.

That close.

He wanted to be able to look at her sometimes and think of her not as Jamie's mother but as a woman. He wanted to be able to think of her as a lover and not feel guilty about it afterward. He wanted to dream about her and smile.

But there she was, swooping down on Jamie and heaving him off the sand, perching him on her hip and sauntering back toward the umbrella, dusting the sand from his fingers and lecturing him on the dangers of chasing dogs he didn't know.

There she was, being a mother. And Kip felt guilty.

THEY CONSUMED A LIGHT supper of sandwiches and soup. Shelley hadn't planned on making dinner, since she'd expected to be dining out in Old Harbor, as they usually did when Kip brought Jamie back to the island. But she couldn't imagine trying to eat a full meal. The longer Kip put off explaining the cartons and his decision to spend a Sunday night on the island, the more anxious she got.

After dinner he cleaned up the kitchen while she gave Jamie a bath. Together they tucked their son into bed. Whenever Kip spent a weekend at the house they collaborated on getting Jamie into bed, but on a Sunday night it felt strange having Kip beside her. He seemed larger, for some reason, a potent presence in the nursery. Shelley felt the warmth of his body as he leaned over the crib rail to run his fingers through Jamie's hair. She smelled the soapy fragrance that lingered on his skin after his shower. Her awareness of him was visceral, and it troubled her.

Once Jamie had stopped shifting and squirming, they tiptoed out. Kip took her elbow and led her into the tiny bedroom and up the ladder stairs to the attic. He gestured her ahead of him, then followed her up.

A gentle breeze wafted through the open windows of the cupola, carrying in the fresh, clean smell of roses and the sea. "Leave the trapdoor open," she said when he started to close it behind them. "I want to be able to hear Jamie if he calls."

Kip eyed her respectfully. "I wouldn't have thought of that. I guess..." He didn't finish the thought.

Expectation mingled with a sense of foreboding inside her. She settled in her corner, drew her legs up toward her chest, closed her arms around her shins and rested her chin on her knees. Kip sat diagonally opposite her and stretched his legs out across the floor, skirting the open trapdoor as well as he could. There was something unsettling in the way he occupied so much of the floor, and the way she folded herself up into such a defensive posture.

Something was about to change in their delicately balanced situation. She knew it, and she braced herself for the worst.

He turned his eyes toward the ceiling and ran his hand through his hair. Through the window came the distant mewing of a gull. After a long, tense minute, Kip offered Shelley a hopeful smile and said, "I want to live here."

Without thinking, she nodded. Somehow she had already known that this was what the cartons were all about.

It would be awkward having him so close, knowing he was under her roof but miles from her emotionally. But what could she do? It wasn't really her roof, after all. It was his. She couldn't deny Kip a place in his own house.

"I see," she said in a neutral voice.

"I'd be using my own room, of course," he clarified.

He didn't have to spell it out, for heaven's sake. She knew he didn't love her, not that way. She knew that the only time he'd ever shared his bed with her was when he'd been confused and emotionally battered, desperate for any comfort she could offer.

He was still in love with Amanda, but he was strong enough now not to require any sexual cures for his wounded heart from the local pharmacist. Of course he'd stay in his own room. No question about it.

"I want more time with Jamie," he continued. "He belongs here, Shelley—I would never dream of changing the custody arrangement. You're a wonderful mother, and he belongs with you. It's just..." He sighed. "I'm his father, and he belongs with me, too."

She toyed with a button on her shirt and tried to collect her thoughts. She wanted to say she was delighted by the idea, but the truth was, it scared her.

"I've been thinking about it for a while," he said. "I wanted to work it out before I discussed it with you."

"What have you worked out?"

"Well, my job, for one thing. Most of the consulting I'm doing now can be done long-distance, with the phone, a modem, fax. When I need to do an on-site I can do one, but I really don't have to be in a downtown office every day. I can set up shop right here, in the house. I was thinking I could wall off part of the cellar and convert the space into an office."

"The cellar? It's so cold and gloomy down there. And all those spiders..."

He grinned. "I'll bring in a space heater and kill the spiders."

"We have power outages all the time—"

"I'll hook into a backup portable generator." He studied her in the dusk shadows, assessing her response. "Do you really *not* want me to do this?"

"No. I mean, if you want to do it, Kip, it's all right with me."

"But?" he prompted her.

"No buts. I think..." She meditated for a minute, then forced herself to speak honestly. "I think there's a lot to recommend it. Jamie misses you during the week. And having you around would lift some of the responsibility from my shoulders. I have no objection to that."

He contemplated her. The evening light waned; darkness crept slowly across the small room, consuming everything in its path. She could guess what he was thinking: that she'd said yes, but her tone didn't support her words. That for all her positive statements, she was besieged with uncertainty. "But?" he pressed.

"But nothing."

"You're afraid I'll get in the way."

"No, of course not. I'm at the pharmacy all day, and Jamie's at Alice's house. Why do you think you'd be in anyone's way?"

"Well..." He shrugged. "This has been your home for two years. You've got your own way of doing things—"

"You know what my way is," she said, managing a faint smile. "No toys allowed on the stairs, and I vacuum whenever the dust bunnies start to resemble an invading army. Laundry twice a week. If you move in, Kip, you're going to get stuck with one of the laundries."

He smiled, too. "I want it clear between us," he said, still selecting his words with deliberation, "that my moving into the house won't change our relationship."

Right. They would be reserved and restrained with each other, all their love and affection directed to Jamie. Kip would find his relationships elsewhere, and Shelley would have her precious independence.

"Okay," she said, averting her gaze.

"I know how you feel about marriage. That's not what this is about. Unless, of course, you think getting married might make things easier."

Her eyes flew back to him. It wasn't the first time he'd proposed marriage, and it might not be the last. But she knew he was raising the subject—as he always did—only because he was well-bred and responsible, willing to accept his obligations.

"No," she said, her voice low but steely. "I don't believe in marriage. It causes more problems than it solves. I don't want it."

He seemed to feel the need to justify himself. "I mentioned it only because I thought it might simplify things."

Her eyes suddenly felt hot with tears, her vision misting. "I know," she murmured. "Maybe that's a good reason to get married—but it doesn't sound like much of a reason to me."

They lapsed into silence. Outside the wind was picking up, whispering through the branches of the red maple. From the east came the moan of the ferry's horn, announcing the day's final departure for Pt. Judith.

Kip wasn't on that ferry. He was here. Shelley hugged her arms more tightly around her legs, wishing she could trust him but knowing she couldn't. He was a man, and she probably loved him, and love and trust, when mixed together, were lethal.

For better or worse, though, Kip was here. She was just going to have to protect herself.

LYING IN BED later that night, he thought about Shelley across the hall from him. He thought about her climbing into her own bed and drawing up the covers, thought about her hair splaying across her pillow. He thought about the way she'd looked in her swimsuit earlier that day—and the way she'd looked naked one night long ago.

He thought about how swiftly she'd turned down his marriage proposal, and a cold, heavy resignation descended over him.

The last time he'd raised the possibility of marriage had been a little over a year ago. She'd said no just as swiftly that time. "I appreciate your kindness, Kip," she'd said, "but your heart belongs to Amanda. You know that."

"I know that," he'd concurred.

If she expressed that assumption now, he wasn't sure he would agree. He wouldn't deny that Amanda was a part of him. He still felt her presence sometimes, still found himself wondering what she would think of his child, whether she would love Jamie as much as he did, whether she would approve of his noble efforts at fatherhood.

Amanda was a part of him—but so was Shelley. Lately when he closed his eyes, the image that filled his mind was Shelley: the joyous radiance of her eyes whenever she glimpsed her son. The tall, regal beauty of her body. Her courage, her competence, her generosity. Her sun-streaked hair and her full, soft lips.

She didn't want to marry him. Whatever her feelings for him, they didn't include a desire for a permanent legal commitment. To be sure, he wasn't sure what the hell they *did* include.

Moving into the house with her might turn out to be one of the most stupid mistakes of his life. But he had to do it, for Jamie. He had to do it because he wanted his child to have a complete, stable family. Whatever was right or wrong between Shelley and Kip, he wanted to be more than a part-time father.

He shouldn't have brought Shelley up to the cupola to discuss his plans, but he couldn't imagine talking to her about them anywhere else. The cupola was where they went, where they'd always gone when they'd had to talk. Ever since they'd been kids.

The first time he'd really kissed her had been in the cupola. And the last time he'd really kissed her, she'd been lying with him right here in this bed.

He wanted her. He wanted her with the same fierce, unadorned hunger he'd felt as a fifteen-year-old boy discovering, to his amazement, that his good old summer pal had breasts and hips and an astonishingly sexy mouth. He couldn't act on that hunger, though, not without jeopardizing everything he and Shelley had built together. He couldn't even talk about his feelings, because the only subject of any importance he and Shelley seemed able to talk about these days was Jamie.

She probably had no idea what he was thinking, what he was feeling, how difficult it was going to be for him to co-exist in the house with her. Given how much she'd done for him, he owed her the privilege of remaining ignorant. She would never have to know his feelings and frustrations. If she ever found out, she might open her arms to him out of pity. Or she might boot him out of the house altogether.

Perhaps she was right, perhaps he ought to forget about marrying her and making their family a legal, spiritual entity. If he needed a woman to love, he'd find one, and he'd leave Shelley out of it. What he had with her was too vital and too fragile to risk on something as painful as love.

Chapter Eleven

Shelley awakened to silence.

Bolting upright in bed, she glanced at the clock on the nightstand beside her: seven-thirty. Sunlight filtered through the curtains, filling the room with a benign glow. Her heart began to pound; anxiety stabbed her like needles of ice, sending shivers down her back.

Where was Jamie? Why hadn't she heard him hollering "Mommy gemme out!" from his crib?

She leaped out of bed, grabbed her bathrobe from the chair and raced frantically out of her room. The door of the bedroom across the hall was open. Spotting the unmade bed, she let out her breath in a long sigh. Kip was here. Although it was Monday, Kip was here. He must have gotten Jamie out of the crib.

She shook her head in astonishment at how far he had come, from his first frantic retreat to the news that she was pregnant until this moment, when he'd moved physically into the house and taken over the job of rescuing Jamie from his crib at dawn. She never would have guessed, two years ago, that someday he would appear at the house and announce, "I want more time with Jamie. I'm his father and he belongs with me."

He'd done all the right things back then: transferring to a new office in Providence, finding Shelley a doctor at

Rhode Island Hospital, meeting her whenever possible at the doctor's office and apologizing profusely for her inconvenience at having to travel to the mainland for her examinations. He'd purchased his parents' house and helped Shelley to settle in, and he'd shipped baby furnishings to her from "America." He'd arranged with the air ambulance service on Block Island to have Shelley transported to the hospital as soon as she went into labor, and he'd sat beside her, holding her hand and murmuring words of encouragement throughout the ordeal.

But she always sensed something automatic and unthinking in his actions, a definite whiff of obligation. Kip was a decent man, and he did what a decent man was supposed to do when he got caught. He hadn't provided Shelley with everything an expectant mother might need because he loved her. He'd done it because it had been the proper thing to do.

Or so she thought, right up to the afternoon she went into labor. She telephoned his office in Providence to alert him, and by the time she'd arrived at the hospital he was there—calm, businesslike, completely in charge. The nurses helped her to undress while he stood on the other side of the curtain with the doctor, speaking soberly about whether he should scrub up now or wait a while, whether Shelley should be strapped to a fetal monitor, whether all the proper health insurance forms had been filed.

The labor was long and tiring. Shelley cursed and cried, counted breaths and sucked on chips of ice. Through it all, Kip was the ultimate gentleman. "Would you like some water?" he would inquire. "Would you like to try standing for a while? I'm sorry it hurts, Shelley."

More than once she found herself thinking he would have done just as well sending her a greeting card.

At three o'clock the following morning, though, everything changed. Especially Kip. At three o'clock, Jamie arrived.

As soon as she heard she'd delivered a healthy boy, Shelley sank into the pillows in exhaustion, only dimly aware of the activity at the foot of the bed: the cord being cut, the baby's face being washed, his mouth and nose being cleared of fluid. She closed her eyes and gulped in deep, relaxing breaths, allowing herself a small grin of triumph that expanded when she heard her son's first tremulous cry. Then she opened her eyes and propped herself up.

The baby had been swaddled in a fleecy receiving blanket. "You rest," a nurse ordered her as she handed the baby to Kip. He pulled off his face mask and peered at the squalling, squirming bundle of life in his arms, and tears streamed down his cheeks.

After so many months of stoic self-control, he cradled his son and kissed him and wept.

Shelley didn't dare to ask whether his tears were tears of joy or of grief and bitterness that Shelley and not Amanda had mothered his child. She assumed they were a bit of both.

At least he had yielded to emotion. At least he'd stopped being so composed and circumspect. Kip Stroud—brooding widower, affluent yuppie, honorable gentleman—had metamorphosed into a fanatically sentimental daddy.

When he returned to the hospital later that day to visit Shelley and Jamie, his wedding band was gone. Shelley had never seen him wear it again.

And now he was here, on the island, moving in. Becoming a part of the household. Whatever unresolved tensions and missed connections existed between her and Kip, she would never stand in the way of what he had with Jamie. He was a dad. He deserved to be here, and Jamie deserved to have him here.

She tied the sash of her robe around her waist, then descended to the first floor in time to see Kip and Jamie entering from the front veranda. They were both dressed, and they both looked far more alert than Shelley felt. Kip held

Jamie high in his arms, making the child appear amazingly light and small on his lofty perch.

"Mommy! We see mitt," he announced proudly.

"Mist," Kip corrected him.

Jamie scrunched his face in concentration. "Mitt," he said.

Shelley smiled. One of her favorite things about Jamie was his sheer enthusiasm for everything, including the mist that floated eerily above the lawn until the sun burned it away. He refused Shelley the opportunity to become blasé about the island's natural splendor.

"Why don't you go get dressed?" Kip suggested. "I'll start Jamie on breakfast."

"Thanks." Still smiling, Shelley turned and headed back up the stairs. To be able to shower and dress at her own leisurely pace on a weekday morning was a luxury she couldn't resist.

Maybe Kip's living in the house wouldn't be so bad, after all. They'd been together nearly all the time as kids, and they'd been wonderfully close. The brief, intense interlude that led to Jamie's conception—they'd seen each other every day then, too, and they'd been intimately attuned to each other.

Shelley had long ago learned to anticipate the worst, to trust only herself and assume that men operated in their own self-interest, without regard for the wreckage they left behind. But Kip... Kip had always been better than that.

Maybe it was time to start trusting again.

"I WANT WABBOOS," Jamie whined.

"There aren't any waffles," Kip told him, returning from the pantry with a box of puffed wheat.

"I want wabboos."

Kip allowed himself a wry smile. A quick survey of the pantry had informed him that Shelley was a lot stricter than he was when it came to Jamie's diet. In Providence Kip served Jamie waffles or pancakes or took him out to Dunkin' Donuts. Judging by the contents of the pantry cabinets, Shelley fed Jamie only healthy cereals for breakfast.

He was pouring puffed wheat into Jamie's plastic Kermit the Frog bowl when Shelley entered the kitchen. Dressed in a flowered cotton dress, with a clean white lab jacket draped over one arm and her purse clutched in the other hand, she appeared refreshed and poised, prepared to face the day. In truth, he preferred the way she'd looked when she'd first stumbled down the stairs in her nightgown and robe, her feet bare, her hair mussed, her cheeks rosy from the warmth of her pillow and her eyes a muted gray color, still half-glazed with sleep.

He was going to have to stop thinking that way.

"I made some coffee," he told her, angling his head toward the coffeemaker on the counter. "I didn't know what else you wanted."

"I haven't got time to eat anything," she remarked, pulling a bottle of orange juice from the refrigerator. "I'm not used to sleeping so late. What time did Jamie wake up?"

Well, then, there it was—a conversation revolving around Jamie. As always.

He fixed himself two slices of toast while Shelley packed Jamie's tote with diapers and wipes, and a change of clothing—all items he might need at the baby-sitter's. "Has he got a sun hat?" Kip asked.

"It's in the front hall closet."

"Do you want me to take him to Alice's today?"

"No, that's okay," Shelley answered. "Her house is on my way to the pharmacy."

"I don't mind taking him. Especially since you're running late." It was with a certain disbelief that Kip listened to the words emerging from him. Not that any of it wasn't important, not that Jamie wasn't the center of his universe, but damn it, why couldn't Kip say what he was really thinking? *You look lovely, Shelley. That dress makes your eyes look almost blue. I want to give you a good-morning kiss and I'm afraid to. Tell me how not to be afraid. Tell me you wouldn't hate me for kissing you.*

"Use your spoon, Jamie," he said instead, forcing the baby spoon into his son's chubby fingers.

"I use hand."

"You're a big boy, Jamie. Use your spoon," Shelley chimed in as she sat at the table with her coffee and juice. Kip carried his toast to the table and joined them. "What are your plans for the day?" she asked him.

"I'm going to organize the stuff I unloaded from the car last night," he told her. "I may spend some time clearing out a section of the cellar. I'll be heading back to 'America' this afternoon, though. I have an appointment tomorrow morning in Providence, and then I'll load up the car and bring some more stuff over on the ferry."

"So you won't be here for dinner," she said.

"Not tonight. Tomorrow night, yes."

"Fine."

Frustration drummed through him. He supposed he would have to get used to it. If he permitted anything personal to enter the discussion, anything that even hinted that his awareness of Shelley extended beyond her role as Jamie's mother, she might feel threatened. She might retreat.

Damn it to hell. When he'd contemplated moving to the island, he had thought only about how wonderful it would be to live with her and Jamie, to create a real family with them. He'd thought that since he'd never had serious qualms about spending the weekend at the house, he'd have no problems spending the week there. But to find himself seated across the table from a woman he desired—on a Monday morning—that was different. Finding himself talking with her about child care when he wanted nothing more than to envelop her in his arms, to feel her skin against his palms, against his lips...

That was torture.

"I'd better be going," she said in a matter-of-fact tone. "Are you sure you don't mind taking Jamie?"

"Not at all," he insisted.

"Look at dis," Jamie broke in. He rested his spoon on the edge of the bowl and heaped a pile of wheat puffs in its curved surface. Then he pounded on the handle of the spoon, turning it into a catapult that sent the puffs flying all over the room.

"Jamie!" Kip and Shelley yelled in unison.

Jamie looked concerned; his demonstration hadn't been greeted with the approval he'd obviously expected. Shelley opened her mouth, ready to chew him out, but before she could say anything her eye caught Kip's.

He laughed.

Shelley's lips twitched into a smile that she tried valiantly but unsuccessfully to suppress. "Don't," she scolded Kip, her voice wavering around her own laughter. "That was really naughty of him."

Kip unstrapped Jamie's high chair seat belt and lifted him out. "Start picking them up, sport," he commanded, then glanced at Shelley and grinned. "Hey, the kid's learning elementary physics."

"The kid's learning that his dad's a softie."

"One of his parents has to be."

Shelley's chuckling abated and her smile became gentle, spreading upward into her eyes. If he wanted, he could almost believe she was happy about his being there. "I've got news for you," she murmured. "His mom's a softie, too, sometimes."

"Then he's either very lucky or doomed."

"He's lucky," she said, then abruptly turned away and reached for her jacket and purse. "I've got to go. Make sure you get all the cereal cleaned up. We've had some ants parading through the kitchen lately."

Kip waved Shelley out of the room, then squatted down beside his son, who, he discovered with dismay, was pick-

ing up the scattered puffs and popping them into his mouth.
"Hey, Jamie, don't eat off the floor."

"Eat wabboos," Jamie declared.

Kip had engaged in enough dialogues with Jamie to understand what the child was saying: if he'd been served
waffles he would have gobbled them down without mishap,
but if he was going to get stuck eating cereal, he intended to
make a mess with it. This was not a good attitude, and even
a certified softie like Kip wasn't going to allow it to stand
unchallenged.

On the other hand, he couldn't deny that it had a certain
appealing logic.

You did the best you could in a situation, and took from
it what joy you could. If you couldn't have waffles, you
found ways to satisfy yourself with puffed wheat. If you
couldn't make love with Shelley, you satisfied yourself with
whatever you could get from her.

You could make the puffs more palatable by adding some
fruit, too, Kip thought once the floor was clean and Jamie
was back in his high chair. As he sliced a banana into Jamie's bowl, he thought about the unassuming touches of
sweetness that made his relationship with Shelley more than
palatable.

He thought about the way her eyes had glowed when
she'd said, "His mom's a softie, too."

Jamie was lucky, all right.

So was Kip. He was lucky to have what he did—a beautiful son, a tranquil home, the clean, salty winds and breathtaking scenery of Block Island. And Shelley, who could gaze
into his eyes and smile in a way that made him feel healthy
and whole and glad to be alive.

It was greedy to want everything; he could learn to be
satisfied with a few sweet slices of fruit.

Chapter Twelve

Cellars were supposed to be cold, but on the most sweltering day of the summer this one unfortunately held the heat. He had opened the door leading out to the side yard and stood a fan on the stairs, which helped somewhat. It also helped that he could wear shorts and an old T-shirt while he worked.

That, Kip had quickly learned, was one of the best things about working out of one's own home.

Two weeks after he'd moved to Block Island, his office was not yet fully operational, but he was further along than he would have predicted. He'd managed to find someone to sublet his apartment in Providence. A few of his furnishings he'd moved to the island; a few he'd donated to his cousin Becky, who was about to start her second year at Yale Law School and was in dire need of furniture for the flat in New Haven she was sharing with a classmate. The tenant who'd taken over Kip's lease had bought a few items from him, and the rest went to Goodwill.

He shuddered whenever he walked past the smallest bedroom on the second floor and saw the stacks of moving cartons stored there, full of his personal possessions. Every morning when he passed the room he promised himself to unpack at least one carton that evening when he was done working—but then the evening would arrive and he would wind up playing with Jamie instead.

At least his subterranean work space was reasonably well set up. Bringing telephone lines down into the cellar had been simple, and the portable generator he'd installed protected him against the fluctuations in electric power that were common on the island. He'd gotten his file cabinets, his desk and his high-back swivel chair arranged in one corner of the cellar, and he'd brightened one wall with the framed Georgia O'Keeffe prints he'd bought from his neighbor in Boston.

Jamie had fallen madly in love with Kip's chair. "Gimme ride! Gimme ride!" he would shriek whenever he came down to the cellar. When Kip complied Jamie would goad him on, "Faster, faster!" until he was reduced to a giggling blur spinning around and around in the chair.

Whatever the inconveniences of working apart from his clients, they were worth the opportunity to spend more time with Jamie. Spending more time with Shelley was quite another thing. They got along well enough, discussing menus and chores, planning Jamie's schedule, occasionally renting a video from the pharmacy and watching it together in companionable silence. They never argued, never clashed. It was all so cordial, so accommodating—as flavorless as the air in the cellar.

He blamed himself. If only he could stop thinking of Shelley as a *woman,* he could enjoy her as a friend. If only he could look at her and see simply a busy mother, a pharmacist, a volunteer with the island's historical society, a neighbor who liked to drop in on the McCormicks or the Durgans for a cold drink on a hot evening....

But he couldn't. He couldn't stop noticing the sleek curves of her calves beneath the hems of her conservative dresses and skirts. He couldn't stop noticing the golden shimmer in her hair, the breathtaking clarity of her eyes, the fullness of her lips. Every evening he would kiss her cheek or pat her arm and say good-night, and he would dive onto his bed and groan over its emptiness, over his loneliness.

He wanted her. Not because he wasn't involved with anyone else, not because he and she lived under the same roof. Not even because she was the mother of his child.

He'd wanted her long before he had relocated to the island. Now that he was there he was forced to acknowledge the truth: he had moved to the house for Shelley as much as for Jamie.

He'd moved because he loved her.

He didn't know how to break through the self-protective layers she'd wrapped around herself. He didn't know how to express his feelings for her, how to convince her they were genuine. More importantly, he didn't know how to deal with the profound uneasiness his love for her caused him.

He didn't know how to say goodbye to Amanda.

Emerging from the cellar at four-thirty, he headed for the kitchen, where a pitcher of lemonade sat waiting for him inside the refrigerator. He rinsed off his face at the sink, then filled a glass with lemonade and ice and went outside.

The front yard baked beneath the merciless July sun. He strolled across the parched grass to the driveway and down to the mailbox at the side of the road. Lowering the hinged door, he withdrew a few bills, a long-awaited check from one of his clients and a personal letter for Shelley. He carried the mail inside, opened the envelope containing the check and left the other letters on the kitchen table. Then he drained his glass, refilled it with lemonade and returned to his desk to see if his printer was done with the spreadsheets he'd labored on most of the afternoon.

The printer had completed its task. Kip settled in his chair, positioned to receive the brunt of the fan's breeze, and scanned his data. It was at times like this, when he submerged himself fully in the job of deciphering a client's pattern of expenditures and investments, that he could forget he was in love with two women, one of whom was dead and the other of whom lived behind an emotional fortress no normal man could breach. He could simply lose himself in the numbers, in the far less dangerous pursuit of salvaging a client's faltering business.

"Daddy! Hi, Daddy! Gimme ride!"

Kip glanced up from the spreadsheets to see Jamie clomping down the stairs to the cellar. His round face was pink from the heat; his hair was curly and damp with sweat; his sunsuit had a mysterious orange stain across the bib front and his feet looked delectably plump in his miniature sandals.

"We home," he declared happily. "I habba ride?"

"What's the magic word?" Kip prompted him.

"Pleeeeee."

"Okay. Hop aboard," said Kip, standing and setting the spreadsheets on his desk.

Jamie clambered onto the chair and let out an anticipatory squeal of delight. "Fast, Daddy, fast!" he demanded as Kip began to swivel the chair around.

Kip spun Jamie until his laughter filled the room, echoing off the hard concrete walls and floor. After a minute Kip was as breathless as Jamie, simply from laughing along with him. He slowed the chair to a halt and hoisted Jamie high into the air. "How're you doing, sport?"

"I have dizz!"

"You're dizzy?"

"Lotsa dizz!"

Kip gave him a hug, then balanced him more comfortably in the crook of his elbow. "Where's Mommy?"

"Upstairs."

"Let's go find her." Kip turned off the fluorescent desk lamp, pushed his chair into the well of his desk, and crossed to the outside steps to turn off the fan. Once he'd locked the outer door, he carried Jamie up the stairs, shouting, "Mommy? Where's Mommy? Here come two hungry boys, and we want to eat!"

"We eat!" Jamie chorused. "Boys wanna eat!"

They found Shelley in the kitchen, seated at the table with her back to the door. Her purse and white jacket lay on the chair next to her. She didn't move, didn't turn, didn't say hello.

Jamie continued to squawk about eating, but Kip sobered at once. He lowered Jamie to his feet and circled the table carefully, aware from the tension in Shelley's shoulders and the arch of her spine that something was gravely wrong.

She looked up when he reached the opposite side of the table. A white sheet of paper covered with a slanting handwriting lay before her. Beside it lay a torn envelope. Kip recognized it—he'd pulled it from the mailbox a half hour ago. Shelley's hands were clasped together on the table next to the letter, her fingers woven into a bloodless clench.

Kip lifted his gaze from the letter to her face. She was pale, her eyes glassy, her lips pressed together as if to contain her emotions. Rage? he wondered. Anguish? Sorrow? He couldn't guess.

"Shell?" he asked softly.

"We eat!" Jamie bellowed as he marched around the room. "Boys wanna eat!"

"Yes—yes, of course," Shelley said, breaking from Kip's inquisitive stare. "Let's eat."

"I'll make dinner," he suggested. She was clearly in no condition to prepare a meal.

She steered her gaze back to him, revealing a glimmer of gratitude along with her agitation. "I'd like to go upstairs and change, and then I'll help you."

"Take your time."

Sending him a grateful nod, she folded the sheet of stationery meticulously along its creases, slid it back into the envelope, stood and left the kitchen, carrying the letter with her.

"I hep," Jamie offered to Kip's combined amusement and alarm. When Jamie "hepped" in the kitchen, Kip generally wound up working twice as hard to get a meal ready.

The turkey-burgers were grilled and on the table before Shelley returned to the kitchen. She refused a roll, poked at her burger with the tines of her fork, sipped her lemonade and stared into space. While engaging Jamie in an assortment of nonsensical dialogues, Kip allowed one part of his mind to focus on her. He longed to question her about the letter she'd received, but he didn't want to pry. She was obviously upset about it; he wished she trusted him enough to confide in him.

After dinner he offered to handle Jamie's bath and bedtime, and Shelley accepted. Jamie splashed in the tub, attacked Kip with his ducky, refused to sit on the potty and then peed all over the bathroom floor while Kip was getting a fresh diaper from the nursery. While Kip mopped the floor, Jamie attempted, with less than stellar success, to apply a dab of toothpaste to his brush. While Kip scrubbed the toothpaste off the wall, Jamie raced up and down the hall, his towel draped over his shoulders like a cape, and shouted, "Soo-pa-man!"

Through it all, no sign of Shelley.

By the time Jamie was tucked into his crib Kip was tired enough to lie down next to him and nod off. Instead he kissed his son's soft, clean cheek, turned on the night-light and left the nursery. He went downstairs, checking every room, the front veranda and the back deck, knowing even as he searched for Shelley that he wouldn't find her there. He still had no idea what was in the letter she'd received, but he knew where she'd go to think about it.

He pulled two beers from the refrigerator, opened them, and climbed the stairs to the cupola.

SHE FONDLED THIS LETTER as she had the one she'd received so many years ago. She touched the paper now exactly as she had then, explored its texture, memorized its surface with her fingertips. She studied the militant scrawl of the penmanship, the indentations the ballpoint had etched into the stationery. One thing was different, though: this time she knew better than to believe a single word of it.

A bilious taste filled her mouth, and she tried to swallow it down. How could he do this? Everything was going smoothly in her life. She and Kip had succeeded in creating a home for their child. The pharmacy's business was strong, and so, apparently, was Kip's consulting enterprise. Other than the daily joy Jamie brought her, her existence had no significant peaks, but it had no deep valleys, either. She was getting along, enjoying the undemanding pace of her days.

She asked for nothing more. How dare he ask so much of her?

She heard the footsteps in the attic. Of course Kip would know to look for her here. She assumed that if he was coming after her Jamie must be asleep. And while she wasn't sure she was willing to talk about the letter— No. She *was* willing to talk about it. The only person she'd told about the last letter was Kip. Now he was with her again, and she would talk to him again, like old times. He was here, and for this one evening when she was just moments from disintegrating she would pretend he was the same friend now as he'd been so many years ago.

He entered through the trapdoor and handed her a cold bottle of beer. She smiled at his thoughtfulness. Remembering to leave the door open, he took his usual seat in the corner diagonally across from her. He lifted his own beer in a silent toast and drank.

Shelley took a sip of her beer, then touched the icy glass of the bottle to her forehead and cheeks to cool her feverish skin. Lowering the bottle to her lap, she noticed Kip watching her. He said nothing, but his dark eyes were full of questions.

"It's my father," she finally said.

"That would have been one of my guesses," he admitted.

"I haven't heard from him in almost fifteen years."

"And now he's hoping for a reconciliation?"

"He's dying," she said.

An instant of horror flashed across Kip's face, and then he let out a long sigh. She knew he was reliving his own grievous experience with death—but he shouldn't be. What she felt for her father was nothing like what Kip must have felt when Amanda had died. Kip had lost his woman. His wife. His one true love.

Shelley, on the other hand, despised her father. He'd died for her long ago. She was all done mourning for him.

"He has pancreatic cancer," she told Kip. "His doctors are treating him with chemotherapy, but his prospects are pretty grim."

"Shelley, whatever you think of him, it's a sad thing," Kip said. "You're allowed to feel sorry for him."

"Thanks," she snapped, then suffered a pang of remorse. Kip didn't deserve her wrath. She closed her eyes and turned away, wishing she could cool her temper with her bottle of beer the way she'd cooled her cheeks.

The dark slashes of her father's handwriting hurtled through her mind, words she'd read enough times to commit to memory: *I know you hate me, and I deserve no better.... I have paid for my mistakes in more ways than you will ever know.... Prison was nothing compared to losing the respect of my daughter.... I've tracked down your mother, and she's told me about you....*

"He wants to visit," Shelley informed Kip in a tone devoid of anger—devoid of life. The only way she could cope with her father was to remain numb.

"Oh?"

"He found out about Jamie. He wants to meet his grandson before he dies."

Kip didn't speak. The setting sun imbued his face with intriguing shadows. Behind the lenses of his glasses his eyes glowed with sympathy; the light's angle emphasized the strong, square line of his jaw. His lips curved in an enigmatic half smile that revealed no hint of his thoughts.

"It's not him I'm worried about," Shelley continued, struggling to vocalize feelings that hadn't yet solidified in her mind. "It's not my father. I don't give a damn whether he gets to meet his grandson or not. He doesn't have the right to ask me for any favors."

Still Kip remained silent, drinking his beer and scrutinizing Shelley through the thickening gloom, listening without judging her.

"It's Jamie," she explained. "How can I foist a total stranger on Jamie? He already has a grampa. He loves your father, Kip. I don't even know my father anymore. How can I force Jamie to accept him? Why should I?"

Kip's gaze softened. He extended his hand, and for that one instant Shelley decided to believe their friendship was everything it used to be. She placed her hand inside his and let him pull her across the tiny room into his arms.

His chest was warm and secure, a solid cushion for her throbbing head. The comfort of his embrace and the soothing sensation of his long, graceful fingers twirling through her hair almost dispelled the oppressive doom that threatened to descend upon her.

"Is it really Jamie you're worried about?" he asked quietly.

She closed her eyes again, longing to let Kip take care of everything. For once in her life she wished she could give in to helplessness and become dependent on a man. She wished Kip loved her, not just as a friend or as Jamie's mother, but truly loved her, the way he had loved his wife. If only he did, she might be able to yield control to him, let him write a response to her father, let him decide what was good or bad for Jamie.

But that wasn't the way it was, and she wasn't going to yield control. "No," she answered in a weary voice. "I mean, yes, I *am* worried about Jamie. But...it's me. I can't give my father anything. I can't even think about him without hurting."

Kip's fingers continued to meander through the soft, silky waves of her hair. "Is he asking you to forgive him?"

"No." Her father's letter had contained confession and penitence, but no plea for forgiveness.

"It's your decision," Kip murmured, his words washing down over her head like bathwater, calm and cleansing. "You have to do what's right for you."

"I don't want to see him," she declared.

Kip stroked her hair in silence.

She resented him for leaving her words unchallenged. They hung in the air, petty and spiteful. If her father were a stranger suffering from cancer, Shelley would treat him with greater charity. But because he was her father, she felt no sadness at his suffering.

Kip had once accused her of being a lady with a long memory. A long memory and a big grudge.

"Even if I did let him come," she muttered, "I sure as hell wouldn't forgive him."

"Does that mean you're going to tell him he can come?"

"All I said was I wouldn't forgive him."

"No," Kip argued gently. "That's not all you said."

A tear leaked out of her eye and she hastily wiped it away. She wasn't going to cry in front of Kip. Now, more than ever, she had to present herself as tough and indomitable. In her youth she might have let Kip witness her tears, but not anymore. Not since she'd learned that no man—especially not her father—was worth shedding tears over.

"You don't have to forgive him," Kip reminded her.

"I know." Her voice emerged faint and hoarse from her effort to stifle her bitterness and the unexpected, very real fear she felt at the comprehension that her father was actually dying. "If I don't let him come, Kip..." A shaky sigh escaped her. "I don't want him to come, but if I don't let him meet his grandchild before he dies, I'll never forgive myself."

She couldn't see Kip's face, but she could picture his smile. She could feel his slight nod of approval, the shift of his shoulders, the constant beat of his heart as she nestled her head against his chest.

"I'll be right beside you the whole time," he promised in a low, earnest tone. "I'll do whatever I can to help."

"That's all right," she said. "I'll get through it somehow. There's really nothing you could do, anyway."

"There's plenty I can do, and I'll do it," Kip insisted. "Trust me, Shelley. Just trust me."

Like a woman with no memory at all, no sense of the past, no recollection of how very hard she'd struggled to travel solo and rely only on herself, she whispered, "I trust you."

HE HOVERED BEHIND HER while she dialed the telephone number her father had written in his letter. He had promised to be beside Shelley the whole time, and that time evidently began the moment she lifted the telephone and started to dial. It was a Connecticut exchange; the return address indicated that he was living in Bridgeport.

What would her father be like? Sick, obviously, but beyond that, what? Kip had met George Ballard only a few times, years ago, and he remembered the man as being tall and broad-shouldered, like Shelley, with her fair coloring. There had been a hardness about him, the sort of laminated veneer one might expect to find on a piece of molded fiberglass. Mr. Ballard had dressed well, favoring knit sport shirts with little alligators on them, pale-hued slacks and expensive loafers.

Without being able to hear anything through the receiver, he knew precisely the moment Shelley's father answered the phone. She flinched, then stiffened, tension stringing her body as tight as a rubber band about to snap.

"Hello," she said. "It's Shelley."

Kip lifted his hands to her shoulders and massaged them, digging his fingers into the knotted muscles.

"I got your letter," she said into the phone. Kip could tell from the dry, faint sound of her voice that each word was a struggle.

He worked his hands down her back, moving his thumbs in soothing circles on either side of her spine. Her legs swayed beneath her, and she leaned back against him. Yes, he thought, he wanted her to lean on him. For once in her life, he wanted her to lean on him.

"He's two years old. He's—" she choked on what sounded like a sob "—he's fine. If you really—What? No, we're not married. We're friends, Dad. You remember Kip. We're friends."

Thank you, Kip mouthed, his lips dancing a fraction of an inch from her hair. At least she would acknowledge that much. He was her friend, always, forever, just as he'd sworn one September morning when he'd discovered he was going to survive Amanda's death—one foggy, wondrous morning when Jamie was already growing inside Shelley.

"Because friends don't do to each other what husbands and wives do. That's why we aren't married," she said into the phone, her tone becoming harsh. "Look, Dad, if you're going to—" She fell silent as her father spoke, then let out a small, shivery sigh. "Okay. Look. You want to come and meet Jamie? Fine. Come. Don't expect any sort of welcome from me, but—"

Kip circled his arms around her waist and hugged her. She rested against him, her head bowed. He saw a streak of moisture on her cheek, a teardrop falling from her chin to land on her blouse, on the soft curve of her breast.

"*This* weekend? I thought, maybe—When? Next Wednesday? Wouldn't you feel better by the weekend? Oh.

I didn't realize... But *this* weekend is so...no, come if you're coming. You're probably better off coming right away, before I can change my mind.'' She listened for a minute, then said, ''Fine. Call me Friday night and let me know what ferry you're taking. I'll pick you up at Old Harbor.'' She recited the telephone number, then mumbled a goodbye and hung up.

Slowly, as if in a daze, she rotated in Kip's arms. Her body shook. He pulled her close.

He wanted to assure Shelley that in time the pain would recede, and she would find she remembered only the happy parts, not the anguish, not the rage. But if he told her that, she wouldn't believe him.

He didn't really believe it himself. No matter how much he loved Shelley, no matter how much he wanted to help her, he didn't believe in miracles.

He could offer Shelley no miracle. All he could offer were his arms around her, holding her while she trembled and refused to cry.

Chapter Thirteen

She went through the motions: counting out a month's worth of Cyclopar 500 mg tablets for Sue Byner's acne; filling his-and-hers bottles of Aldomet for Ed and Lucille Burkholtz and their matching hypertension; refilling John Rucci's prescription for Amphojel and Hedda Foster's prescription for Ativan.

Given how distraught Shelley was, she almost wished she could set aside a few tranquilizers for herself.

Her father would be arriving tomorrow. She would have preferred that he come later in the month, but the following week he was scheduled for a round of chemotherapy, so she'd agreed to let him come now.

She pulled an adhesive label from her computer printer, proofread it, and affixed it to the bottle of Cyclopar. After placing the bottle aside for Sue Byner, she left the glassed-in drug area to ring up a candy purchase for a couple of summer kids in swimsuits and rubber sandals. As soon as they left the store, Shelley started back to the glass enclosure. She wanted to lock herself inside, to hide there until Sunday night. She didn't want to have to leave the pharmacy, go home, wake up tomorrow and confront the man who had ruined her life.

Before she reached the enclosure, the door at the front of the store opened. Stepping back to the counter, she shaped another artificial smile for the customer. The moment she saw who it was, however, she stopped pretending to be cheerful. She slumped against the cash register and shoved her limp hair back from her brow. "Hi." She sighed as Kip sauntered down the aisle to her.

He'd been awfully good to her since she'd received her father's letter, doing more than his share around the house, keeping Jamie occupied whenever Shelley succumbed to a bad mood. But that afternoon, with the dreaded reunion less than twenty-four hours away, even Kip's gentle smile and luminous brown eyes couldn't allay her gloominess.

"Rough one?" he asked once he reached the counter.

She nodded sullenly. "This store needs a bigger air conditioner. I'm burning up in here."

Kip gave her a meaningful look. They both knew that Shelley's discomfort had little to do with the heat.

"Has it been unbearable in the cellar? I've been thinking, maybe we ought to move your office up to the attic."

"The cellar's fine," he said, reaching across the counter and taking her hand. He closed his fingers around it, then cupped his other hand over it so his palm rounded her knuckles. She was assailed by an unexpected memory of the agility in his hands when he'd sanded and varnished the stairway railing three years ago. She remembered the way his smooth businessman's fingers gradually acquired the rough texture of a laborer's, the way his skill and dexterity had illuminated hidden aspects of his personality. She remembered the way, a couple of days later, his hands had felt on her skin, on her body, making love to her.

She wished his kindness during the past week was a result of love, but she knew it was more a matter of repayment. She had pulled him out of his despair three years ago; now he was trying to do the same for her.

"Did you finish work early today?" she asked, appalled by the catch in her voice. Would she ever stop dwelling on that one extraordinary night she and Kip had made love? Would she ever stop wanting more than he could give her? He was giving her so much, particularly now, when her nervous system was more overheated than the stifling summer air. She simply had to learn to stop wanting so much.

He gave her a pensive smile. "I just got off the phone with your father."

Her fingers tensed within his hands. He refused to let go. "I don't suppose he called to cancel his trip," she muttered.

"He said he's going to take the 10:00 a.m. ferry out of New London tomorrow. He should be arriving in Old Harbor around noon."

Shelley swallowed and ordered herself to nod. Her father was truly coming. She was going to have to accept it.

"We haven't really worked out all the details," Kip noted.

"Details?" She could scarcely grasp the big picture. How was she supposed to think about details?

"Do you want me to buy something special for dinner tomorrow night?"

"No. I don't care. We'll grill hamburgers or something."

"Okay," Kip agreed, still holding onto her hand, still perusing her. "The other thing," he said slowly, "is the sleeping arrangements."

"He can sleep on the couch in the living room," she decided. She hadn't given much thought to it, but she couldn't imagine where else her father would stay, except at a hotel.

"I think he should have my room," Kip suggested. "I'll take the living room couch."

"Absolutely not." Her father didn't deserve to have people inconveniencing themselves on his behalf.

"Shelley. I know you're angry with him, but..." Kip paused to consider his words. "Your father isn't young and he isn't well. My room is private, and he would be much more comfortable in my bed."

He was right, of course. She reluctantly admitted that if she was going to extend any hospitality at all, she might as well extend a little more and not force an ailing man to spend the night on a sofa in the living room. "It's not fair for you to have to put yourself out that way, Kip," she said. "I'll take the couch. My father can have my room."

"You should be near Jamie," Kip argued.

"But you shouldn't get stuck on the sofa."

Kip's eyes met hers for a moment, and then he glanced away and shaped a lopsided grin. "Call it my punishment for cluttering up the small bedroom with all my junk. If only I'd gotten around to unpacking those cartons, we could have set up a cot in there for your father."

Shelley allowed herself an equally crooked smile. "Your punishment has been to put up with my horrible temper this past week." She moved her hand within his, rotating her wrist to lace her fingers through his. "I don't want you stuck on the couch," she said.

He steered his gaze back to her, and as she absorbed the dark beauty of his eyes she recalled not only how talented his hands were but how safe and comforting his embrace could be.

"You can stay in my room," she whispered, lowering her gaze to their intertwined fingers.

His grip tightened on her—almost imperceptibly, but she felt the change in him, the ripple of tension. She wondered whether he believed she was trying to unbalance things, risking destruction of the fragile harmony they'd worked so hard to achieve. "What I mean," she clarified, "is . . . It's a big bed, and it's not—I'm not saying—"

"I know exactly what you're saying," he said, his voice level and amiable although his grip remained numbingly tight.

"This isn't an—an invitation or anything—"

"No. It's the ravings of a desperate woman," he joked.

She lifted her eyes to him. His smile comforted her. But his hand was still binding, possessive, sending a distinctly unfunny message up her arm.

He didn't want her, she convinced herself. He didn't want her *that* way. No doubt if she happened to be conveniently stretched out beneath the covers beside him he wouldn't object to availing himself, but he didn't want her. She was his pal.

"You're right," she said, offering him a feeble smile. "I'm desperate."

"It's a big bed," he murmured. He leaned across the counter to kiss her cheek, then let go of her hand, turned and strode down the aisle to the door.

She watched his departure, resentful of his easy grace, his appealing lankiness, his serene response to the proposition of spending a night in bed with her. The tensing of his fingers around her hand had been simply a male reflex, not an expression of desire. He didn't love her. He didn't need her. She was merely someone to talk to over dinner, someone to diaper Jamie, someone who'd consoled him in his grief and sweated and bled so he could have a son.

She gave her head a sharp shake. Kip didn't deserve that bitter judgment. He was a good man, and he was going to help her survive the weekend, and he was going to prove himself the ultimate gentleman—whether or not she wanted him to be one—when he lay in bed next to her on Saturday night.

Letting out a weary breath, she moved back to the glass enclosure, ready to measure out some more prescriptions, resolved to stop thinking about Kip and concentrate on her father. It was easier to focus on him. She knew what she felt; the emotion was uncluttered and unmistakable.

That was the best strategy: put Kip out of her mind and think only about how much she despised her father.

CRUISING ALONG the winding road leading east to Old Harbor at noon on Saturday, he began to whistle. Objectively he was sorry for what Shelley was going through, but from a selfish point of view... this was his chance.

Kip *did* feel sorry for her. She was a wreck. She'd spent most of the previous evening with Jamie, clinging obsessively to him even when he'd wanted to scramble off her lap and play. She'd lingered over his bath until he'd hauled himself out of the tub, and she'd sat in the rocker by his crib in the dimly lit nursery, riding the chair back and forth, back and forth, for hours after Jamie had drifted off to sleep.

That morning her breakfast had consisted of a scarcely touched cup of coffee, and she'd set about cleaning the house. "Don't knock yourself out," Kip had said. The house wasn't that dirty, and anyway, no one expected a house with a two-year-old residing in it to be spotless.

"I'm not doing it for him," Shelley had informed Kip, not having to identify whom she was referring to. Kip realized her housecleaning was therapeutic, a way to channel her tension into a productive activity, just as he'd caulked the windows and refinished the banisters three years ago.

At eleven-thirty Kip reluctantly reminded her of the time. She'd cringed and her eyes had misted over with tears. "I've got to wash up," she'd murmured, her voice tremulous. "I'm a mess. Kip..." She'd sighed and given him a plaintive look. "Would you pick my father up for me?"

She was only delaying the inevitable, but he'd granted her wish. "Sure. Do you want me to take Jamie along?"

"No, leave Jamie here. I want to be with him when he meets my father."

Kip had given her a smile, intending to boost her spirits. She'd smiled back, but it was the saddest, most poignant smile Kip had ever seen. He'd wanted to envelop her in his arms, to whisper that he loved her, to assure her that no matter how awful the weekend was she wouldn't regret having allowed her father to come.

He couldn't say that, though; her father's visit might prove to be a disastrous mistake. As for the other part, telling her he loved her... He doubted that was something she was in any mood to hear.

Even so, her father, bless his blighted soul, had forced Shelley to lean on Kip this weekend. He harbored a strange, probably groundless notion that the trauma of seeing her father might somehow cause an emotional meltdown inside her, burning away her defenses and freeing her to feel again. She might pass through hell and emerge stronger for it. She might acknowledge that through it all Kip had been with her, behind her, beside her, wherever she needed him to be— and that when all was said and done, that was as good a definition of love as any.

He parked in the asphalt lot adjacent to the dock and got out. The sweltering heat of the past several days had abated and the sky was clear, adorned by just a few high, tufted clouds. Within a minute of his arrival he heard the deep, resonant moan of the New London ferry's horn. The slow-moving vessel glided around the stone breakwater and into the harbor.

Kip leaned on the front bumper of his car, waiting and wondering whether he would recognize George Ballard. It had been so long since he'd seen the man.

The dock workers tied the ferry to its moorings and the passengers streamed off, some in cars, a few walking bicycles onto the island, many carrying suitcases or knapsacks. Kip searched their faces, pausing to examine every passenger older than middle age. A hale silver-haired man bounded off the boat, swinging a leather satchel; before Kip could approach him, the man hurried over to an attractive woman at the other side of the lot.

He turned back to the boat and felt a sharp twinge of déjà vu as his gaze snagged on a tall, bony man with whispy gray hair and parchment-yellow skin. The man walked with a hesitant gait, his trousers baggy enough to flutter in the breeze as he stepped off the boat. He carried an old suitcase in one hand; the other shielded his eyes as he surveyed the dock. Kip noticed the man's gray eyes, the high forehead, the breadth of his shoulders beneath his cotton-knit polo shirt. He noticed the surprising fullness of the man's lips, bracketed with deep creases that emphasized his hollow cheeks.

He pushed away from his car. "Mr. Ballard," he said, extending his hand.

The man regarded him for a moment, his thin brows dipping in a frown. Then he gave Kip's hand a shake. "You must be the Stroud boy. Kip, is it?"

"That's right," Kip said, smiling at the comprehension that no matter how old he was, Mr. Ballard would undoubtedly think of him as the "Stroud Boy" forever.

Shelley's father glanced past Kip and his frown deepened. "She didn't come?"

"She's home with Jamie."

The older man digested this news, his thoughts hidden behind an impassive expression.

"Let me take your bag," Kip offered, easing it out of George Ballard's grip. It was lighter than he had expected. He imagined that Mr. Ballard would be lighter than he looked, too. He had an aura of fragility about him, despite his height, his wide shoulders, long legs and large hands.

Kip tossed the bag into the back of the car, then opened the passenger door. Before sitting, Shelley's father gave the harbor a slow perusal. Kip recalled his own return to the island after so many years away. He wondered if, like him, Mr. Ballard was tallying up the changes, feeling the weight of his years, measuring the passage of time in the newly named shops and freshly planted flower boxes.

Once they were both in the car, Kip revved the engine and drove out of the lot. Shelley's father continued to gaze out the window. "Did you have a good trip?" Kip asked.

"It was all right," Mr. Ballard said.

The traffic on Water Street was heavy, cars creeping along while bike and moped riders wove in and out around them. "I bet it feels strange to be back," Kip hazarded.

Shelley's father gave him a sharp look. "Everything feels strange to me these days."

"I'm sorry about your illness, Mr. Ballard."

"It's cancer, and you can call it that," he snapped. Subsiding in his bucket seat, he added, "And you can call me George."

"If that's what you want."

Shelley's father folded his arms over his chest and glowered at Kip. "What I want is for you to be able to call me Dad. I don't understand this situation, Kip. You get my daughter pregnant, you live with her but you don't marry her."

Kip refrained from informing George that he had asked Shelley to marry him several times, and that she had turned him down. He didn't want to cause friction between Shelley and her father before they had even seen each other.

"Shelley and I have worked things out between us," he said vaguely. He would do whatever was necessary to avoid quarreling with George. The key to surviving the weekend was to keep things calm and civil.

"I know what she's afraid of," George muttered, staring forward, his high brow creased with lines. "She thinks if she does anything like her mother and I did, she'll suffer the same consequences. Honest to God, Kip—if I could undo one thing of it, if I could teach her anything..."

Kip ground his teeth together. Less than five minutes since George had set foot on the island, he was already subjecting Kip to a lecture about marrying Shelley and some chest-thumping repentance for his own sins. "Listen," Kip said carefully. "You've come here to meet your grandson, not to rehash the past. I've got to warn you, George, Jamie is a terrific kid. You're going to like him. You're going to have a good time with him. Let's focus on that, okay?"

George eyed him speculatively, a grudging respect shining in his gray eyes. "I don't remember you being such a wise-ass," he remarked, his tone implying that this was a compliment.

"Oh, I've been a wise-ass all my life," Kip insisted with a grin.

They reached the lushly overgrown stone wall marking the beginning of Kip's property, and he turned onto the driveway, coasting to a stop near the front porch. He hadn't expected Shelley and Jamie to be waiting eagerly on the front porch, jumping up and down with excitement over their guest's arrival. But he hadn't expected the house to look deserted, either.

Sighing, praying that he would be able to help Shelley though this ordeal, he climbed out of the car. A mild breeze swept across the yard, carrying with it the trilling commentary of several blue jays perched on a high branch of the red maple. He pulled George's suitcase out of the hatchback, glancing at the empty-looking house again, searching the windows for a sign of Shelley.

Abruptly he realized where she would be. Craning his neck, he spotted two shadowy figures in the open window of the cupola, one small and mobile and one tall and still. Through the screen he heard a gleeful yell. "They here, Mommy! They here!"

SHE HAD BEEN WORKING herself into a state for so many days, stockpiling her rage, preparing herself to hate him, girding to protect her precious son from him. Now, as his arrival time drew close, she figured she was as ready to see her father as she'd ever be.

Which wasn't very ready at all.

"We're going to have company," Shelley told Jamie as she brought him up to the cupola. "Daddy went to pick up our company at the ferry."

"We have company," Jamie said. "We have chips!" Given the casual nature of life on Block Island, Shelley's entertaining generally extended to serving beer and potato chips whenever someone dropped by.

"Maybe later," she said.

"I hear car! I hear Daddy car!"

Shelley also heard the hum of an engine growing louder as the car neared the house. Glancing out the window, she spotted the Saab pulling into the driveway. Kip climbed out. Then, from the passenger side... her father.

He looked dreadfully old and frail, moving in small, stiff steps across the lawn. Even from her distance four stories above him, she could see his hair had thinned, his complexion had paled. When a gust of wind flattened his shirt against his chest she could see how much weight he had lost.

He's dying, she thought. *That man ruined my childhood and destroyed my idealism, and now he's dying.*

Jamie was already wrestling with the trapdoor latch, and Shelley nudged him aside and lifted the door. She preceded him down the ladder steps, guiding his sandaled feet on each step so he wouldn't fall. Reaching the attic, he scampered ahead, scooting down the attic stairs, past Kip's unpacked cartons in the small bedroom, along the hallway, down the stairs to the first floor. The front door opened as Shelley descended the last few steps. The moment her father stepped across the threshold Jamie fell back shyly, pressing back against her legs and staring up at the stranger looming in the entry.

Shelley lifted her gaze from her towheaded son to her father. It was a struggle not to wince at his haggard appearance, at the pallor of his complexion, the pockets of shadow under his eyes and the gauntness of his cheeks. His eyes, once alert and radiant, seemed flat and rheumy to her. Deep lines grooved the sides of his mouth and spanned his forehead.

She could ascribe his physical decline to his cancer, and then she would feel sorry for him. She chose, instead, to ascribe it to the years he'd spent in prison. He'd brought his deterioration on himself for having betrayed his wife, his employers, the federal government—and his daughter.

His eyes met hers for a moment, searching for something. Affection? Absolution? Welcome? Whatever he was looking for, he apparently didn't find it, because he didn't address Shelley, didn't thank her for allowing him to come, didn't apologize, didn't even say hello.

He squatted down in front of Jamie and smiled. "Hey, there—you must be Jamie," he said in a surprisingly gentle voice. It was more gravelly than she'd remembered, but sweeter than the voice she'd heard on the telephone a few days ago. He used to speak sweetly to her, hadn't he? Once upon a time, when she was a naive little girl, she was pretty sure he used to speak in a sweet voice to her.

She clung to the newel post behind her to keep from shivering. Holding her breath, she waited to hear what Jamie would say. He only gaped at the balding, skeletal man hunkering down in front of him.

"Do you know who I am?" Shelley's father asked.

"You company," Jamie said.

Her father's smile widened. "Yes, I suppose I am."

"This is your grandfather," Kip said when it seemed obvious that Shelley wasn't going to introduce him.

Jamie looked bewildered. "My Gramma Grampa in Chester Hill."

"Chestnut Hill," Kip corrected, moving to Jamie and placing his hand gently on the boy's shoulder, easing him away from Shelley's legs. "That's your other grampa. You've got that grampa and gramma, and then you've got your other grandmother in Texas, right? And this is your other grandfather."

Jamie twisted to give Shelley a quizzical look. It took every ounce of strength in her body to nod in confirmation.

Turning back to Shelley's father, Jamie tilted his head and appraised the stranger. "You my other grampa."

"How about if you called me something different, say, Granddad?" he suggested. "That way you won't get confused."

"Granddad," Jamie said.

"I've got some surprises for you in my suitcase. Do you like surprises?"

"Soo-pri!" Jamie whooped. Shelley's father had spoken the magic word; he had won Jamie's eternal devotion. "Mommy! Company bring soo-pri!" Unable to contain himself, he pranced into the living room and out again, clapping his hands and shrieking for joy.

Shelley's father opened his suitcase and pulled out several clumsily gift-wrapped packages. Jamie flopped down on the hardwood floor and tore the wrapping to shreds.

Kip inched closer to Shelley and discreetly slipped his arm around her. His touch seemed to drain her of what little energy she had left; her body went limp against him. Watching Jamie rhapsodize over his presents—a plastic dump truck and a clown doll that beeped when its stomach was squeezed—was almost unbearable. This felon, this cruel,

selfish, deceitful man who had broken his vows and abdi-
cated his responsibilities, who stood for everything Shelley
abhorred, had won over her son with five dollars' worth of
toys.

"Are you hungry, George?" Kip asked, covering for
Shelley's lapse in manners.

Her father glanced up from his position on the floor next
to Jamie. "No, thanks. I'd just like to spend some time with
Jamie."

"Maybe we could go to the beach. Would you like that?"

"Beach!" Jamie bellowed. "Go beach!"

Shelley closed her eyes and swallowed. "I don't feel too
well," she whispered.

Kip peered at her, his eyes shimmering, his arm snug
around her quaking shoulders. "I could take your father
and Jamie down to the beach for a while," he suggested. "If
you really aren't up to it—"

She almost wished she could ask her father to take Jamie
and let Kip stay home with her. She wanted to bury herself
in his embrace, draw strength from him, let him shelter her
from this agony. She wanted to lose herself with him, the
way she'd lost herself one fog-shrouded September night,
when his love had carried her far away from reality, from
venal parents and lost wives and all the pain she and Kip had
ever suffered.

But she couldn't abandon her son to her father. "If you
wouldn't mind," she mumbled. "Please take them to the
beach. I'll . . . I'll just rest awhile."

"Sure." He gave her a comforting squeeze and then released her. "Come on," he said brightly to the others.
"Let's get some stuff together and go to the beach."

Shelley watched as the men in her life joined forces to
prepare for their outing. Hanging onto the newel post as if
it were a crutch, she observed them, three generations, three

men who had inhabited her heart in their own individual ways. One she had loved with all her heart and now hated beyond measure. One she loved now and would love always.

One was Kip, and as difficult as it was to have her father back in her life, trying to figure out her relationship with Kip was even more difficult. She almost cried out as he lifted her father's bag and ushered him and Jamie up the stairs. She almost cried out, "Don't go, don't leave me!"

She had sworn to herself that she would never become dependent on a man. But today, as she watched him vanish upstairs with her father and her son, she comprehended that she had broken that vow. She was utterly dependent on Kip—and the realization frightened her to her soul.

HE TOOK THEM to Scotch Beach. Some twenty or so other people were enjoying the sunny afternoon there—a mob by Block Island standards, but really not much of a crowd. Kip had brought along a beach umbrella, two beach chairs, a blanket, towels and a tote full of toys. Taking Jamie to the beach was a lot more complicated than taking Shelley used to be. So much more equipment was involved.

Before they'd driven to the beach, George had wanted to wash up from his long trip. He hadn't changed his clothes, though. Now he pulled his shoes and socks off and rolled up his trousers.

Kip lounged in one of the beach chairs while George and Jamie played in the damp sand near the water's edge, building a sand castle and trying out the new toy dump truck. The sun was high, the water placid. He gazed at the white sand, the stalky reeds of grass climbing the dunes, the clear line of the horizon and the deep blue-green of the waves rolling toward the shore in a gentle rhythm. Scotch

Beach wasn't as pretty as the secret cove Kip and Shelley
favored, but it was special in its own way.

It was here that he had first met Shelley, more than two
decades ago. They had circled each other, sized each other
up, and tramped through the grass together to examine a
dead snake. They had been so fearless back then.

Jamie trudged across the sand to Kip. George followed,
lugging the toys. As soon as Jamie reached the shade of the
umbrella he tore off his sun hat and let out a whimper.
"Dirsty," he said.

Kip suspected he was more tired than thirsty, but he dutifully pulled a juice box out of his bag. The child took two
sips, then handed the box back to Kip and sprawled out on
the blanket.

Kip lowered himself from the chair to lie beside Jamie,
who happily nestled in the curve of his arm. His skin smelled
of salt and sand and the baby-oil fragrance of sunscreen. In
short time he was fast asleep.

George had settled into the other beach chair, adjusting
it so the umbrella would shade him. "That's a great kid
you've got," he remarked.

"I know," Kip said, not boasting but simply stating a
fact.

"You've done a good job with him."

"Shelley's done most of it," Kip asserted. This, too, was
a simple fact. He saw no reason to hype Shelley to her father. If George didn't realize what a great kid his daughter
was, that was his problem.

George meditated for a while, squinting as he surveyed the
vast expanse of the sound. "I don't get it," he finally said.

"Don't get what?"

"The two of you make this wonderful child. You've got
a nice house, you've got money, you seem to like each
other..." He fixed an accusing look on Kip. "You don't

want to talk about marrying her, Kip, so we won't talk about that. But she's my daughter. She's beautiful and smart. She's a woman of quality." Obviously George *did* realize what a fine daughter he had.

"So, what is it?" he went on in his scratchy voice. "You put my suitcase in that bedroom, and I saw it was filled with your things. I could understand if she took over the closet in her room so you had to hang your things in another closet. Her mother used to take up three-quarters of the closet space—I understand how women are. But . . . it's not just the closet, Kip. That's your room. It's where you live. Am I right?"

"Yeah," Kip said, focusing on the horizon to avoid meeting George's inquisitive gaze.

"I could tell. You don't share a room with Shelley. You don't *live* with her."

Kip closed his eyes and prayed for patience. This was not a conversation he'd planned for—and certainly not one he wanted to have.

His feelings must have been evident because George continued. "You're thinking it's none of my business. You're thinking I'm way out of line, discussing my daughter's relationship with you, questioning the sleeping arrangements. And you're right, Kip. It's none of my business."

"Then let's not talk about it," Kip muttered. Beyond the basic awkwardness of discussing such a sensitive subject with Shelley's father, Kip was disturbed by his own desire for things to be different between him and Shelley. He himself questioned the sleeping arrangements almost every night. When he climbed into Shelley's bed tonight, he would still be questioning them. He knew he would be there not as a lover but as a comforter, something for her to hold onto, something she needed the way Jamie needed his teddy bear and his night-light. He wanted her body, her soul, the warmth of her around him—and she wanted security. For one night. Tomorrow he'd be safely back on his own side of the hall, aching with hunger for her but too scared of jeopardizing what little he had with her to demand more.

"I'll tell you, Kip, at this stage of my life, I don't give a damn whether something is my business or not, whether I'm stepping on toes or getting on people's nerves. I've done so much damage to my loved ones, at this point it doesn't matter anymore. You want to hate me? Be my guest."

"I don't hate you."

"I'm not a fool. I've done some foolish things in my life, but I'm not a fool. I've got a business degree from Columbia University. Just because I work as a motel desk clerk doesn't mean I'm an idiot."

Kip groaned inwardly. "No one's calling you an idiot."

"So, what is it, then? What do you find so distasteful about my daughter? You won't marry her, you won't sleep with her. What is it? Are you gay?"

Kip let out a short laugh. "No, I'm not gay. Believe me, if Shelley was interested, I would be very happy to sleep with her. And marry her."

"You mean, *she's* gay?"

"No."

George ruminated. "All right. Maybe I *am* an idiot. I just don't understand the situation."

Kip's wry amusement at George's confusion vanished, replaced by a healthy surge of anger. "I'll explain it, then, George. It's *you*. Shelley sees what you did and she doesn't trust men. She sees the agony you caused her mother, and she refuses to open herself to anyone. You scarred her, George. You hurt her so badly she's afraid to love anyone."

Kip's enraged accusations seemed to bounce off George. "She loves Jamie," he pointed out.

Kip lowered his gaze to his son, warm and slumbering, his chest rising and falling as he snored. "Jamie hasn't betrayed her."

"And you have?"

"No, I—" Falling silent, Kip glanced away. Two teenagers, a boy and a girl, were playing in the water, splashing and dunking each other, sending silver arcs of sea spray into each other's faces. Flirting. Falling in love.

The way he and Shelley had fallen in love so many years ago.

A profound sadness filled him. "She thinks I'm in love with someone else," he said quietly.

"Are you?"

"No. I was, but... The woman died."

"And now?"

"I love Shelley."

"And she doesn't know that?"

He shook his head.

George cursed. "Damn it, boy, why don't you make sure she finds out? What the hell are you waiting for?" When Kip turned back to him, too astonished to speak, he added, "She's my daughter, and I love her, and I came back to make sure she finds that out before I die. You may think an old ex-con doped up on painkillers has no good advice to give a young hotshot like you, but you're wrong. Tell her you love her. Let her know before it's too late. Make my daughter happy."

Kip turned back to the horizon, his mind reeling. George made it sound so simple—and perhaps, when one was old and sick and had nothing left to lose, things did become simple.

What did Kip have to lose? When it came to Shelley, all he had to lose were his heart and his pride and the loneliness of his bed at night.

She already had his heart. His pride was worth risking. And he could think of nothing he'd rather lose than the lonely torment of having to confront each night without Shelley in his arms.

Chapter Fourteen

Shelley emerged from the master bathroom, clad in a demure cotton nightgown. She'd kept her shower brief in order to save hot water for her father and Kip, and the five minutes she'd spent under the spray had done little to calm her. Her nervous system was suffering a critical overload; the only thing that kept her from falling apart completely was the understanding that by the same time tomorrow night her father would be gone, and Kip would be back in his own bed.

He was seated on the edge of her bed now, his back to her. He'd already removed his shirt, and as he hunched over something on his lap her gaze took in the smooth, masculine arch of his sun-darkened skin, the rugged breadth of his shoulders and the trim span of his waist above the belt of his jeans. In any other context Shelley would have reacted to his naked torso with a sigh of longing.

Damn it, she *was* sighing. Despite her frazzled nerves, despite the anguish wringing her soul, she suffered a searing pang of sexual awareness at the realization that this man was going to be spending the night beside her.

She shook her shoulders—as if she could shrug off her longing—and announced, "I'm all done in the bathroom, if you want it."

Kip turned and smiled at her. He was pulling a crisply folded royal-blue garment out of a rectangular plastic bag. Standing, he crumpled the bag and discarded it in the garbage pail, then unfolded the cloth.

"New pajamas?" Shelley asked.

"I bought them Friday afternoon. I thought you'd feel more comfortable if I wore them."

His smile was apparently meant to ease her distress. His words, however, conveyed that he generally didn't wear pajamas, and the image that notion provoked only cranked her tension up another notch.

To distract herself, she concentrated on her father in the room across the hall, visualizing his wasted body and his haunted eyes. She recalled the stilted conversation at dinner, during which he had sketchily described his job manning the desk at a motel—thank God for the health insurance, he'd said—and his apartment with its panoramic view of the Connecticut Turnpike, and his pet cat, named Joey after his closest friend from his days at the federal prison in Danbury. Fortunately he'd been discreet in front of Jamie, avoiding the actual word "prison."

Jamie had exclaimed jubilantly over the news that Granddad had a cat. "We get cat?" he asked over and over to Kip's amusement and Shelley's irritation.

Less than a day left, she reminded herself. Less than eighteen hours, and her father would be out of her life once more.

Kip removed his eyeglasses and set them on the night table. Then he went into the bathroom and closed the door behind him. Shelley brushed her hair, rubbed moisturizer into her hands, listened to the rush of the shower through the closed door and gazed compulsively at the eyeglasses on the night table, next to the pillow that would be Kip's.

Unable to sit still, she left the bedroom to check on Jamie. He was fast asleep, his thumb in his mouth and his teddy bear clutched in his free hand. One of his feet poked out from under the blanket, and she rearranged the soft coverlet around his body. Then she leaned over the crib railing and kissed his cheek. He made a faint sucking noise, his cheeks flexing and his lips tightening around his thumb.

Only eighteen more hours, she thought, and it would all be over.

She tiptoed back down the hall to her own room. Her gaze was drawn to the door across the hall from hers. The narrow crack between the door and the hallway was dark.

Kip always had his light on when she returned from the nursery after her final good night to Jamie. Shelley had never consciously paid attention to that, but it must have registered on her in some subliminal way because the darkness filling the space under the door startled her.

She had absorbed Kip's presence in so many subtle ways. In the few weeks since he'd moved permanently into the house, she had grown accustomed to his scent, his footsteps, his voice. She'd grown used to seeing the light under his door before she retired for the night. She'd drawn comfort from knowing he was near—but not too near.

Sighing again, she turned and entered her own bedroom. As she closed the door Kip stepped out of the bathroom, running a towel through his thick brown hair. He had on the new pajamas. Spotting Shelley, he tossed the towel onto a chair and struck a comical modeling pose. "Well? How do I look?"

"Very dapper," she told him with a smile.

He combed the damp waves of his hair loose with his fingers, then extended his hand to her. "Come here," he murmured.

She experienced another pang, this one comprising both curiosity and annoyance. If he did anything more than kiss her on the cheek, she would scream, or crumble, or burst into tears. She couldn't handle anything beyond a friendly hug from him, especially not tonight.

Warily she placed her hand in his. He led her to the bed and nudged her to sit. "Lie down, Shelley," he said.

"Kip." Her voice carried a firm warning.

"Just lie down." He sat beside her and forced her shoulders down to the mattress.

"Kip—"

"Roll over. On your stomach. That's it," he said, helping her into a prone position. He shifted higher onto the mattress, then leaned over and dug his thumbs into the knotted flesh at the base of her neck.

A back rub. Exactly what she needed. How could she have doubted him? How could she have questioned his motives?

She lifted her face slightly out of the pillow so he would hear her when she said, "Thanks."

"You were expecting something else," he needled her.

"Just keep rubbing. It feels wonderful."

"Don't mention it."

She groaned, feeling him rout out the knots in her muscles, draw her stress to the surface and sweep it away with the deft motions of his fingertips. She was ashamed of herself for having suspected him of attempting a seduction. He had been her champion all day, her savior, her protector.

"You've been too good to me," she mumbled, succumbing to the soothing spell of his massage.

"I know," he agreed.

She measured his tone, searching for amusement in it. He'd sounded surprisingly serious, though.

"Well—I appreciate it," she said.

"Do you?"

Puzzled, she raised her head and shoulders, twisting to glimpse his face.

He pushed her back down. "I'm not done yet," he said, inching his fingers down along her spine, loosening the clenched muscles of her back. A minute passed in silence and then he said, "You've treated your father terribly, Shelley."

"What?"

"You heard me." His voice was low and even, devoid of rancor. "You've been awful to him. You've treated him like dirt. You've been acting like a first-class bitch."

She drew in a sharp, angry breath. If he hadn't been giving her such an effective back rub, she would have reared up and slapped him. How could he say such a thing? He knew what her life had been like, thanks to her father's venal actions. He knew the way she'd been wounded, the scars she carried. What was she supposed to do, treat her father like visiting royalty?

Kip's hands continued to move on her back. "You didn't come to the beach with us. Over dinner you scarcely said a word to him, and then the minute we were done eating you raced off with Jamie to get his bath and put him to bed. Then you came back downstairs and pretended to clean the kitchen, even though I had already put everything away. And finally, when you condescended to join your father and me, you sat at the opposite end of the living room and glowered at him until nine-thirty, at which point you came upstairs. You didn't even say good-night."

So what? She hadn't even wanted her father to come. She'd done her good deed by letting him meet his grandchild. How dare he—or Kip—demand more of her?

She rolled away from Kip so he wouldn't be able to subdue her with his massage. Sitting, she glared at him. "Well, I guess he's lucky he had you for company all day. He's obviously won you over to his side."

Kip's expression was stern, his mouth shaping a grim line as he met her hostile stare. "This isn't a game, Shelley. Nobody's choosing sides."

"That man—" she waved a furious finger in the direction of Kip's bedroom "—is a convicted criminal. He's an adulterer. He destroyed my family out of greed and selfishness. He made us pay for his sins, and I'm not talking about the money. I'm talking about my heart." She jabbed her chest with her thumb. "I'm talking about how much I've paid, right here, inside me."

"Fine. You've paid. It's time to close out the account."

"Don't throw your financial consulting language at me."

"I'm not throwing anything at you, Shelley. I'm trying to talk some sense into you."

His patronizing attitude honed her already frazzled nerves to razor sharpness. "Thanks," she snapped, her voice taut and her spinal muscles coiling with tension again. "Thanks a heap. I thought I could depend on you this weekend. I should have known better. You're just a man, throwing your lot in with another man."

"Stop," Kip said with disarming gentleness.

She wasn't fooled, not anymore. This wasn't a good time to have to learn that even Kip couldn't be trusted, that in a crisis he wouldn't shore her up. But he'd forced the lesson on her. She was learning.

He extended his hand and she shrank from him. "Shelley," he said, "I'm just trying to open your eyes—"

"Thanks. They're wide open." A few tears leaked down her cheeks, but she wouldn't give Kip the satisfaction of seeing her close her eyes against them.

"He's come to work it out with you before he dies. Don't you see? He didn't come here just to meet his grandchild. He came here to make amends with you."

"I haven't seen him trying to make amends—"

"You haven't *seen* him, period."

"I let him come here. I never promised I'd greet him with open arms. He ought to be happy I let him enter my house."

"You let him enter your house, and ever since he walked through the door you've been running from him. You're evading him. You're shutting yourself off from him."

"Because he ruined my life!"

"Ruined it?" Kip put an incredulous spin on the words. "Whatever he did to your life, Shelley, you've managed to rise above it quite nicely."

"What is going on here, Kip? What the hell are you doing?"

"I'm fighting with you."

"You've got a hell of a nerve—"

"Shelley—"

"Criticizing me, lashing out at me—" Her words became disjointed, mirroring her fragmented state of mind. "Just stop it, okay? Leave me alone."

Kip examined her for a moment, gazing across the bed as if it were a great chasm. He took a deep breath, then said, "Let's talk about it."

"I don't want to talk about anything," she railed, twisting away and fluffing her pillow in the hope that he'd turn off the light and shut up.

Instead he reached across the bed, gripped her shoulder and turned her back to him. His touch ignited an unknown rage in her, an emotion as raw and blind as the fury she'd felt when she'd first found out about her father's crimes. Without thinking, she curled her hand into a fist and swung, her only desire to hit Kip, to hurt him the way he was hurting her.

He easily blocked her punch and manacled her wrist with his hand. Neither of them spoke; they simply stared at each other, breathing hard. At that moment, his dark eyes stabbing her, his hand squeezing until her fingers began to tingle, Shelley hated Kip more than she'd ever hated anyone before.

Her eyes burned with tears. She needed Kip's strength this weekend. She needed his support. Why was he undermining her, cutting her down?

"Kip, please," she said softly, unable to quell the tremor in her voice. "I don't need this."

"Yes, you do," he said just as quietly, his tone as firm and certain as hers was faltering.

She turned away, knowing it was a sign of defeat to do so but no longer able to meet his piercing gaze. Her anger seemed to drain from her, leaving behind only a hollow, throbbing pain as she absorbed the profound grief of Kip's betrayal. "Why are you doing this to me?" she asked querulously.

"Because I'm your friend," he answered.

Her tears broke loose, spilling down her cheeks. Kip released her hand and she jerked away from him, rolling into a self-defensive position, her back to him and her head buried in her pillow to muffle her sobs.

She wouldn't accept comfort from him, not when he'd been so determined to undermine her in the first place, not when he'd picked a fight with her so deliberately, at a time when she was so vulnerable. *I'm fighting with you,* he'd practically boasted—as if it were an act of heroism.

She and Kip never fought. They hadn't had a single argument since he'd moved back into the house. They hadn't argued three years ago, when Kip had returned to the island and found her living there. In fact, as she thought about it, the last time they'd actually fought was when they'd been children together, and teenagers.

When they'd been true friends, trusting each other so much they weren't afraid to disagree.

Now, as adults, they discussed things, took each other's feelings into consideration and treated each other with respect. They didn't trust each other enough to risk their relationship on an honest fight anymore.

Hours later, after the lamp had been turned off and Kip had stopped shifting on his half of the bed, Shelley lay awake in the darkness, huddled at the edge of the mattress, listening to the steady rhythm of his breathing. Why was he even in her bed? Why hadn't she kicked him out of her room? She loathed him for attacking her, tonight of all nights. She despised him. She had trusted him, and he'd let her down.

No. He *hadn't* let her down. He'd forced her to face the truth, even though it hurt. Even though he knew she'd hate him for it.

Even though their friendship might not survive his honesty.

SHE ROSE AFTER a few hours of fitful sleep. The sky had faded from black to gray as the sun crept closer to the eastern horizon. Kip was still asleep, lying on his side, facing away from her. His disheveled hair appeared almost black in the early morning gloom, stark against the white linen of the pillowcase. Sometime during the night he had unbuttoned the shirt of his pajamas, and when Shelley circled the bed she caught a glimpse of his bare chest with its lean muscles and shadow of hair.

What she felt toward him no longer resembled anger—or even desire. Rather, she was dazed, and more than a little awed by his courage in taking her on last night.

His timing had been wretched, his words brutal. If he had intended to wound her he'd succeeded. But he had spoken his heart. That was the important thing: he'd said what he felt he had to say. He had taken a chance. He'd goaded her, infuriated her—*because I'm your friend,* he'd said.

The room was warm, but she put on her robe before leaving. Silence filled the upstairs hallway. It was too early for Jamie to be bellowing for someone to get him out of his crib.

The door across the hall was open, the bed made.

Shelley glided down the stairs. She could tell from the angle of the shaft of light spilling into the hall that the lamp above the kitchen table was on. She entered to discover her father at the counter, stirring milk into a mug of coffee.

"Good morning," she said.

He set the spoon down and turned to her. "I hope you don't mind," he said, gesturing toward the coffee pot, which was filled with freshly brewed coffee. "Kip said I should help myself."

"Of course I don't mind." She filled a mug for herself and carried it to the table. Her father took a seat facing her, lifted the coffee to his mouth and sipped.

His fingers appeared almost fleshless. She felt her stomach tighten, not in resentment but in pity. But what could she say to him? When she didn't even know what she was thinking, what on earth could she say?

He bailed her out by speaking first. "You're a good mother, Shelley. Jamie is a fine boy."

"Thank you." She orbited the rim of her mug with her finger, groping for some clever quip, some all-purpose statement that would solve everything.

"I'm proud of you. What you've accomplished—I know it's been hard. Putting yourself through school, having a baby, holding down a job... I'm very proud, Shelley. I don't suppose I can take any of the credit for the way you've turned out, but... a father couldn't hope for more."

"A father could hope for his daughter's love," she whispered, aching to give him that, knowing she couldn't.

"Not when he squandered it the first time around." He exhaled. "You've got a lot of love in you, Shelley. Give it to the people who deserve it."

She lifted her gaze. Her father's eyes seemed animated in the pre dawn light, dense and shimmering like mercury. She had seen that glow before: when, at five years old, she swam the width of a neighbor's pool all by herself. When, at seven, she brought home a stellar report card. When, at three, she plucked a perfect buttercup and scampered across the grass to give it to him.

Back in ancient times, when the Ballards were a loving family, she'd seen his eyes glow for her. She was filled with a consuming hunger for the security of her father's love once more, a hunger to know she was more important to him than money or professional advancement or extra-marital affairs.

"Maybe you won't die," she said.

Her father appeared bemused. "We're all going to die someday."

"No—I mean, your cancer. Maybe the chemotherapy will work. More and more people are surviving cancer these days."

His lips spread in a crooked grin. "You're still an optimist, aren't you."

The observation brought her up short. She had been so bitter for so long. Yet perhaps, buried beneath the layers of cynicism she'd accumulated over the years, a spark of optimism still burned.

Deciding to mother Jamie had been impractical; a realist might have put him up for adoption. But Shelley had become Jamie's mother as an act of faith, and her faith had been rewarded. Jamie had renewed her idealism. He'd proven to her that it was all right to hope, and that things sometimes did work out.

"All I'm saying," she explained, "is that some people go on and on for years after they've been diagnosed. Some people go into permanent remission. Maybe you'll be one of the lucky ones."

He issued a short grunt of a laugh. "I haven't been lucky in a long time," he reminded her.

"You were lucky to find out you had a grandchild. You were lucky to come here before it was too late."

He studied her for a wordless minute, his smile fading from his lips. "I don't know, Shelley. Is it too late?"

"I don't know, either," she said, ignoring the quiver in her voice. "I want to forgive you, but I don't know if I can. I need more time. You can't die, Dad. I need more time."

The light in his eyes grew brighter. For the first time since he'd set foot in her house, she had called him "Dad." "I'll give you as much time as I've got," he said.

She suddenly felt reckless. If her father was willing to give her time, maybe he could also give her answers. "Why did you do it?" she asked. "Why did you do what you did to us?"

He sighed, then drank some coffee, his eyes never leaving her. "Which part of it?"

"The adultery. The embezzlement. Any of it. Just tell me why. I loved you so much, Dad. I idolized you—"

"I wasn't God, Shelley. I'm a human being. I made mistakes."

"Mistakes," she echoed sardonically. "Forgetting to put a stamp on a letter before you mail it is a mistake. Giving Jamie a box of crayons and leaving the room is a mistake. Cheating on your wife and stealing money from your boss— that's a little different."

"What do you think, these things happened in a vacuum?" He scowled, gazing out the window at the drifting morning mist and collecting his thoughts. "I loved your mother, but I couldn't be what she wanted me to be. She was a working-class girl who wanted to move up in the world. She pushed and pushed and pushed. I couldn't keep up. I wanted to, but I couldn't."

"Not legally, anyway."

Her father turned back to her so she could receive the full force of his frown. "I gave her what she wanted, but it was never enough. I worked as hard as I could. I clawed my way up the ladder for her. But it wasn't enough." He let out a weary breath. "Did I stop loving her? Yes. Did I have an affair? Yes. I wanted a woman who would love me without making those kinds of demands on me."

"And you went and bought her a condominium, and—"

"Look at me! I don't know how to love a woman without giving her things. Your mother had me convinced that a woman expects these things, so I did them. I bought her what she needed. At least she never asked for them, not the way your mother did. There weren't contingencies and unwritten contracts. She was divorced, and she needed a place to live. I helped her out."

"*Mom* was divorced and she needed a place to live, too," Shelley retorted. "You didn't help her out."

"I was under indictment," he reminded her. "I didn't want a divorce, but your mother did, so I went along with it. I didn't want any of it to come out the way it did. What can I say, Shelley? I'm lousy at human relationships. So now I live with a cat."

Shelley tried to lift her mug, but her hands were shaking too much. Clasping them together, she hid them in her lap. "I don't know what went wrong with you and Mom," she conceded in a low, tight voice. "But *I* never did anything. I was an innocent bystander."

"I know," her father said, his frown transforming into a rueful smile. "I know. It probably doesn't matter if you forgive me. I'll never forgive myself for the way you got hurt."

She felt a sob rise up, filling her throat. She unfolded her hands and lifted them to her cheeks.

To her relief, her father remained in his chair. She didn't want him to comfort her. She wanted to weep until her tears eroded the small, stony node of pain deep inside her, dissolved it and washed it away.

"What can I do?" he asked sadly. "Tell me, Shelley. What can I do to make it better? What can I give you to make up for everything I took?"

"A gold necklace," she blurted out, then succumbed to a fresh spate of tears.

"A necklace?" He sounded surprised—and disappointed.

She shook her head and wiped her eyes. "It was a simple gold chain—you probably don't even remember it. You gave it to me for my fifteenth birthday, and I loved it. Not because it was expensive, but because you gave it to me."

He nodded, his eyes sharpening as he remembered. "It was a little choker, wasn't it?"

"Yes. And when—" she sniffled and steadied her voice "—when you were sentenced, and there were so many debts and we had to sell everything..." She didn't want to seem petty, but it had meant so much to her at the time. It had symbolized every sin her father had committed, everything she had lost. "Mom had to sell it for the money. She took it along with all her jewelry to a broker who dealt in estate sales, and he gave her a few thousand dollars for the whole lot. I don't remember the exact amount—it all went to the bank and the IRS." She wiped away the tears that lingered on her lashes. "It was just a little chain, I know it couldn't have been worth that much..." Except that her father had given it to her, and that had made it priceless in Shelley's eyes.

Evidently her father understood the necklace's significance. "I can't ever give you that again, Princess. I wish I could. I could go right out now and buy you a necklace ten times prettier and more expensive. But I can't give you the necklace you want."

She nodded. When she'd lost that necklace she'd lost her faith, her trust, her youth. They were gone forever. No one, not even a father desperate for his daughter's forgiveness, could bring them back.

"I can't give you anything as good as what you have now," her father continued, his voice gaining strength and conviction. "You've got a son, and this fine house on Block Island. You always loved Block Island."

"I used to nag you to spend more time here," Shelley recalled. "Maybe it would have done you some good. It would have kept you out of trouble."

He chuckled grimly. "I doubt it, Shelley. But it did *you* good, that much is clear. It's still doing you good." He extended his arm across the table, and slowly, hesitantly, Shelley slipped her hand inside his. His grip was stronger than she'd imagined, his skin warmer. "You've got a man here who's doing you good, too. I remember Kip as a scrappy little kid with big eyeglasses. But he's grown up, Shelley. He's a good man."

"I know."

"He's a better father than I ever was."

"I don't know about that," Shelley debated him, feeling a shy smile shape her mouth. "He's only been a father for two years. The jury's still out."

Her father smiled, as well. "I look at you, Shelley, and I think maybe your mother and I did something right. You didn't turn out so badly."

Outside the bay window the mist was brightening from gray to white as the sun broke over the eastern edge of the island. From upstairs came Jamie's shrill command, "Gemme out! Mommy, gemme out!"

"My master's voice," she joked, sliding her hand from her father's and mopping her damp cheeks as she stood.

"Can I come with you?" he asked.

She didn't forgive him. She hadn't stopped hurting. One intense, tear-soaked early morning conversation couldn't undo years of sorrow and anger.

But even though her father had cheated her out of it a few years too soon, she would have lost her youthful naïveté eventually. She would have come of age, like the heroes and heroines of the books she and Kip had read one summer during their youth. She would have learned that even in the best of circumstances a person underwent metamorphosis, that even the happiest of people lost their innocence, and that one could have one's optimism crushed—but sometimes it came back in a new shape.

For years she had dwelled on her losses. But in the opalescent light of an early midsummer morning, everything she'd lost seemed no more valuable than a gold chain necklace.

What she had now was infinitely better: a man who had cared enough to pressure her into facing her father, and the child she and that man had brought into this world.

"Mommy!" Jamie hollered impatiently. "Gemme out!"

"Yes," she murmured, taking her father's hand. "Come with me."

Chapter Fifteen

At four o'clock she drove her father to Old Harbor. It was their final time alone, their last chance to say whatever remained to be said. "I'm glad you came," she admitted as she stood with him on the dock, waiting for the ferry to begin boarding. "At least, I think I am."

Her father smiled. "As visits go, it could have been worse."

"I still don't know if I can forgive you," she said. "I just can't erase everything that happened—"

"It's our history, Princess. You don't have to forgive me or erase anything. All you've got to do is keep the memories in the past, where they belong."

"Maybe I'm just not able to do that."

"Try harder," he said. A dock worker began to collect ferry tickets. Shelley's father gave her a quick, awkward hug. "I'll send you a necklace."

"A piece of string will do," she told him. "And don't send it. Bring it." Then, before she could retract the invitation, she spun on her heel and jogged back to the Blazer.

Unspoken words hung between her and Kip throughout the evening. He didn't comment on what had occurred to change Shelley overnight. He didn't ask how her farewell with her father had gone. Both he and Shelley concentrated on Jamie as they usually did, cutting his pizza into tiny pieces and taking turns refilling his cup whenever he shouted, "Deuce! Deuce, *pleeeeee.*"

The questions hovered, though, deafening in their silence. Kip's questions and Shelley's confessions. All through Jamie's bath, through his futile attempt to use the potty, through his bedtime story and lullaby and good-night kisses, thoughts of her father, Kip and her own life lurked like shadows, haunting her, waiting until she mustered the courage to acknowledge them.

After bestowing a final kiss on her slumbering son, she left the nursery. She reached her bedroom door just as Kip approached it from inside the room. He was holding his pajamas. "I left these here," he explained.

She and Kip had to talk. She had to tell him that, because of him, she had begun to shed the oppressive burden of her hatred, that because of what he'd done to her last night she was a better person today. She had to tell him that, while she could not exonerate her father, or even understand why he'd done what he'd done, she could accept him.

She had to thank Kip for being her friend.

What she said was, "Make love to me."

As soon as the words slipped out she shrank back a step, astonished. Why had she said that? Where had it come from? She had meant to *talk* to Kip.

But staring at him across the threshold of her bedroom, her vision filled with his tall, athletic body and his square face, the strength and beauty of his deep-set brown eyes meeting hers, and behind him her bed, the bed she'd shared with him so chastely and angrily last night... She had spoken not her mind but her heart.

He had stripped her soul bare last night. Now, tonight, she stood before him, her soul still exposed, wanting him. Loving him.

The fabric of his shirt shifted as he breathed; his fingers clutched his pajamas. As a minute ticked by in silence, it dawned on Shelley that perhaps Kip didn't want her, that spending last night in her bed had meant nothing to him, that he could desire her only when he was in mourning for another woman.

"Are you sure?" he asked.

She lowered her eyes. "Not really."

He pondered her candid answer, then tossed his pajamas onto a chair and reached for her. "I'm sure enough for both of us," he whispered before pulling her into his arms and covering her mouth with his.

The potent hunger of his kiss told her he did want her, as much as she wanted him. The force of his tongue filling her mouth, stroking and teasing and bathing her with the heat of his need told her that last night had been as difficult for him as it had been for her. The nearly desperate strength of his arms binding her to him, his hands flat against her hips as his hardness found the crevice between her thighs, told her that no conversation, no confession or explanation or expression of gratitude was as important as this.

With a hushed groan, he ended the kiss and moved to the door to close it. "If Jamie needs us he'll shout," he said before Shelley could protest, and she knew he was right. As he returned to her, she lifted her hands to the buttons of his shirt.

They undressed each other hastily, carelessly. The bedside lamp spread an amber glow through the room, giving Shelley a view of Kip's body she hadn't had the last time, when they'd made love in the dark. It gave Kip a better view of her body, too—and pregnancy had left her body less young and firm than it used to be. She modestly crossed her arms over her breasts.

Kip took her hands in his and eased them away. "You're beautiful," he said, easily comprehending her bashfulness. "Don't hide."

"Maybe I'll look better without these," she remarked, pulling off his glasses and turning to place them on the night table. He glided behind her, slipping his arms around her and filling his hands with her breasts. He cupped his palms beneath their womanly weight, then arched his fingers upward to touch her nipples, fondling them until they were taut and burning.

His caress sent waves of heat down into her hips, causing her legs to weaken. His lips found the sensitive skin below her ear and she moaned. "Kip..."

He spun her around and pressed her down onto the bed, then lay down beside her. He kissed her throat once more, exploring the smooth underside of her jaw with his lips and tongue, nibbling to her collarbone and then downward. "Oh, Shelley—I've been waiting so long..." He captured one swollen nipple with his mouth and sucked. "I've wanted this for so long..."

"One night?" she asked, bewildered. Before last night, neither of them had dared to breach the hallway that separated their rooms, their beds.

"Weeks," he whispered. "Years."

Before she could question him further he closed his mouth over her other breast, drawing the nipple deep into his mouth. She clung to him, overwhelmed by the continuing surges of heat within her, the seething, building tension rippling down from her breasts to her belly, to her hips and thighs, making some parts of her tighten and other parts melt into liquid softness. She loved him, not because he'd forced her to deal with her father, not because he'd fathered her child, not even because he was kissing her so sublimely. She loved him because he was Kip—because she'd always loved him, because, as frightening as it was to admit, she needed him.

At that moment he needed her just as much. She hugged him, caressed him, raked her fingers through the hair of his chest and down, brushing lightly over his aroused flesh. She reveled in the clenching of his abdomen, in his breathless groan of encouragement as she wrapped her fingers around him. He lifted his mouth from her breast and closed his eyes for an instant, flexing his hips in response to her touch. Then he reciprocated, sliding his hand down her body to find her, to arouse her fully, to stroke and tantalize and feed her yearning for him until her body ached for more.

"I have—" She gasped, her hips writhing from the erotic cadence of his fingers on her. "Kip..." She struggled to clear her mind. "In the drawer. I have something, I thought..." Her voice dissolved into another broken moan as his thumb traced a thrilling circle over her tender flesh, sending a spasm of sensation deep into her.

He bowed to kiss her lips, an unbearably sweet, gentle kiss. "What?"

"Protection. There's a box in the drawer—"

He kissed her again, his tongue silencing her with a swift, demoralizing lunge. "No." His lips moved against hers as he shaped the words. "Let's make another baby."

She should have been shocked. She should have brought things to a halt, sat up and demanded a serious discussion of the subject. This wasn't the sort of decision to be made when her mind could accommodate nothing but love and longing. She should have stopped Kip, pulled herself together, made room in her heart for reality.

But she didn't. Perhaps she was too aroused to act sensibly, too eager for Kip's complete possession to pull back and analyze the pros and cons of having another child. Or perhaps she was unable to object because there was something irrefutably right in his suggestion, something crazy and impetuous but overwhelmingly optimistic about it, something as glorious as the act of making love itself.

Without a word she drew him back to her, urging him onto her, welcoming his weight, his hard male strength. He locked himself to her in a deep, conquering thrust that brought a moan to her lips, a prayer, a sigh of blissful surrender.

She had experienced something this profound only twice before: the night Jamie was conceived, and the night she and Kip had first kissed. He was skillful and sensitive, an astonishing combination of patience and impatience, ardor and control, savage power and exquisite tenderness. But Shelley responded to him not only because of his talent as a lover.

She responded to him because she trusted him.

She trusted him to feel the changes in her body, to adopt her rhythm, to move at the right angle, with the right pressure. She trusted him to watch and listen, to wait when he had to and surge faster, harder when her body arched in frantic need. She trusted him to deliver her to ecstasy, to follow close behind her, to be there to protect her when the thundering beauty of it stormed through her.

She felt him go rigid as she peaked, her flesh pulsing in stunning undulations of pleasure and her breath escaping her in a faint, ragged cry. Only then did he give in to his own release, his body wrenching in a final burst of energy, spilling his essence into her.

He sank down beside her, his skin damp, his respiration shallow. When she started to shift away he reached out and gathered her to him, holding her in an unbreakable embrace. "Don't move," he whispered, his voice muffled by her hair as he brushed his lips over her temple. "Just stay here. I need you. Just stay."

She did. Long after his breathing grew deep and regular, long after his body became motionless and his arm felt like a dead weight across her ribs, long after she'd turned off the light and settled back into the pillow and drew the blanket up over them, she stayed.

Kip slept, and she thought. About her father, about her son, about bearing another child. About keeping her history in the past, and facing the future.

About why Block Island and Jamie, security and tranquility and the first glimmerings of a rapprochement with her father weren't enough to satisfy her. About why Kip's friendship wasn't enough.

Even the intimacy they'd just shared wasn't enough. Kip had wanted their lovemaking; Shelley wanted his love. She wanted him to love her as much as he'd loved Amanda, so much that Shelley would always be with him, permanently lodged in his soul, an eternal, indelible part of him, something he could never escape—and would never wish to escape.

She used to believe that even though he would never love her that way, she could be content. She still believed he would never love her that way.

But she could not longer convince herself that what she had was enough.

HE DREAMED she was slipping away from him, eluding him, obscured by the mist. He struggled to see her, searching through the swirling haze for her black curls, her pale heart-shaped face, her Cupid's-bow mouth. But there had been no haze on Geary Street that evening, and just before the fog swallowed the woman forever he glimpsed dark blond hair and dazzling gray eyes.

A voice filled his head, a hoarse rasp of sound: *Let her know before it's too late.*

He bolted upright in the bed, gasping for breath, his skin covered by a film of perspiration and his pulse pounding in his temples. He was alone.

Throwing off the cover, he reached for his jeans and tugged them on. Then he hurried down the hall, moving instinctively to the small bedroom, to the attic stairs, through the attic to the ladder.

The trapdoor was open. Maybe she'd left it that way in order to hear if Jamie awakened, but Kip wanted to believe she'd left it open for him.

He found her kneeling on the floor of the cupola, clad in her bathrobe, her elbows resting on the windowsill and her chin balanced on her arms. Wisps of fog blurred the stark brilliance of the moonlight, giving it an ethereal glow.

At the sound of his footsteps she turned her head. An enigmatic smile crossed her lips.

"I'm sorry," he said.

Her eyebrows rose. "About what?"

He approached her, kneeled beside her, tucked an errant strand of hair behind her ear. Her cheek was soft and warm. He wanted to keep touching her, caressing the lobe of her ear. He wanted to kiss her, to know she was still with him, where he needed her to be.

"What I did to you." He grappled with his vague, enveloping fear. "Downstairs. I shouldn't have done that."

"Make love to me, you mean?"

"Without protection." His voice was low, halting. "I shouldn't have just tossed the idea at you the way I did. It's such a serious decision, having another child. I should have given you some time—"

"I didn't need time," she said, her smile widening slightly. "I think it's a wonderful idea."

"Even so, I shouldn't have railroaded you like that, when we were both—"

She brushed her index finger over his mouth to silence him. "At least we talked about it first. With Jamie we didn't even do that much. And look what happened."

What happened was a miracle. What happened was that Kip and Shelley both learned how much love they had to give.

"I want another child," she assured him, her eyes luminous and her voice calm.

"This time it will be easier," he promised. "I'll be with you the whole time, and—"

"You don't have to talk me into it." Her gaze was constant and certain. "I've cleared a lot of stuff out of my heart, Kip. A lot of anger and resentment. I've cleared it out, and now there's this space just waiting to be filled."

He knew what "stuff" she was referring to. There would be time later to ask her how she'd rid herself of it, why she had finally decided to make peace with her father. If Kip had helped in any way, he was glad—but what mattered was that she'd done it.

What mattered even more was that she cared enough about Kip to be willing to have another child with him.

It took all his willpower not to take her in his arms and crush her to him. He hadn't completely recovered from his nightmare; he hadn't yet convinced himself that she would never vanish in the fog. "It might take more than one try," he pointed out.

She erupted in a hushed, throaty laugh. "Meaning, you want to spend more time in my bed?"

"Meaning, I want to think of it as *our* bed. I want to marry you, Shelley."

Her smile ebbed and she turned away, gazing through the window at the hazy moon. For a long moment Kip heard nothing but the distant chorus of crickets, the faint rustle of leaves, the constant rhythm of his breath and hers. She smelled of baby shampoo and talcum powder, of heat and sex. He longed to run his hand through her hair, to pull back the lapel of her robe, to bare her throat and breasts, to touch her, to love her.

Her silence closed around his heart, cold as stone.

"I love you," he said.

"Not the way you loved Amanda," she whispered. There was no jealousy in her voice, no reproach. She stated the words as if they were a simple, irrefutable truth.

He shut his eyes and waited. Amanda appeared in his mind, young, full of hope and promise, her eyes sparkling and her cheeks stretched by her smile as she stood at the corner and waved at Kip. But instead of stepping into the street, she kept smiling, kept waving, her outlines receding as fog rolled in.

Block Island fog.

And suddenly he realized she was waving goodbye.

"You're right," he said, opening his eyes and taking in the magnificent vastness of the night sky, the symphony of island sounds, the delicate caress of the wind. "I don't love you the way I loved her. The way I loved her was like a sunset, one of those gorgeous sunsets at the cove, when the sun sinks below the water and drags the daylight down behind it. It ended in darkness, Shelley. It was beautiful, but it ended in darkness."

He curved his arm around her shoulders, needing to feel her against him, to hold onto her so she wouldn't flee. "The way I love you is different. It's more... like a sunrise. It's warm and clear, and it fills the world with light. It makes me want to wake up and live. That's how I love you."

She rotated in his arm and gazed at him. Her eyes shimmered with tears. "I don't know, Kip..."

"Is it that you don't love me?" he asked apprehensively.

She laughed. "Oh, Kip—I've loved you since...probably since the day you showed me that dead snake at Scotch Beach."

"Really?"

"In different ways at different times, but yes. I love you." Her smile waned. "I promised myself I'd never get married."

"Some promises are meant to be broken."

"I promised myself I would never become dependent on a man—"

"And some promises can't be kept, no matter how hard you try. It works both ways, Shelley. I'm dependent on you, too."

"Because I helped you get over Amanda."

"Because I love you," he corrected her. She *had* helped him recover from his grief, she *had* helped him to pull himself out of his depression. But that was behind him now, and he still needed Shelley, still depended on her. They anchored each other, relied on each other, understood each other. Trusted each other—he hoped.

"You do trust me, don't you?"

A tear skittered down her cheek, but she didn't avert her face. "Once, when we were up here," she reminisced, "when we were fifteen years old, you kissed me."

He smiled. "I remember."

"Afterward, you said you would never do anything bad to me." She swallowed, then took his hand in hers, holding tight. "You never have. I've always trusted you. Even when I was angry or scared, I've always trusted you."

"Then marry me."

She leaned toward him and touched her lips to his. "I'll marry you."

He closed his arms around her, drew her back to him and kissed her deeply. He remembered that first wonderful kiss, so many, many years ago. He remembered how excited they'd both been, and how frightened. He remembered how Shelley had broken from him in panic, how she'd trembled in his arms, terrified by how close she had come to being swept away.

She was no longer trembling, no longer afraid. Her hands cupped his cheeks and she held him to her, matching his passion, his confidence, his love.

An eternity seemed to pass before they drew back, breathless. He searched her face and saw joy there, and serenity. He didn't know whether they had conceived another child that night, but he knew that something had come to life inside them both. It was flourishing, blossoming, spreading its leaves and sheltering them. It was part friendship, part trust, part understanding. Part need and part choice, and it was love.

In the moonlit cupola, high above the island, above Old Harbor and New Harbor and the ocean beyond, Kip held Shelley and felt the seeds of his new life take root and grow.

PENNY JORDAN

Sins and infidelities . . .
Dreams and obsessions . . .
Shattering secrets
unfold in . . .

THE HIDDEN YEARS

SAGE — stunning, sensual and vibrant, she spent a lifetime distancing herself from a past too painful to confront . . . the mother who seemed to hold her at bay, the father who resented her and the heartache of unfulfilled love. To the world, Sage was independent and invulnerable— but it was a mask she cultivated to hide a desperation she herself couldn't quite understand . . . until an unforeseen turn of events drew her into the discovery of the hidden years, finally allowing Sage to open her heart to a passion denied for so long.

The Hidden Years—a compelling novel of truth and passion that will unlock the heart and soul of every woman.

AVAILABLE IN OCTOBER!
Watch for your opportunity to complete your Penny Jordan set.
POWER PLAY and SILVER will also be available in October.

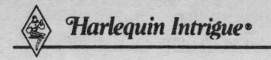

"INDULGE A LITTLE" SWEEPSTAKES

HERE'S HOW THE SWEEPSTAKES WORKS

NO PURCHASE NECESSARY

To enter each drawing, complete the appropriate Official Entry Form or a 3" by 5" index card by hand-printing your name, address and phone number and the trip destination that the entry is being submitted for (i.e., Walt Disney World Vacation Drawing, etc.) and mailing it to: Indulge '91 Subscribers-Only Sweepstakes, P.O. Box 1397, Buffalo, New York 14269-1397.

No responsibility is assumed for lost, late or misdirected mail. Entries must be sent separately with first class postage affixed, and be received by: 9/30/91 for the Walt Disney World Vacation Drawing, 10/31/91 for the Alaskan Cruise Drawing and 11/30/91 for the Hawaiian Vacation Drawing. Sweepstakes is open to residents of the U.S. and Canada, 21 years of age or older as of 11/7/91.

For complete rules, send a self-addressed, stamped (WA residents need not affix return postage) envelope to: Indulge '91 Subscribers-Only Sweepstakes Rules, P.O. Box 4005, Blair, NE 68009.

© 1991 HARLEQUIN ENTERPRISES LTD.   DIR-RL

- -

"INDULGE A LITTLE" SWEEPSTAKES

HERE'S HOW THE SWEEPSTAKES WORKS

NO PURCHASE NECESSARY

To enter each drawing, complete the appropriate Official Entry Form or a 3" by 5" index card by hand-printing your name, address and phone number and the trip destination that the entry is being submitted for (i.e., Walt Disney World Vacation Drawing, etc.) and mailing it to: Indulge '91 Subscribers-Only Sweepstakes, P.O. Box 1397, Buffalo, New York 14269-1397.

No responsibility is assumed for lost, late or misdirected mail. Entries must be sent separately with first class postage affixed, and be received by: 9/30/91 for the Walt Disney World Vacation Drawing, 10/31/91 for the Alaskan Cruise Drawing and 11/30/91 for the Hawaiian Vacation Drawing. Sweepstakes is open to residents of the U.S. and Canada, 21 years of age or older as of 11/7/91.

For complete rules, send a self-addressed, stamped (WA residents need not affix return postage) envelope to: Indulge '91 Subscribers-Only Sweepstakes Rules, P.O. Box 4005, Blair, NE 68009.

© 1991 HARLEQUIN ENTERPRISES LTD.   DIR-RL

INDULGE A LITTLE—WIN A LOT!

Summer of '91 Subscribers-Only Sweepstakes

OFFICIAL ENTRY FORM

This entry must be received by: Sept. 30, 1991
This month's winner will be notified by: Oct. 7, 1991
Trip must be taken between: Nov. 7, 1991—Nov. 7, 1992

YES, I want to win the Walt Disney World® vacation for two. I understand the prize includes round-trip airfare, first-class hotel and pocket money as revealed on the "wallet" scratch-off card.

Name _____

Address _____ Apt. _____

City _____

State/Prov. _____ Zip/Postal Code _____

Daytime phone number _____
                             (Area Code)

Return entries with invoice in envelope provided. Each book in this shipment has two entry coupons—and the more coupons you enter, the better your chances of winning!

© 1991 HARLEQUIN ENTERPRISES LTD.   CPS-M1

INDULGE A LITTLE—WIN A LOT!

Summer of '91 Subscribers-Only Sweepstakes

OFFICIAL ENTRY FORM

This entry must be received by: Sept. 30, 1991
This month's winner will be notified by: Oct. 7, 1991
Trip must be taken between: Nov. 7, 1991—Nov. 7, 1992

YES, I want to win the Walt Disney World® vacation for two. I understand the prize includes round-trip airfare, first-class hotel and pocket money as revealed on the "wallet" scratch-off card.

Name _____

Address _____ Apt. _____

City _____

State/Prov. _____ Zip/Postal Code _____

Daytime phone number _____
                             (Area Code)

Return entries with invoice in envelope provided. Each book in this shipment has two entry coupons—and the more coupons you enter, the better your chances of winning!

© 1991 HARLEQUIN ENTERPRISES LTD.   CPS-M1